"Are you aski...
your m...

"Yes. That is what I am asking you, Lillian."

Her lip trembled. "Why?"

That was the one question he hadn't expected. "You have stated many times that you are not suitable for me, and yet this desire courses between us whenever we are near each other. I propose that we allow it. Surrender to it."

"I see," she said so softly he almost didn't hear it.

He moved forward, aching to touch her. "Have I not made it clear enough that I want you? This request is a selfish one. I make it because I ache to feel your body next to mine in bed."

Romances by **Jenna Petersen**

WHAT THE DUKE DESIRES
HER NOTORIOUS VISCOUNT
LESSONS FROM A COURTESAN
SEDUCTION IS FOREVER
DESIRE NEVER DIES
FROM LONDON WITH LOVE
SCANDALOUS

What The Duke Desires

Jenna Petersen

AVON

An Imprint of HarperCollinsPublishers

This is a work of fiction. Names, characters, places, and incidents are products of the author's imagination or are used fictitiously and are not to be construed as real. Any resemblance to actual events, locales, organizations, or persons, living or dead, is entirely coincidental.

AVON BOOKS
An Imprint of HarperCollins*Publishers*
10 East 53rd Street
New York, New York 10022-5299

Copyright © 2009 by Jesse Petersen
ISBN 978-0-06-147082-0
www.avonromance.com

First Avon Books paperback printing: November 2009

Avon Trademark Reg. U.S. Pat. Off. and in Other Countries, Marca Registrada, Hecho en U.S.A.
HarperCollins® is a registered trademark of HarperCollins Publishers.

Printed in the U.S.A.

10 9 8 7 6 5 4 3 2 1

This book is for Miriam. There are a myriad of hats a good agent wears, from brainstorming partner, to first reader, to hand holder and "snap out of it" sayer, not to mention career nurturer. You do all of them with style and polish and infinite kindness. Thank you so much for all you do and who you are.

And for Michael, who makes everything all better with hugs, sound advice, and occasionally ice cream. You are my hero, and I'm so lucky to have you as my partner for the rest of my life.

What The Duke Desires

Chapter 1

1816

She had never had a face. Since Simon was a boy, that was how he knew she was part of a dream. Not a nightmare, for she wasn't phantom. No, he wasn't quite sure how he would describe her. Perhaps a feeling, rather than a figure, and that feeling was comfort.

He couldn't remember a time when the woman hadn't been a part of his dreams, floating through the ever-changing landscape of his nocturnal fantasies and soothing the occasional nightmare.

And yet, when she spoke, she always said the same thing.

Wake up, child.

On cue, Simon Crathorne, Duke of Billingham, jolted awake, disoriented and foggy. He stared through the darkness of his chamber, searching as if the mysterious figure would somehow remain in his presence, only this time she would be flesh and bone.

Of course, she was not.

With a curse, he threw back the covers and paced through his chamber to the cloaked window. He yanked the curtains open with violence and winced as bright morning sunshine slapped him in the face.

He glared at the clock on the mantel across the room. It was still early, he had at least an hour before his valet would come to assist in his preparations for the day. And he'd had a late night, drinking a bit too much with his best friend, Rhys Carlisle, the Duke of Waverly, who had come out to the Billingham shire to offer moral support during the dreaded house party that would commence today.

And that was probably why the troubling dream with the faceless woman had come to him yet again. She normally appeared when he was out of sorts, worrying over something. And really, this party was quite important, wasn't it?

After all, in a few short hours, at least a dozen well-appointed carriages would pull into the drive below and deposit a veritable gaggle of young ladies and their mamas or other chaperones. Before a fortnight of merriment was finished, one of those same ladies might very well be his intended, with the Billingham diamond, worn by every Duchess of Billingham for eleven generations, sparkling on her finger and announcing to the world that the new duke had at last found his bride.

He groaned as he yanked the curtains shut and flopped back onto his bed. If he was already dreaming of the faceless woman, it was going to be a very long party indeed.

"Are you quite certain your aunt is asleep?" Lillian Mayhew whispered as she elbowed her best friend, Lady Gabriela Watsenvale, in the ribs. "I think her eyes are open."

Gabby gave a delicate shudder as the two girls stared across the jolting carriage at the empty, glazed-over gaze of their chaperone.

"Yes, she does that," her friend murmured as she looked away. "It is quite disturbing, is it not? But I promise you, Auntie Isabel is asleep. Even if she wasn't, she's stone deaf. We could scream out the entire *Dictionary of the Vulgar Tongue* and she would never so much as stir."

Lillian smothered a giggle with her palm. "Do we have a copy of the *Dictionary* at hand to scream out? I would greatly like to expand my vocabulary. Wouldn't it be delightful if I could march right up to the Duke of Billingham and tell him exactly what I thought of his so-called saintly father in terms that would color his ears blood red?"

Gabby's forehead wrinkled. "To do such a thing would be a bit obvious, don't you agree? The entire purpose of your visit is to quietly obtain evidence that the man's father wasn't the paragon of virtue the *ton* believes. If you offend the new duke within five minutes of our arrival, you shall be sent packing before teatime, and that won't get you anywhere."

Lillian folded her arms and scrunched down lower in her seat. "Well, I suppose you're right. Leave it to you to consider this logically instead of indulging my fantasies. You know, sometimes I forget that I am the elder of the two of us by four years!"

Gabby laughed. "I have an old soul."

Lillian stuck out her tongue playfully before she sighed. "I shall skip memorizing vulgarities then and stick to my original plan."

The lines in her friend's forehead deepened and her teasing gaiety faded away. "Again, I must mention my lingering concerns about this plan of yours, Lillian."

Lillian shut her eyes with a groan. She'd heard this sermon a dozen times or more.

Her friend ignored her expression and said, "You do not like to hear it, but Billingham is one of the most powerful men in the country. If you cross him . . ."

Lillian shrugged. "I don't think Simon Crathorne can do worse to me than his father did to my mother."

At the same moment, Gabby and she both shivered. Her friend shook her head. "I cannot believe your father would tell you such a thing. It is not for a woman's ears."

Lillian blinked back tears. Her father had died just over six months before, and on his deathbed, he had revealed such a secret . . . such a horrible revelation that every time she thought of it, her blood boiled and her hands shook with the force of her upset and anger.

"He wasn't telling me, I only overheard him," she murmured. "He told my brother. He asked Jack to get revenge on the duke for our family. Instead, my brother dissolved into a bottle of whiskey with his pain. Which leaves only *me* to fulfill my father's last wishes."

"Revenge is not a woman's duty, Lillian," her friend whispered as she touched her hand. "It's too ugly and often dangerous, are you certain you cannot leave it be?"

"Leave it be?" Lillian snapped before she shot a glance at Aunt Isabel. But Gabby was right, the older woman had not so much as stirred despite the spirited conversation taking place six inches away from her.

"I cannot leave it be!" Lillian continued. "Five years ago, Roger Crathorne, the Duke of Billingham, found my mother alone at a party and he . . . he . . ." She could hardly say it. "He raped her.

Within a month, she had killed herself, driven to suicide rather than live with the shame of what he had done to her. Since that night, I have lost everything I held dear. My mother, my father, now my brother. Not to mention that people whisper of the rumors surrounding her death. Because of it, *my* family is looked down upon and my own chances at a decent match are limited, at best."

Gabby frowned, but Lillian did not allow her to interrupt.

"All this occurs while Roger Crathorne's memory is exalted. Why, only two weeks ago I overheard someone malign my family and in almost the same *breath* she spoke of how wonderful a man the late Duke of Billingham was. How can I leave that be? How can I let that stand?"

"Your father did," Gabby argued. "He had five years to take revenge and he didn't."

Lillian shook her head as she thought of her father. After her mother's death he had disappeared into his grief. He had hardly been able to get up in the morning, let alone turn his thoughts to vengeance.

"My father regretted his weakness every day!" Lillian said as she thought of his deathbed words once more. "He told my brother so and begged him to find revenge before the duke died."

"Then let your brother do it," Gabby begged, grabbing her hands.

"I have waited months for him to do so, but you know my brother. He is too like my father, he would rather drown his sorrow in a bottle than avenge it. But those were my father's requests, and that is what my mother deserves. So I am here and I intend to do as he asked, even if it wasn't me he asked it of."

Gabby held her stare for a long moment and then nodded. "I do understand. It must be horrible to hear people go on and on about how wonderful the duke was when you know the truth. I hear they are going to erect a statue to him for all his good works."

Lillian clenched her jaw. "You see. *That* is exactly why this must be done even though he is dead. I will not have one more Season pass where that man is lauded a saint."

"I understand," her friend whispered.

Lillian nodded, but her conscience pricked nonetheless. "In truth, it is more *you* I worry about. After all, if I am successful in proving that the great and glorious Roger Crathorne died not a saint, but as a hideous liar and sinner, then I will, as you say, make powerful enemies. If you had any designs on finding a match amongst the duke or his friends—"

Gabby lifted a hand to cut her off. "I've told you more than once, I could never want a man whose family was responsible for so much of your pain."

Lillian squeezed her friend's fingers and ended the subject by turning to look out the window as the lush green countryside rolled by. As much as she appreciated her friend's loyalty, Lillian was one of the very few people who understood the true financial straits of Gabby's family. Her friend would have to marry well, so Lillian had to keep the Watsenvale name clear of wherever her ultimate plans took her.

"Do you *really* think you'll find some kind of proof that the late duke did the sort of things your family accused him of?" Gabby asked, drawing Lillian's attention back to her. "The *ton* will turn on its heroes like vipers, it's true, but not without strong proof."

"I know." Lillian rested her head against the leather seat behind her, suddenly tired, and she had not even begun her quest. "The bastard . . ."

She trailed off to cast a quick glance at Gabby's aunt Isabel, but though her eyes remained eerily open, a low snore escaped her lips.

"The bastard was so well-liked, he had so many people fooled that it will take a great deal to make them see him for what he truly was. But if I could find enough evidence, I think I could convince them. Even if they would not hear it from me, then the papers would print the truth. They couldn't ignore that."

Gabby swallowed hard. "The papers? They will

most definitely require solid proof of something wicked to print it and risk the ire of the Billingham family."

Lillian nodded. "Yes. Since the man spent almost every moment he was not in London at this particular country estate, I think it is as good a place as any to find his Achilles' heel."

Gabby arched a brow. "Not to mention that it is the *only* Billingham home you have been invited to."

Lillian gazed outside a second time. It was not an unkindly meant comment, but it did remind her of her place in the world. "You are correct. I'm not exactly being invited to balls by dukes, but perhaps luck will be on my side."

Gabby flinched as if she realized her statement had cut, but then she nodded. "I'm sure it shall be. You will find what you need here, I know it. And I'll do anything in my power to assist you."

Lillian grasped her friend's hand and squeezed it gently. If there was one good truth that remained in her world, it was that Gabriela was the best and most loyal friend she had ever had.

When Lillian's father died and her younger brother went wild, it had been Gabby who had convinced her father to allow Lillian to stay with their family and take part in the Season as her guest. It had been Gabby who had somehow managed to get herself included in the new Duke of Billing-

ham's house party. And it had been Gabby who
had written in the guise of her father to the duchess, asking that Lillian be included as well. All
because her friend knew how desperately Lillian
wanted to right the wrong done to her family.

The carriage slid to a stop and there were a
few voices outside. At that moment, Aunt Isabel
snorted awake, sitting up from her slightly cock-
eyed position and giving the two girls a flighty
smile before she peeked out the curtain on the
window beside her.

"Ah, we are here at last! They are opening the
gate for us," Aunt Isabel said, her voice still thick
with sleep.

No sooner had the words been spoken than the
carriage began to move and they entered the main
estate area where the Billingham dukes had kept a
home for eleven generations. Twelve, now, Lillian
supposed. After all, there was a new duke.

Rumor had it that father and son had been quite
close, so the son was probably as corrupt and false
as his father before him. At least Lillian assumed
so. If he was not, it would certainly make her quest
all the more uncomfortable.

Such an odd situation, to be hoping one's host
was a scoundrel.

She straightened up as the carriage wound its
way down the road leading to the main house.
Now was the time to pull herself together and pre-

pare for every contingency. The man she was about
to meet could never guess that she had come to his
country party not as a guest, but as the harbinger
of his doom. Or at least of the end of his late father's highly respected name.

No, she would have to be sweet and empty and
forgettable, but never cold or bitter. Then the new
duke would put his focus on the other poor women
he intended to court and forget about her, leaving
her to conduct her search in peace.

The carriage pulled to a stop, and instantly there
was a hustle and bustle of activity as footmen rat-
tled down from their seats. The door was pulled
open and Aunt Isabel stepped out first, calling her
greeting to seemingly no one in particular. Gabby
followed after a brief but meaningful glance in Lillian's direction.

Once her friend was gone, Lillian drew in a
final breath of strength and took the gloved fingers
that were offered by the servant outside. Stepping
down, she made to join Aunt Isabel and Gabby. But
as she moved around a footman to begin this charade, she came to a sudden stop. The two women
were not alone. They had been joined by a man.

And not just any man, but possibly the most
beautiful man she had ever seen in her twenty-
seven years on this earth. He was tall, probably a
head and a half taller than she was, with broad
shoulders that fit perfectly into his impeccably tai-

lored waistcoat and jacket. He had thick, black hair that was just a touch too long and curled over his forehead in little tendrils that she had the strangest urge to smooth back. He had a firmly defined jaw and full lips that, when she looked at them, gave her an odd little thrill low in her stomach.

But it wasn't those things that made everything else around her fade away. No, those were features any handsome man might possess. The attribute that stood out above all others on his uncommonly beautiful face was his eyes.

She had never seen a man with eyes the color of jade. Pale and bright, filled with intelligence and humor and just a touch of suppressed mischief. The best part was that those eyes were locked with hers in a stare so intense that she felt hot even though the late spring breeze still had a lovely coolness to it.

"And this is my niece's traveling companion and friend, Miss Lillian Mayhew," Aunt Isabel said, the only one oblivious to the impact of this meeting. Certainly Gabby was staring back and forth between the two of them, her face pale and lips thin.

Lillian stepped forward, trying to remember to breathe, trying to remember herself at all.

"Good afternoon," she whispered, glad that her voice did not tremble and betray how much this stranger had moved her with just a fleeting glance.

He reached out and took her hand lightly in his. He wore gloves, as did she, but the warmth and strength of his fingers still radiated through the two layers of fabric.

"Good afternoon, Miss Mayhew. Welcome to my home. I am Simon Crathorne"—Lillian sucked in a breath, her smile actually rolling off her face like a waterfall as he completed the sentence—"the Duke of Billingham."

Chapter 2

"S o now that you've had a chance to examine them, what do you think of your potential brides?" Rhys asked as he settled into a comfortable leather chair in Simon's office.

Simon didn't move from his place standing before the window, staring out at the green lawn behind the estate. The women had gathered there a short time ago to share tea with his mother. The duchess had returned to the estate to host this gathering at his side. It wasn't a situation she relished, as the two had never been close, but she was good at carrying through the motions for the sake of the continuation of the title, and he appreciated the act.

"You speak of them as if I were examining cattle, Waverly," he finally responded, referring to Rhys by his title, as his friend preferred.

Simon strained to see the women in the distance, and one stood out to him. Lillian Mayhew with her honey blond locks that were currently just peeking out from the edge of her bonnet. He had felt the strangest connection to her when they met, an electricity that made his stomach jump . . . as well as other, *lower* parts of his anatomy. But when he introduced himself, she had snatched her hand away, her face suddenly pale. Oh, she'd covered her reaction quickly enough, but it lingered in his mind.

"It is as good a comparison as any," Rhys said, interrupting his thoughts. "Livestock are an asset. So is the proper wife. Why should you not examine her as carefully as you would a mare or a goat?"

Simon shook off his thoughts of Lillian and spun away from the window with a snort of derision. "Is that how you think of Anne, then? As a goat that will increase your holdings?"

Rhys folded his arms as his nostrils flared slightly. "You purposefully misunderstand me. You know I do not think of my fiancée as a goat. No one ever could. Lady Anne has breeding, beauty, and grace. She will make an excellent duchess, be the best hostess in London, and ultimately raise sons I shall be proud of."

Simon stared at his best friend. He was all for propriety and marrying within his sphere, but sometimes he thought Rhys took it a bit too far.

"But shouldn't a marriage be about more than just those things?" he asked with a shake of his head. "You speak of it as if it is merely a business transaction."

"Don't mistake it for a moment, my friend." Rhys took a final sip of his tea and got to his feet. "It *is* a business transaction. Anyone who claims otherwise is trying to justify a poor match."

"But attraction, friendship, passion . . ."

His friend waved him off. "Of course you'll be attracted to the woman you wed. All the girls you have invited to the party are more than pretty enough to make fulfilling your husbandly duties a pleasure when the time comes. As for friendship, why is it necessary? You have friends aplenty, you have little need for another. And passion is why you'll have a mistress."

His friend clapped a hand on his shoulder as he joined Simon at the window to stare down below at the women of their party. "Now tell me, is there anyone in particular whom you have singled out?"

Simon shifted. Although he and Rhys had very different ideas about marital happiness, he respected his friend's opinion. He shrugged one shoulder.

"It is too early to truly know anything about them, but I did feel a connection to one woman."

"Excellent. Which one?"

"Lillian Mayhew." Simon flicked a finger toward her, sitting across the courtyard chatting with some of the other women.

Rhys wrinkled his brow as he stared blankly at the group. "Mayhew . . ."

"She came with Lady Gabriela, the Earl of Watsenvale's daughter."

His friend turned on him with a look of horror lining his expression. "Dear God, man, *that* one? Now I know why the name is familiar."

Simon drew back in surprise at the contempt in his friend's voice. He hadn't been expecting that, and now burned with curiosity as to the reason. "You speak so strenuously about a girl you have yet to meet."

Rhys shook his head. "Meeting her is unnecessary. I can already tell you she is entirely inappropriate on so many levels I can hardly name them all."

"Try." Simon folded his arms.

His friend ticked off one of his fingers. "For one, her father was of little importance. Just a younger son of a younger son. No title, very little money. Normally you might be able to overlook such a thing if there were other benefits to the match, but there is more to be held against her. Her brother is rumored to be quite wild since their father's death six months ago. But most importantly, there is her mother. You must know about *her*."

"No." Simon shook his head.

His friend rolled his eyes before he paced away. "Christ, man, you are a *duke*. You're leader of one of the most respected families in England, not to mention you are now responsible for upholding the legacy of honor and esteem you inherited from your late father. You *must* make yourself more aware of those below you, as well as those of your own rank. Especially when you consider a match."

Simon felt his frustration rising. Although he liked Rhys a great deal, was probably closer to him than any other friend in his life, sometimes he could not abide Rhys's pompous attitude.

His friend had always been obsessed by bloodline. He had formed "The Duke Club" when they were in Eton, excluding any young man who did not come from a ducal family or have a chance to inherit that exalted title. And from the moment Rhys's father passed and he inherited the title of Duke of Waverly, his arrogant attitude seemed only to grow.

But Simon remained friendly with him because of one powerful reason. Once one was within Waverly's circle of friends, the other man was more loyal than anyone Simon had ever met. Rhys had almost gotten himself killed standing up for Simon during one drunken brawl years ago. His friend might take a bullet for him if the situation arose. That was a rare commodity in the circles they ran in, where friendship was often tossed aside for personal gain, so Simon had found ways to ignore the parts of Rhys's personality that were less attractive.

"What about the mother, Waverly?" he pressed.

Rhys leaned forward. "There were whispers she was a . . ." His voice dropped even lower. *"Suicide."*

Simon flinched as he paced away from his friend, but not for the reasons Rhys intended. Rather than making Simon less interested in Lillian Mayhew, this new information only solidified his awareness of the young woman. After all, he had only recently lost his own parent, a father he had looked up to and adored his entire life. He could only imagine what Lillian felt, losing both her parents, and perhaps one to a suicide.

He found himself seeking Lillian out again at the next window down the wall, away from Rhys's disapproving stare. She was laughing now, and her smile was so wide and genuine that his lips twitched with a desire to join in her pleasure.

Why shouldn't he?

At thirty-two, he was not in his first Season examining the young ladies around him and trying to determine if they would make an appropriate bride. In all the years since he had been old enough to look at them with real intent, very few had sparked his interest. The ones who had were a disappointment upon closer inspection.

So despite Rhys's warnings about a lack of

standing, money, and Lord knew what else, Simon intended to get to know Miss Mayhew a little better. After all, if she was friendly with the Earl of Watsenvale's family, that meant she had *some* connections, and certainly many a man had elevated through marriage a lady from an untitled family.

Since his father's death, there had been more pressure than ever to find the woman who would be his duchess. He needed to provide the family with its next heir so everyone could breathe a bit easier, including his nearest cousin, a vicar who repeatedly reminded him how little he desired to become a duke by default.

"You are determined to pursue this, aren't you?" Rhys snapped, his sharp tone interrupting Simon's thoughts.

He glanced at his friend with a smile. "Indeed, I am. There was an intensity to her stare, Rhys. A determination I have rarely seen in a lady. It interests me, and I would like to see if there is something more there. Likely there is not and that will be the end of it."

His words seemed to comfort his friend somewhat, but Rhys still looked concerned as he gave the woman across the courtyard a final glance.

"Just be careful, Billingham," his friend said as he returned to his seat and his abandoned tea. "A woman who reaches beyond her sphere is often looking for something. You are my closest friend and I would hate to see you snared in a trap."

Lillian folded a chemise carefully and set it in the chest of drawers in the large chamber she was sharing with Gabby. From her position sprawled across the bed, her friend watched her with a frown.

"Maggie will do that for you."

Lillian shrugged. Her friend's maid had been very accommodating since Lillian had been forced to let go of her own due to a lack of funds, but at this country party the servant was overworked. Even more so since it had been discovered that Gabby's favorite gown had a small stain on it. Maggie had rushed down to the laundresses to oversee the washing herself.

Even if the servant hadn't been busy, Lillian was loath to allow the girl to add to her work. It was rather humiliating, if nothing else, to have to beg the services of someone else's maid because one could not afford one's own. But she couldn't tell Gabby that. With her friend's teetering financial status hanging over her head, it would only be cruel to give her a glimpse into her possible future.

"I'm restless," Lillian explained as she closed the drawers. She left the trunk where it was for a footman to remove later and moved toward the bed, where she worried a loose thread dangling from the edge of the coverlet.

"I see that." Gabby stifled a yawn into her palm. "We could call for some warm milk or a bit of brandy. Perhaps it would calm you enough to join me for a nap."

Lillian tilted her head to examine her friend. "You *do* look exhausted after the long journey. I'm sorry, Gabby, I'm keeping you from your rest. Why don't I go do a bit of exploring—"

"Snooping," her friend interrupted as she let her eyes close.

"*Exploring,*" Lillian insisted with a laugh. "And I'll come fetch you in an hour or so."

"Thank you, dear," Gabby said as she shifted into a more comfortable position. "I think a nap would be quite restorative. Don't get into any trouble, though."

Lillian ignored her friend's playful parting shot as she slipped from the room and closed the door behind her quietly. In the hallway, she took a long, calming breath before she gazed around in wonder. After months of trying to figure out how she could get her revenge on the man who had all but murdered her mother, now she was here in his home.

And it was overwhelming. She had no idea where to start her search. In truth she didn't even really know what she was looking for. After all, Roger Crathorne had spent decades carefully crafting a public image of piety and goodness, fidelity and decency . . . it wasn't as if he would leave details of his evil deeds just lying about for her to stumble upon.

And then there was her earlier encounter with his son, the *new* Duke of Billingham. Simon Crathorne had thrown her mightily. She had been out in Society long enough to recognize the signs when a man was attracted to her, and she certainly knew herself well enough to feel when she was attracted in return. Outside on the drive, both had been abundantly clear.

But Lillian didn't *want* to be attracted to the new duke, not with the ugly history their families shared. She certainly didn't want him attracted to her. His interest meant he would watch her. He might even seek her out, which would all but devastate her plans to quietly search his home without detection.

She would have to be careful how she handled him from here on out.

Shaking off her troubling thoughts, she moved through the halls. Unlike earlier in the day when the guests had been arriving in noisy waves, all was quiet now. After sharing tea, almost all the female guests had retired to their chambers to organize their things, take naps . . . and probably gossip about their handsome host. The men were likely off drinking port or whatever it was men did when they left the ladies and had a few rare moments of peace.

Which meant this was the perfect time for Lillian to discover the lay of the estate house. Even if she was caught snooping, she had the perfect and *true* excuse that Gabby was napping and she was restless and hadn't wanted to keep her friend from her sleep. As long as she didn't behave suspiciously, no one would question her intentions.

Moving down the long, curving staircase into the foyer, she looked around. There were so many doors, so many corridors, one could hardly choose. But finally she picked one randomly and pressed it open slowly, just in case there were people within.

Happily, the room was empty, but it was only a parlor decorated with a floral motif. Pale pink furniture, bright curtains, it was clearly a ladies' gathering place. She winced at the cloying prettiness of it and shut the door again. The next room was another parlor, then a sunny breakfast room. She made a mental note of each chamber, in case she had a chance for a deeper search later.

She moved to the next door, ready to do a brief perusal and move on yet again, but when she pushed the heavy wooden barrier aside, she caught her breath and couldn't help but move into the chamber and gaze about in wonder.

A library! And fully the most beautiful one she had ever seen. High cherrywood shelves stretched up to the vaulted ceilings, so elevated that there was actually a terrace to reach the higher books and a wheeled ladder on each level for the same purpose.

A fireplace sat along the back wall, with a cheery fire dancing invitingly to warm and brighten the room. Two chairs were positioned before it, with a table in between. One side of the room had a high, broad window, its panes polished to a gleaming shine to allow the most light in for reading. Finally, a window seat covered in a soft, light green fabric beckoned her to sit and lose herself in story for the next few hours.

Lillian found herself gliding along the shelves, sliding a finger across the spines as she read every title from Shakespeare to medical journals to foreign tomes she didn't even recognize. Better yet, the books appeared to have been *read* rather than simply collected there for show. In fact, a few were obviously well-read, for their spines were worn and cracked from being opened and shut so many times.

"Are you also an admirer of the Bard?"

Lillian jumped and spun around to face the voice that had shocked her from her reverie. There, leaning negligently in the doorway, was her host, the Duke of Billingham. Lillian drew in a breath of surprise. Not a quarter of an hour before she had been vowing to avoid him and here he was. Yet her first reaction was not regret or displeasure, but something else. Something she shoved away as he gave her a crooked smile that invited her to join in the expression.

But she didn't. Instead, she stepped away from the bookshelf and folded her hands in front of her demurely.

"I am British. Is it not law to be an admirer of the Bard, Your Grace?" she replied.

Instantly she regretted her words, for the duke's crooked smile widened into a full grin and his jade eyes danced with humor. Both stuttered her heart. Damn, she had amused him. Not the right path if she wanted to become forgettable in his estimation.

"Perhaps that law *is* on the books," he mused as he stepped toward her. "If it is not, I shall propose it to the House of Lords when we next meet in a few weeks. I'm certain there will be much support for such a thing from all parties."

A clever retort danced on Lillian's tongue, but she forced herself to swallow it back. Playful banter was not in her best interest, no matter how tempting it was.

"I did not mean to intrude," she said, purposefully avoiding Simon's pointed gaze as if she could not be less interested in him. "My friend Lady Gabriela decided to take a nap, but I was too restless to sleep."

"I see," he said, looking around with a contented sigh. "Well, if there is any room in this home to soothe you, this library is the one. It has long been my favorite place to gather my thoughts."

Lillian found herself staring at the man for a long, charged moment. If not for his familial ties, he would be very attractive to her at present. Physically, yes, for no one could deny he was a fine specimen of his sex.

But there was more to it than that. After just a few moments spent together, she could sense how intelligent he was. And apparently well-read, which had always been appealing to her. Not to mention that whenever he smiled, she couldn't help but look at his mouth. And that made her tingle a little too much for comfort.

With effort, she shook off his strange effect on her. "But you have come here to enjoy some privacy, Your Grace. I would not dream of intruding."

She moved for the door, but he took a quick sidestep and suddenly he was blocking her path. Just as she had when he took her hand outside a few hours before, Lillian couldn't help but swallow hard and look up into his face. His very handsome, very friendly face.

"I did not come here for privacy," he said softly. "I came because the door was ajar. And I did not ask you to go, Miss Mayhew."

Lillian blinked. The fact that he recalled her name after meeting so many other ladies that day only underscored the problem that she was apparently memorable to him. And if she dug in her heels and ran from the room to escape him, she would only become more memorable.

So dull she would have to be, although it did not come naturally to her.

"Well, books can be so dusty, can't they?" she said, trying hard not to take a forlorn look behind her at the rising shelves. She might never again have the chance to explore this amazing room, and it hurt her heart to leave it behind.

His smile fell at her apparent distaste for the books. She almost sighed in relief. With any luck, he would now think her quite stupid and that would be the end of it.

Instead, he shrugged. "Ah well, if you are not comfortable in this room, then come, I shall give you the grand tour of the rest of the house. I'm certain we can find at least *one* chamber to your liking."

He held out an elbow and Lillian found herself staring at his arm. A very nice arm it was, too. Even through his jacket, she could see the faint definition of muscle. Why could he not be soft and lazy and unattractive?

"Miss Mayhew?"

She blinked and looked up to find Simon staring down at her with a small smile tilting up one corner of his lips. His arm still hovered between them and finally she took it, trying desperately to ignore the spark of awareness that crackled through her when she touched him.

They walked into the hallway together at a leisurely pace, as if Simon had nothing better to do than to show her around his home. Obviously that could not be true. He was a duke, after all. He had many responsibilities, so why was he so focused on her?

"I understand that you and Lady Gabriela are very good friends," he said as he motioned her into a lovely parlor with a piano near a large window overlooking the rolling hills of the estate.

She tried not to suck in her breath with pleasure. Whatever else his family was, they certainly had nice taste. The piano was beautiful and obviously well cared for if the shining black surface was any indication. Perhaps later Gabby would play on the instrument. Her friend was remarkably talented.

"Gabby is my dearest friend in the world," she said as they departed the room and continued their travels up the hall. "She is closer of an age to my younger brother, but our mothers were once friendly, so we've known each other all our lives. We became close despite the disparity in our ages."

He leaned back a fraction. "Tsk, Miss Mayhew. There cannot be much of a disparity to overcome! You are not so much older than your friend."

Despite herself, a little blush of pleasure tinged her cheeks. She had been on the shelf so long she sometimes felt ancient. And especially next to Gabby, who was so fresh and pretty.

"Lady Gabriela is four years my junior, Your Grace, which is an eternity to most in our circles." She smiled despite herself. "And *you* should know that a gentleman never speaks to a lady about the number of her years."

"My apologies."

He gave a playful bow as they entered a billiard room. She released a faint sigh. Billiards always put her to mind of her late father. He had loved to play and been quite good at the game. He'd even taught her a little, over her mother's laughing objections. Those were such happy times.

"How did you two become so close with so *many* years between you?" Simon asked, his tone still playful and teasing.

Lillian stopped walking. The whisper of pains long past squeezed around her heart. "We—we shared a few common experiences."

"Such as?" He tilted his head, but he seemed a bit more serious now, as if he was aware of her shift in behavior and manner.

"We both lost our mothers within a year of each other," she explained after a long pause.

As much as she hated to say anything about her mother to this man, especially, it wasn't as if that fact was a great secret. Rumors and whispers still echoed through the *ton* about her mother's demise. Since she'd mentioned it, he would probably uncover some of the details, and that would certainly end his interest in her. It had ended the interest of countless others like him.

She forced herself to continue, "That common experience made Gabby older than her years and bonded us forever."

Simon flinched slightly. "My apologies, again, and this time sincerely," he said, reaching out to briefly take her hand. This time she was not wearing gloves and neither was he. His skin was warm and slightly rough against hers. "I was playful about a painful and personal subject. I hope I have not offended you."

Lillian swallowed. Simon seemed so sincere in his apology. But was it real? Had his father been so adept at false kindness if he wanted a woman? She didn't know, but it was all very confusing.

She finally shook her head. "You could not have known, my lord. It was a very long time ago."

He squeezed her fingers gently. "I do not think there is enough time in the world to fully overcome the loss of a parent. My own father died just over six months ago, and the pain is just as raw to me now as it was the day of his passing."

At the mention of Roger Crathorne, Lillian jerked her hand away from his.

"Excuse me, Your Grace," she said, her breath short. "I promised my friend I would come back and wake her to ready for supper. It is far past time I do so. Thank you for the tour."

Then she turned on her heel and walked away.

Chapter 3

And then he went so far as to *dare* compare his father's death to my mother's! As if the two of them should be put in the same sphere in any way."

Lillian paced across the chamber yet again, arms folded and high emotion bubbling from every pore in her body. She was practically shaking from the force of it.

Gabby watched her with a worried expression. "But dearest, you must remember that to him the two losses *are* similar. You lost both your parents and he lost a father. The death of a parent *is* a common bond you share."

Although there was truth to her friend's words that she could not deny, Lillian couldn't keep herself from shaking her head violently.

"Never say that! I have no bond with him. I will *never* have a bond with him." She blinked at the sudden tears that burned her eyes. "My

mother was good and decent and kind. His
father was a hypocrite and a fiend who would
take what he could not earn without regard for
the consequences."

"You forget," Gabby said as she got to her feet
and moved toward Lillian. "Simon Crathorne may
be as in the dark about his father's true character
as everyone else was. You said yourself that Roger
Crathorne hid his true self well. Simon could have
no idea in the slightest about what the late duke
did when no one was watching."

At that, Lillian stopped pacing and flinched.
In her darkest hours, when she had planned and
plotted against the late Duke of Billingham's good
name, she had been able to pretend away the effect
her actions could have on innocents. It was harder
now. The pang of guilt she had felt when considering the impact of her quest on others had been
steadily growing since her arrival.

If the family truly didn't know of the late duke's
predilections and lies, it would be devastating for
them.

But could that be true? Could Roger Crathorne's
family live with him and not have some awareness
of what a bastard he was? Wouldn't he have revealed it somehow, some way?

No, it was far more likely that the family, including Simon, had simply looked the other way,
taking the benefit that his lies and public persona

had created and never thinking one moment about the cost to those the late duke hurt.

That thought made her shake away the guilt. Her mother deserved the justice no man in her family had been able or willing to provide. And Roger Crathorne deserved whispers of horror when his name was spoken, not flowery declarations of sainthood and goodness. Only Lillian could fulfill her father's dying wish, the least she could do was try now that she was here and had the opportunity.

"Now tell me, before you stormed out of the room, did you determine anything of interest about Simon or his father?" Gabby pressed.

Lillian shrugged. The two girls had decided to refer to Simon by his first name when they were in private to reduce confusion about which Duke of Billingham they were referring to. But thinking of him in such an intimate way only made the entire exercise more difficult.

"Simon was definitely aware of me," Lillian said with a sigh. "In the library, especially, he was quite flirtatious. And then later in the billiard room before I told him about my mother."

Gabby winced ever so slightly, and Lillian knew she was thinking of her own mother. "I see."

Lillian scowled. "I think it goes to show that Simon might be exactly like his father."

"Because he flirted with you a little?" Gabby's laughter was incredulous.

She nodded, shoving aside the fact that he had seemed sincere. All that could have been an act, no matter how real it felt in the moment.

"Come now, Lillian, that is a bit uncharitable to you both. How many men have flirted with you harmlessly? And you have never thought the worst of *them*. Do not censure Simon so blindly only to make yourself feel better."

"It is one thing for the second son of an earl to flirt with me, or even a baronet," Lillian reasoned. "But for a duke to express an interest in someone like me . . . well, it leaves me a bit suspicious. He could not be marriage-minded, so he must desire something else entirely."

A bright blush colored Gabby's cheeks as she realized what the "something else" Lillian had made reference to was.

"So you do not allow that he could simply have been as attracted to you as you were to him that first moment he saw you this morning?" her friend asked with a frown. "And that he simply wished to speak to you further. Must it be marriage-minded or mistress-minded and nothing in between?"

"You are so willing to assume the best of others," Lillian said with a sigh and a smile toward Gabby. "I admire it, even if I do think it a bit naïve at times."

She thought again of the seemingly honest apology Simon had made to her in the billiard room. That and the intense way he had looked at her while they spoke.

With a shrug, she said, "Perhaps you are correct, perhaps the new duke *isn't* nefariously plotting against me and my virtue. But either way, his interest, whatever its motive, puts me in a difficult position. He will likely watch my every move very carefully."

When she glanced over her shoulder, she found Gabby had sunk into a chair with a frown. "Yes. I hadn't thought of that."

"I tried to be dull and spiritless. Perhaps it was enough." Lillian sighed. "And the mention of my mother may lead to further investigation on his part. Certainly when he hears rumors of her suicide, that will end his curiosity."

"Lillian—"

She waved off her friend's sympathy. "I'm only being truthful, Gabby. It is a scandal most families want to avoid."

"And what if this man is different?" Gabby asked softly.

Lillian closed her eyes briefly. How many times had she fantasized about finding a man who *could* be different? Who could overlook a past that was entirely out of her control and want her regardless.

But Simon Crathorne was not that man. He *could*

not be. And if word of her mother's suicide did not make him pull away, it would only make her more wary. His rank would not allow him to overlook that past unless he had less than savory plans in mind for her.

"If those things do not deter him, I shall be forced to be openly rude to him."

Her friend barked out a laugh of derision. "Great God, Lillian, that is the most foolish thing I have ever heard!"

"Why?"

"Because if you are rude to one of the most important men in Society you will make not only him, but *everyone* watch your every move, if only for the gossip they can take back to London when the Season officially opens after the party!"

"Damn." Lillian sat down hard on her own chair and glared at her friend. "How I despise it when you are right."

Gabby laughed.

"But whatever shall I do? How do I make him leave off his pursuit if my attempts today do not force his hand?" Lillian held up her hands in silent plea.

A smile was her friend's reply. "I realize this is not your strong suit, dearest, but I think you will just have to be patient. Allow his interest to play out naturally."

"You mean do nothing at all?" Lillian said, pulling a face that left little doubt of her feelings on the subject.

Gabby shook her head. "Yes. Exactly. At the worst, you will come to know Simon a bit better."

Lillian couldn't help but shiver at that thought. She had never had such a strong physical reaction to a man immediately after meeting him. Even if he wasn't the son of a man she despised, she wasn't certain she would *want* to get to know him better. That kind of powerful connection seemed a bit . . . dangerous.

"Don't look at me that way," Gabby said with a scowl. "As much as you hate to admit it, if you find your way into Simon's confidence, you might learn information about him and his father. Things you would have had to search for on your own if you hadn't caught his eye. If Simon *was* party to his father's true character, a friendship with him could be lucrative."

Lillian bit her lip. Gabby was right, of course. And yet her friend's suggestion went against every fiber of her being. She had come here hoping to avoid as much contact as she could with Simon and the rest of the late duke's family. Forging a relationship with any of them would only complicate matters.

"And what is the best I can hope for if I simply allow his interest to play out naturally?" she asked.

Gabby shrugged. "He'll bore of you. If he does, he shall be just as happy that you are ignoring him and trying to fade into the background. You'll have more freedom to break free of the group and conduct whatever searches you think you must."

Lillian found her forehead wrinkling. Although she didn't want Simon's attention, the idea that he would simply bore of her wasn't exactly a pleasant one. She shoved the reaction aside.

"Yes. I suppose you're right," she admitted with a playful glare for her friend. "Patience may be an even greater virtue than usual in this situation. It cannot hurt to wait out the natural direction of his apparent interest."

Gabby nodded. "Very good, I'm glad you agree. And now I suppose we should ring for Maggie. We are expected downstairs for supper shortly and I am going to need extra help getting into my amethyst gown."

Lillian nodded and got up to ring the bell for the servant. Of course Gabby would want to look pretty tonight. There would be several eligible men in attendance besides the duke. And if Lillian could do nothing yet to pursue her own reasons for being here, at the very least she could make an attempt to help Gabriela catch the eye of someone perfect for her.

Even as she hoped Simon would find someone *else* who interested him.

* * *

It appeared that Simon's mother had taken the same side as Rhys had when it came to the subject of Miss Lillian Mayhew, for she had been placed frustratingly far away from him at supper. His only consolation was that she had been seated between the enormously fat and married Squire Martin and the extremely talkative Lady Swanlea, so it wasn't as if she was being pursued by some of the handsome and eligible dinner guests.

Of course, Lillian never looked in his direction, either. It was a strange thing. He had felt her interest when they met, but then she had gone cold after their introduction. The same had happened in the library. She had been warm, but then pushed him away after she mentioned her mother's death. Now it was as if he wasn't even in the room.

He couldn't read Miss Mayhew, and it made her all the more interesting to him.

He sighed as the young woman beside him began to talk to him at an alarmingly fast rate about the advantages of a high-flyer phaeton over a caned whiskey gig. Obviously someone had told her a man would be impressed by her interest in racing vehicles. Unfortunately, that same person *hadn't* told her that those sorts of things held very little interest to *him*.

He examined her face as she spoke. She was a fetching thing, there was no denying that. Lady . . .

Amanda, he thought it was. She was the daughter of someone important, obviously, for his mother had put her and her very quiet mother right at his elbow. A marquis, perhaps it was?

At any rate, she was very pretty. And yet there was no spark that caught his interest. No light of intelligence in her eyes, no hint of quick wit and laughter about her mouth. She was just so very . . . ordinary. Another rich girl, another titled family, they were all alike.

Truth be told, he had never found himself particularly interested in their ilk. Despite his upbringing, the kind of *life* a woman like that represented didn't appeal to him. Even with all the time his father had spent here when he wasn't in parliamentary session, the opulence of this home was more his mother's style than his father's. Almost as if she had designed it to spite him.

Sometimes when Simon looked at it, he felt uncomfortable.

In fact, the only place he had ever felt fully at home was in the House of Lords. He'd been an active member of the Parliament from the first moment he was old enough to take a seat. He had watched in awe as his father fought for reform there. And he looked forward to doing the same.

The rest of being a duke . . . well, he would do it, of course. But it wasn't innate to him and he wondered if it ever would be.

"Your Grace?"

He started as he turned toward Lady Anne Danvers, Rhys's future bride, who had arrived just a few hours before. He smiled at her, and it was genuine. He liked Anne, not for her appropriateness as a lady, which Rhys forever waxed on about, but for her genuineness. He always knew where he stood with Anne, and that honesty, coupled with her kindness, appealed to him greatly. He had long considered her a friend.

"I am sorry, Lady Anne, forgive my rudeness."

He cast a quick glance at the young woman on his opposite side. She was now chattering at her mother, who was still chewing, staring straight ahead, as if she had mastered the ability to block out the constant stream of noise. He shuddered. If he married Lady Amanda, he wondered if he would eventually do the same.

"It's no bother," Anne reassured him softly. She smiled at Lady Amanda and then dropped her voice to a whisper. "She does prattle on, doesn't she?"

He stifled a laugh into his napkin, but did not rise to the bait and reply.

"Actually, I wanted to inquire after *you*," Anne said. "You seem distracted. Are you well?"

He looked at her once more. Yes, Anne was everything perfect in a bride, and yet she was still likable and intelligent. Sometimes Rhys's intended was Simon's only lifeline that he could find both suitability and happiness in the same woman.

In reality, he simply didn't want to end up in a marriage like the one between his parents. His mother and father had been separate people, with a strange current of animosity forever coursing below the surface, though they were never so common as to hash it out where others could gawk at their discord.

If it had taught Simon anything, it was that he needed more than just "appropriateness" when it came to a woman he would spend the rest of his life with. The woman who would raise his children and stand beside him at events, not to mention bear witness to his most private moments. His greatest hope was that he might find a wife who inspired a sense of connection, and perhaps, if he was lucky, passion.

"Your Grace?" Anne pressed, her brow furrowing.

Simon shook off his thoughts and smiled. "I'm fine," he said. "Thank you. Just distracted by the details of this gathering, I suppose."

"Well, there is much to consider. Rhys tells me you are searching for a bride amongst the ladies. This time in earnest." Anne leaned closer, conspiratorial. "Is there one who has caught your eye?"

He couldn't help but laugh, as her question to

him was the same as Rhys's earlier in the day. He found his gaze flitting down the table to Lillian. For the first time since they had been seated for supper, she was staring back at him, eyes slightly narrowed as if she was looking at something she didn't particularly care for.

She blushed as she realized he was staring at her and turned her face away.

"She is very pretty," Anne said.

Simon blinked as he returned his attention to his companion. "Who?"

Anne stifled a laugh. "*Miss Mayhew.*"

Simon looked at her with a sheepish shrug. "Rhys has already regaled me with reasons why she would never be an appropriate bride."

Anne continued to smile, but Simon thought he saw a brief flash of strong emotions in her green eyes. Anger, perhaps, mixed with a deep sadness he had never seen in her normally steady and happy face. Then it was gone. She picked up her fork and tapped it against the vegetables on her plate without looking at him.

"You and Rhys are like brothers, I know you trust him and have faith in his judgment." She looked up. "As you should in many things, for he is intelligent and can offer very good advice. But when it comes to matters of the heart . . ."

She trailed off with a heavy sigh before she continued.

"Don't listen to him. He can be enormously stupid about them."

Simon blinked in surprise. He had never heard Anne come even close to making a disparaging remark about Rhys. He wasn't sure how to respond to it now. He opened his mouth, but she glanced up with a smile, as if the conversation had never happened, and motioned to the man seated to her right.

"I know you were interested in the plight of the child workers, Your Grace. Did you know that Lord Hartvale here has been putting together information about just that issue?"

Simon nodded as the man began to speak about a topic he was truly passionate about. But even as he listened to Lord Hartvale, he found himself looking down the table at Lillian.

Anne was right. When it came to love or marriage, he and Rhys had opposing views on the subject. And since he would only have one chance at happiness with a bride, he would be foolish not to pursue the first strong interest he had felt toward a woman in a long time.

After all, he had two long weeks to get to know Miss Mayhew. Perhaps during that time he would uncover why she glared daggers into his chest, even as she blushed when he smiled in her direction.

Chapter 4

The last thing I wish to do is picnic. It isn't why I'm here," Lillian said with a groan as she watched Maggie tie the sash on Gabby's gown. After the maid was finished, she gave both girls a quick curtsy and exited the chamber.

Her friend turned on her. "You must be more careful, Lillian, the servants do talk below stairs, you know."

Lillian snorted out laughter. "Good, perhaps I can show them whatever evidence I uncover about Roger Crathorne and let *them* talk. Their gossip is how the *ton* hears half their news."

"Lillian . . ." Gabby's tone was a warning.

"Very well," she said through clenched teeth. "I understand your concerns. Still, I have no wish to tromp through the estate and spend an afternoon listening to the woman coo over Simon and purr over his father's memory. It was ridiculous enough at supper last night. Even his best friend's fiancée was laughing at every word Simon said like he was the most interesting man in the country."

She folded her arms as an unbidden image of the very pretty Lady Anne Danvers entered her mind. The young woman had a beautiful smile, and Simon had seemed quite engrossed in their conversation.

Her friend's eyebrows both lifted gently. "I see."

The two words hung heavily between them and Lillian stared at her friend in confusion. Whatever did *that* tone mean?

Finally Gabby shrugged one shoulder. "Well, if you do not wish to attend, I could give your excuses. A slight headache should free you from any obligation to join us."

Lillian lifted her fingers to her brow dramatically. "I *do* feel a twinge of pain."

Gabby laughed before she reached out and squeezed Lillian's arm. "Very well. I shall make the explanations. But will you promise me one thing?"

Lillian tilted her head. "Yes?"

"If you suddenly recover from your ache and decide to search the house . . ."

Lillian laughed, for it seemed Gabby knew her far too well for her own good.

Gabby continued, "Be careful. Yesterday the

servants were busy and the guests resting. That was as quiet as this house will likely ever be, and yet you were still discovered by Lord Billingham. Once the guests are gone today, the household servants will be more alert to someone roaming the halls. I wouldn't want to see you get yourself into trouble."

Lillian nodded. Her friend was only voicing the worries she herself felt. When the opportunity had arisen for her to come here and search, she hadn't really thought through what that would entail, entirely. She had no experience in intrigue, and in actuality she wasn't certain she *could* find what she sought.

"I will be very careful," she promised. The last thing she needed was for someone to mistake her search for an attempt at robbery or some such nonsense.

"I must go down now. Wait at least a quarter of an hour before you start on whatever your plans are." With a quick kiss on Lillian's cheek, Gabby hurried from the room.

Lillian moved to the small sitting room that was part of their chamber and sank into a chair beside the fire, so she could watch the time tick by on a clock that sat on the mantel. It seemed to take an age for each moment to pass.

Finally she threw herself from the chair and

began to pace restlessly, moving up and down the chamber in long strides as she cast glances at the clock every few moments.

Ten minutes had gone by since Gabby departed. Lillian had promised to wait a quarter of an hour before she started on her search, but it had been a while since she heard any of the guests buzzing about. Surely they were gone and she was safe.

And the patience Gabby kept encouraging had never been her strong suit. She rushed to the door and had just begun to turn the knob when there was a loud rapping on the other side. Out of pure instinct, she jerked the barrier open and found herself face to face with a very surprised-looking Simon Crathorne.

"Miss Mayhew," he said, staggering back a step. "That was very smart of you, were you awaiting my arrival?"

He grinned, but Lillian didn't return the expression. What was he *doing* here?

"Of course not," she snapped, then tempered her tone. "I thought you had already departed for the picnic."

He cocked his head slightly. "I was told you were unwell."

Lillian took a step back. Was Simon actually concerned for her? That was ridiculous! He barely knew her, and it wasn't as if she was an important guest. From the way his mother had shot daggers at her last night, she wasn't even a *wanted* one.

He had to care about all those things, so why did he continue to pursue her?

"There was no need for you to check on me," Lillian said, wrinkling her brow.

"I wanted to."

With those three simple words, Lillian was completely set on her head. Once again, she was struck by how genuine he seemed despite all her misgivings about him.

She stared at him blankly, only managing to squeak out, "Oh." She shook away her shock. "Well, I hope you did not hold up the party for me. It is only a headache, nothing to worry yourself about."

He shrugged, but made no move to turn away. "The party went ahead with my mother and the Duke of Waverly. I am to join them after I'm certain of your health." He looked at her a little more closely. "But I could easily stay with you. I don't know if I can enjoy myself when one of my guests is unwell."

She folded her arms. Well, that would certainly ruin all her plans. "Stay with me in my chamber? Goodness, Your Grace, you do know how to ruin a girl's reputation."

A little high color stained his cheeks, and momentarily there was a flash of something dark and sensual in his eyes, but then he smiled again, that infectious expression that she hated herself for wanting to return.

"Not in your chamber, of course. That would be entirely inappropriate."

His response belied her assumption that he was after her virtue. Wouldn't a true cad jump at the chance to seduce her while everyone was away?

She looked at him evenly. "So you are suggesting that I come downstairs and sit with you, despite my headache?"

His eyes narrowed, but there was no malice in them. Just a challenging light that matched her own. From the sparkle in his expression, he enjoyed sparring with her. Unfortunately . . . she felt the same way.

"Well, that wouldn't really make sense, either," he admitted with a low chuckle that seemed to reverberate in her very blood.

"So you would like to go downstairs and sit, while I stay here and rest?" she asked, unable to suppress a small smile. "You are correct, Your Grace, I'm sure that will make the pain go away."

"I see that my exalted title inspires no respect in you," he said with another deep chuckle.

She stiffened at the reminder of that title, but managed to maintain her smile. "None at all, my lord."

"Still, even if I only sit downstairs while you convalesce, at least I'll know that I didn't abandon one of my lovely guests in her time of trial."

Lillian rolled her eyes. It seemed he could not be deterred. And yet if he stayed here, she could make no search and would only pace around her room, feeling his presence like a heavy cloak.

"Truth be told, I'm starting to feel a bit better," she said with a small sigh. "Perhaps it would do me some good to take a walk in the sunshine and breathe fresh air."

"Are you certain?" he asked, and that genuine concern that so troubled her lit his eyes again.

She nodded. "Quite."

He cocked his head to examine her for a long moment and then said, "Well, then I think that is a very good idea. The group is likely moving slowly to accommodate some of the older chaperones, so we should be able to catch up quickly enough."

Lillian nodded. "Very well."

And as she slipped into the hallway at his side, she tried to tell herself that she had no choice but to join him. She also tried to tell herself that a little thrill that he wanted so much for her to do so did not work through her.

When Simon offered his arm, Lillian pretended she didn't see it. It was obvious it was pretended because her gaze flitted very pointedly toward him before she darted it away and began to walk down the hallway toward the staircase.

He cocked his head as he lengthened his stride to catch her. There was that dichotomy again. Their conversation a moment before had been thick with smart banter and he had greatly enjoyed engaging with her. It seemed she had felt the same, but now she refused to touch him. He might explain that as missish shyness, if he hadn't felt a sense that dislike and interest were warring within her.

He wondered which one would win in the end and if he would ever determine the cause for her reticence.

Not today, likely, so he put the thought out of his mind. They walked down the stairs and out the front door, where he led her down the winding drive and finally off the path through the green countryside.

Once they had walked a little while, Lillian seemed to relax a fraction. She drew in a deep breath. He did the same, smelling the fresh combination of green grass and soft late spring breezes. After so many winter months in stuffy, cold, closed London, this respite was heaven.

It seemed the same was true for her, for her eyes fluttered shut for a brief moment and she let out a tiny sigh of pure pleasure that seemed to ricochet through his body. He shifted uncomfortably. Clearly he needed a woman if a mere sigh could inspire him to lust.

As if she sensed him looking at her, she cleared

her throat. "We have been lucky in the weather these last few days. The roads were dry and there isn't any mud despite everyone walking this way earlier today."

Simon almost laughed. It seemed she was determined to strike upon the dullest subject possible. She had done the same yesterday when she pretended a disinterest in books. Did she really think she could cover up her delight at his library or the obvious intelligence she possessed?

And did she do so to snare him or push him away?

"It is uncommonly good weather," he agreed. Before she could continue upon this tedious topic, he hurried to fill the gap in conversation. "I remember you saying you have a brother, Miss Mayhew. Younger, is he not?"

Apparently that was not a good subject, for her spine stiffened and her steps became jerky. After a long silence, she said, "Yes. My brother, Jack, is younger than I am."

"And where is he now?" he pressed, watching her reactions very carefully. She was like a porcupine, spines extended, making it clear she wanted him to stop, to go away, to be warned.

Her jaw worked like she was grinding her teeth. "London, Your Grace," she bit out. As he had a few moments earlier, she filled the small gap in conversation before he could ask more. "But what of your family? I'd be very interested to hear about them."

Simon cocked a brow. Rhys had mentioned that her younger brother was a wastrel, and it seemed that fact was discomforting to her. Still, he wished he could coax out any hint of confidence. Any tidbit of information that he did not have to wring out of her.

He sighed. Perhaps if he shared a bit about his own family, it would help her open up in the future. Give her some reason to have faith that he wasn't prying, but truly interested.

Certainly he had nothing to hide.

"I also have one sibling, although mine is an older sister, Viscountess Naomi Westford. She will join our party one week from now."

She nodded. "I've seen your sister at events, though we have never met formally. She is a very pretty woman."

He smiled. "Yes. Naomi was a diamond of the first water when she came out. The years have not stolen her beauty, but her kindness and charm are her greatest attributes. We have always been close."

Lillian turned her face as if to examine the waving blades of grass as they passed. "And of course *everyone* knew of your father."

His smile faded a fraction. "Yes. He was a great man and a most excellent father. I do miss him and I sometimes worry about the shoes I shall fill now that I am duke. I worry I won't live up to his example."

Her gaze darted to him. "I'm sure it will not be as difficult as you think."

He looked at her. There was a certain sharpness to her tone that almost seemed sarcastic, but she wasn't looking at him as they walked, so he dismissed his initial reaction.

"I hope you are correct. We shall see once the House of Lords begins meeting in a few weeks. I'm to give a speech on the opening session." He pushed away the twinge of nervousness that accompanied that thought.

"And what of your mother?" Lillian asked. "I've not yet had occasion to speak to her personally since our arrival."

Simon sped his step. Normally he would have been happy to change from the anxiety-inducing subject of his career in the House of Lords, but the topic of his mother was hardly a pleasant one.

"Ah, look," he said, relief washing over him as they crested a hill. "There are the others."

As they neared the group and he raised his hand to wave, the entire mass of heads turned to face them almost in unison. Simon flinched. In all his life, he had never grown fully accustomed to the attention his title brought.

It seemed Lillian was uncomfortable with the inspection as well, for she instantly took a long step away from him. Without looking into his eyes, she murmured, "Thank you for your concern today, Your Grace. And for walking me here. I see Lady Gabriela and our chaperone. I shall join them. Good afternoon."

Before he could speak to argue, agree, or say farewell, she darted away, practically sprinting from his side to join her companions. And as he joined the group himself, seeking out a spot beside Rhys and Anne, he couldn't help a small smile. Miss Lillian Mayhew was a fascinating creature indeed, and spending extra time with her today had done nothing to deter his interest in finding out more about her.

Lillian heaved a great sigh of relief as the party began to trudge its way back across the fields toward the Billingham manse in the distance. It had been a long and trying day, and the headache she had feigned earlier was beginning to become a reality.

"He watched you all afternoon," Gabby murmured at her side.

There was no need to clarify which *he* in the party her friend referred to. Simon was the only man whose stare had flitted to her on a regular basis. Sometimes he smiled, acknowledging that their eyes had met.

And sometimes he simply stared. Later in their

chamber, when she could speak freely about the day with her friend, Lillian would say that Simon's scrutiny made her uncomfortable. Or that she was angry that he was obviously as much of a lecher as his hated father.

But those statements would be untrue. Even though she tried to ignore it or judge it, every time Simon looked at her, she thrilled at his attentions. She felt his eyes on her even when she wasn't looking at him, and she quivered inside at the thought that he remained interested in her beyond the mere politeness of a host to his guest.

Self-directed disgust filled her. Was she so easily swayed by the attentions of a handsome man that she would forget the duty that brought her here? Her father's dying wish and her mother's honor had to be worth more than that.

The two of them fell behind the group a bit, and Gabby linked her arm through Lillian's. "Do you want to tell me more about it?"

"There is nothing to tell," Lillian said quietly, seeking out Simon in the group.

He was walking with one of the other young women and her chaperone. A strange tension made Lillian's stomach clench, but she refused to look away and acknowledge, even to herself, that she didn't like him turning his notice toward anyone else in the group.

"Of course there is something to tell," her friend

pressed. "He stayed behind specifically to check on you, somehow convinced you to come with him, and then you two walked alone down to the picnic site. *Something* of interest must have occurred in that time."

Lillian squeezed her eyes shut for a moment and tried to block out the memory of everything Gabby described. It was impossible, just as it had been all day. Those same thoughts had plagued her since she parted ways with Simon a few hours before. Thoughts of how entertaining it had been to tease him when he offered to stay behind and tend to her. Or how genuine his concern had seemed when he asked after her welfare.

But mostly she had spent the intervening time pondering his words about his family. She had been moved by his kind sentiments about his sister. Once she and her brother had been so close, and she missed Jack terribly.

Simon had also spoken highly of his father, which did not surprise her. That was the common opinion about the late duke, after all, that he was everything decent and good. But when Simon said those words, it seemed he truly believed them.

Which meant he was totally naïve about his father, and if she succeeded in revealing the truth, she would devastate him. *Or* it meant Simon was just as accomplished a liar as his father had been and was determined to keep up the charade that Roger Crathorne had been everything commendable.

Neither option pleased her overly much.

"It was the usual chatter," she said when she realized Gabby was waiting for her to speak. "Nothing of interest."

She didn't know why she was so reluctant to share her moments with Simon with her most-trusted best friend, but somehow it seemed wrong.

Ahead of her, Simon's mother, the Dowager Duchess of Billingham, made her way through the crowd toward her son. Lillian stared as the two women accompanying him moved away and the mother and son stepped aside from the moving group to the right of the path. They spoke for a brief moment, and then the dowager duchess walked away, leaving Simon to stare after her.

When he turned his face back into Lillian's view, she saw that his mouth was pinched with displeasure. She thought of her final question to him about his mother. At the time she asked, she'd thought his avoidance of the topic had to do with the fact that they'd found the picnicking group.

Now she wondered if there was something more to his hesitance to share information about his one living parent. She had yet to see any warmth between them since her arrival at the estate. In fact, the duchess spent little time conversing with Simon at all.

Interesting, indeed.

Suddenly Simon turned toward her and their gazes met. Heat suffused her cheeks at his focused stare, and she couldn't help but draw in a breath as his eyes darkened with emotions far different from the troubled ones reflected there after his discussion with his mother.

Reluctantly she glanced away, but felt his eyes on her for several more seconds before he fell back in with the crowd and they reached the house.

"Nothing at all interesting, eh?" Gabby whispered as they entered the foyer and a servant took their wraps. "It seems to me that if you don't define that significant glance you just shared as *interesting*, you may not be familiar with the meaning of the word."

But as her chuckling friend followed the ladies of the group up the stairs, Lillian covered her eyes. The last thing in the world she wanted was any more *interesting* encounters with Simon Crathorne.

And yet it seemed they were destined to occur.

Chapter 5

Simon looked around the spacious room that was his father's office. With a shake of his head, he corrected himself. *His* office. This was his space now. Or at least it would be once he managed to wade his way through the towering mounds of paperwork and correspondence his father had left behind.

The late duke had been a fastidious man in all ways but this. He had never been able to throw away a paper in his life and kept meticulous notes about anything he thought important. Which was an excellent thing when it came to his thoughts and recollections about an important piece of legislation or letters pertaining to an historic event.

But not so much so when the notes were about the birthing of foals on another estate or the letters were from his father's peculiar and long dead aunt Paulette, who rambled on about her sewing group and the scandal of men who no longer wore wigs and buckled slippers.

Yet both kinds of paperwork were here, stacked haphazardly across the desk, in piles behind the chair, teetering on the bookcases.

And part of Simon's duty, before he left for London, was to sort through these things and determine what to do with it all. He was actually thinking of putting together a memoir of his father's life, and he was certain some items in this room would be of great use for that purpose when the time came.

He would have liked to dive into the business of sorting straightaway since there were duties as host he would have to perform in a few hours, but he couldn't. The previous day after the picnic his mother had requested . . . well, rather *demanded* an audience with him this morning. So he awaited her before he moved to the piles.

As if on cue, the door to the office opened and his mother stepped in. She shut the door behind her and looked around with a sniff.

Once she had been considered a flawless beauty. Stories still circulated about her coming-out year and how men had fought over a chance to simply touch her hand. But Roger Crathorne, who would soon become the eleventh Duke of Billingham, had staked his claim to her early, and everyone knew that Crathorne always got what he wanted one way or another.

Simon sighed as he thought of how their relationship had deteriorated. He looked at his mother. There was no denying she was still quite lovely. Her dark hair had only a hint of gray and her skin remained smooth and blemished by only a few wrinkles.

And yet there was something lacking in her. Her brown eyes were never very happy, and bitterness made her lips flat and harsh. When Simon looked at her, he was put to mind of every time she had turned away from him. Every time she had stared at him with unmasked disdain.

He had never determined what he'd done to invoke such ire from her. His father had always shrugged it off as if the question wasn't important, though the late duke had certainly showered Simon with enough love and affection that Simon knew his father somehow recognized the deep void her disinterest created.

"How many times I told him that his office was a disgrace," she said, snapping Simon from unpleasant memories.

He forced an indulgent smile. "It is a mess. But I'll clean it up somehow."

Her gaze jerked to his unexpectedly and held there for far longer than she normally looked.

"Yes. I expect you will," she said softly.

"Is that what you wished to speak to me about this morning?" he pressed, suddenly uncomfortable beneath her deeper examination. "Are there items you'd like to inspect yourself or keep as mementos?"

She shook her head and paced away from him. "Nothing. I have no interest in his things."

Simon wasn't surprised by her answer. In truth, he blamed his mother more than his father for the breach between his parents. The late duke had always been patient and kind toward her even in the face of her contempt. Still she shunned her husband, just as she shunned Simon. Nothing was good enough for her.

"No, your father is not the reason I wished to speak to you." His mother turned with folded arms. "It is about that girl, Simon."

He blinked. He had expected to avoid this conversation until at least after the welcome ball that was scheduled for the next evening. His interest in Miss Mayhew must have been obvious indeed, for his mother to broach the subject so early.

"Girl, Mother? Which one, there are quite a few here, you know."

He supposed his response was childishly purposeful baiting, but there were times when her coldness stung. If she didn't care about his life, why dictate it?

Her eyes narrowed. "Please do not play games with me. I don't appreciate, nor have time for it. You know I am talking about Lillian Mayhew."

"I see."

"And so do I," she said, her head tilting. "The way you looked at her all day yesterday during the picnic made it clear you have some interest in her."

He shrugged, unwilling to lie, but also unwilling to discuss the subject until forced.

"And even if I hadn't seen it, the Duke of Waverly brought it to my attention himself." His mother's eyes lit with some kind of petty triumph.

Simon sighed. Rhys knew how uncomfortable his relationship with the dowager duchess was. His friend would have to be highly concerned to bring her into the discussion about the worthiness of potential brides.

He leaned against the desk, barely managing not to tip over any of the piles of paperwork.

"Is this not why the ladies are here, Mother?" he asked, controlling his tone carefully. "You've made it abundantly clear that now that I have ascended in title, I have a responsibility to the family name to marry and produce heirs as quickly as I can. This party serves some part in that purpose, does it not? If I have an interest in one of the women here, should you not be delighted?"

His mother moved on him a few steps. "Great

God, Simon! She wasn't even invited in the first place. It is only out of respect for the specific wishes of Lady Gabriela's father, the Earl of Watsenvale, that I agreed to allow her to attend at all."

"How charitable of you," he murmured.

She pretended not to hear his interruption, though by the angry twitch of her lips, he was certain she had.

"She is entirely inappropriate in every way. You must see that."

He shook his head as he thought of the spark in Lillian's gaze and the fascinating dichotomy in her actions, not to mention the arousing perfection of her countenance and soft body.

"I'm sorry, Mother, but I don't see it. I find her both intelligent and interesting."

"As if such things matter when making a match!" his mother burst out in exasperation. "Her father was untitled, and had no great fortune to leave her as a dowry. Even if he had, their family connections are questionable! Her brother . . ."

"Rhys mentioned he was a bit wild," Simon said with a shrug. "But few men of his age are not. I refuse to judge him simply because he is overindulging his senses at present."

"Then think of her mother! The rumors, Simon, the implication that she might have taken her own life . . . those things are unconscionable!" She held up her hands. "I forbid a match between you. I cannot support it!"

Simon almost laughed. He wondered if she knew that her distaste for Lillian only made the girl all the more alluring to him. Certainly it did not deter him.

He rose from his perch against the desk and moved forward. His mother held her ground, but he could see she wished to step back.

"You forget, madam," he said softly, "that I am no longer a reticent child who you can control with the flick of your wrist. I am the duke now, whether you like that fact or not. What I do, who I pursue, and where I go . . . those things are my affair and mine alone."

Her eyes widened and her nostrils flared with rage that was so powerful when it flashed through her eyes that it took Simon off guard. But then it was gone.

"Yes. I suppose that is true," she said through clenched teeth.

He stepped away. "However, I do appreciate your concern. I shall certainly take your uneasiness into account."

"Thank you," she ground out.

He tilted his head. "Will that be all?"

His mother jerked away from him toward the door. "Yes. Good day."

And then she was gone. Simon let out a sigh. His entire life he had been trying to please the woman, but he'd learned years ago that it was a losing battle. Certainly he wasn't going to base his choice in bride or friend or lover on what she said was right or true.

No, in matters of the heart, he was going to listen to his own instincts and no one else's.

Croquet had never been a strength of Lillian's, no matter what kind of rules the game followed. She always whacked the ball far too strenuously. It was no surprise to her, then, that she was put out early in the second round of the tournament-style game arranged for entertainment that day and forced to watch the rest of the match from the sidelines.

It wasn't as if she minded. She didn't want to play. She could learn much more when observing from outside to see how everyone interacted. So much personality was revealed by chance in a game.

Gabby was excellent, of course. It seemed there was little she could not do, and Lillian couldn't help but smile at her friend's enthusiasm and laughter. She was equally pleased to note her friend had caught the gaze of a few gentlemen in attendance.

The others who remained in the game had varying levels of play. She noticed that Lady Philippa, an earl's daughter, pretended to lose her balance every time she shot because she was standing next to Simon and he would right her when she went off kilter.

The daughter of a marquis, Lady Theresa, was hitting such poor shots that Lillian couldn't believe they weren't purposeful. It appeared the foolish chit didn't wish to outperform Simon or any of the other eligible men; after all she had fared just fine in the first round that had matched her against the other ladies of their party.

Lady Anne, the Duke of Waverly's fiancée, played just the opposite. She was careful and steady in her play, but each time she hit a perfect shot, Lillian noticed her eyes lit up with pure triumph. She *almost* liked Lady Anne for that.

And then there was Simon. He calculated his every move carefully, never executing a shot with anything less than the perfect pressure or exact placement. He was always in control, always calm.

He moved in to make his next play and leaned over the ball to line up his mallet for the shot. But suddenly his eyes lifted and she found him looking at her. Staring, really, was the word for it. He gave her a half smile and then he cracked the ball.

It spun out of bounds, smashing through low brush until it came to rest out of sight.

"Lost ball," he called out with feigned exasperation. "By our tournament rules, it appears I am out of the game."

Lillian's jaw dropped open in shock, and it seemed she was not alone in her reaction. A few of the young women still playing looked genuinely distressed, the Duke of Waverly hardly acknowledged the statement, and Lady Anne rolled her eyes slightly.

Simon handed off his mallet to another player and began across the lawn toward her with purpose in his expression. Lillian stiffened. Just as had occurred the day before when they entered the picnic together, his obvious attention drew every eye on the lawn toward her. And many of them were not approving.

The blasted man was making her the center of attention and ruining everything!

And yet her heart leapt as he stopped before her with a smile.

"Do you mind if I join you, Miss Mayhew?" he asked, then stepped in beside her without awaiting her answer.

She cocked an eyebrow as she looked him up and down. "If you truly missed your shot by chance, I shall eat my bonnet."

He barked out surprised laughter, and his strange green eyes twinkled in a way that was quite mesmerizing. Lillian had to force herself to look somewhere else.

"The whole bonnet?" he asked, leaning back as if he was examining the hat perched on her head. "Including the feather?"

"*Especially* the feather," she retorted with a smile she had not bidden.

She pressed her lips together in frustration the moment she had spoken. It seemed she was too willing to abandon her plans the moment Simon turned his charm her way. Gabby said she had to allow his interest to play out, but that didn't mean she should *like* the way he looked at her or smiled at her.

"Well, I would not want to be the cause of your indigestion," Simon said with a shrug. "Therefore, I concede I missed my final shot on purpose."

"Whatever for?" Lillian asked. "You were doing quite well."

"I was more interested in speaking to a young lady who is apparently one of the worst croquet players to ever pick up a mallet."

He tilted his head, and though his words were teasing there was a heat in his stare that made Lillian's very blood tingle and all her objections to his attentions fade away. She swallowed hard.

"That would be *you*, by the way, Miss Mayhew," he whispered.

"You are very rude. I am certainly not the worst croquet player I know." She tried to maintain a light tone, but her voice was suddenly husky.

His eyes widened. "You know worse? Good Lord." His arm came out to fill the space between them and hovered there. "You must tell me more about this crime against sport and nature. Perhaps while we take a turn about the gardens?"

Again, Lillian swallowed. It seemed her body was determined to war with her mind; for she found herself leaning toward Simon, even as her brain screamed at her that he was the son of a man she hated.

But how could she refuse him with everyone watching? And even if they were pretending not to, they were *all* watching. Resistance could only bring trouble. In truth there was little choice in the matter.

Suppressing a sigh, she slipped her fingers through the crook of his elbow and allowed him to lead her away from the croquet field into the garden, which was edged by a shrubbery that came up to her waist.

"And now I have another confession to make," Simon said as they walked slowly down the path through beautiful flowers and carefully trimmed bushes.

"And what is that, Your Grace?" she asked, her mouth suddenly dry.

"I do not wish to talk about croquet," he said with a light laugh. "Unless that is a true passion of yours."

She stopped in the middle of the pathway and glided her hand away from him. It felt warm as she clutched it to her breast.

"Your Grace, forgive my impertinence, but why in the world do you insist upon pursuing *me*?" she burst out. Immediately she wished to snatch the words back or recall the moment.

Years of rejection rose to the forefront of her mind. Men who had seemed interested, but ultimately pushed her aside when they uncovered the rumors of her past. Simon had to know about her mother by now. Someone certainly must have *let* him know if only to discourage him. And yet he continued down this unexpected and unwanted course.

Simon looked at her long and hard before he spoke, but his expression was not one of disappointment or even shock. He seemed to be truly considering her question before he said, "Because, Miss Mayhew, unlike the other women who have gathered here, you interest me. And truth be told, you confuse me. Not many people manage that feat."

"Confuse you?" Lillian repeated.

He nodded. "One moment you are playful, the next you seem determined to get as far away from me as humanly possible. I saw a love of books reflected in your eyes when you stumbled upon my library, but you pretended disinterest when I asked you about it. I don't know what to think of you or how to read you and I like that. I *like* the uncertainty."

Lillian blinked. His reply was entirely unexpected. She didn't think any man had ever been so straightforward with her. Most danced around with pretty words and never really gave an answer. But this . . . *this* was an answer.

"Not to mention the fact that you are quite beautiful, Miss Mayhew," he continued, and now he took a small step closer. "Lillian."

She was suddenly aware of how tall he was. And that he smelled faintly of pine, as if he spent a great deal of time outside in the fresh air. She found herself breathing him in subtly. But then she shook her head and backed away, desperate to break the strange spell he had woven around her with pretty words and heated glances.

"There are at least a dozen beautiful women here, Simon." She flushed as she realized her slip. It seemed her private use of his given name had instilled bad habits in her. "Your Grace."

But a light of triumph had already brightened his eyes. Her use of his name was only encouragement to him.

She hastened to add something else, to counteract her inappropriate statement with a fact that would crush his interest.

"Those other women are far more appropriate than I am, as well," she finally whispered. "If you are on this path to court me, I would bring nothing to you, Your Grace. No money, no alliance with a powerful family, in fact, my connections would bring you down in the estimation of some. I did not come here to pursue that kind of connection to you; I have no illusions that I shall marry, perhaps at all."

He smiled again, but this time there was a gentleness to it. "All that you say may be true. However, I find that I don't really care that much. I do find you interesting, Lillian, whether you like it or not, whether you expected it or not. And since I have the power and the access and the time, I intend to pursue my interest."

Lillian's lips parted as he moved even closer. She felt his body heat now, suffusing her fine linen gown, warming her beneath in a way that suggested naked skin and writhing bodies. With a start, she turned away, but he caught her wrist and held her steady.

"You are a riddle I intend to solve," he whispered, his gaze holding hers.

Before she could find her voice to reply, there was the sound of a throat clearing from behind her. Lillian shook off his hand and turned to find the dowager duchess, Lady Billingham, standing with her arms folded, staring at them. Staring at Simon was actually more accurate. She did not spare Lillian so much as a glance.

"You are neglecting your guests, Your Grace," she said, her tone chilly. "Why don't you join us?"

Lillian thought she heard just the faintest sigh from Simon before he moved forward. "Yes, Mother."

As his mother left the garden, Simon turned back to her. "Will you return with us?"

She shook her head. "No. I'd like to remain in the garden for a few moments."

He smiled. "Good. I hope you shall find something interesting to consider."

She watched his retreating back for a moment with a silent curse. Because of him, all she would think about for some time was the feel of his fingers around her wrist, of the sound of his words while he stated his intention to pursue her, and of the way he had looked at her with such heat that it had warmed her to her very toes.

All she would think about was him.

Chapter 6

The next evening, as she readied herself for the welcome ball, Lillian found her thoughts returning again and again to Simon and their encounter in the garden. She had tried to forget it, ignore it, even curse it, but it leapt to the forefront of her mind despite all attempts to squelch the memory.

"You are thinking of him again," Gabby said as she fastened the clasp of a pretty string of pearls around Lillian's neck.

Lillian's lips thinned. She could only hope she would not be so transparent to Simon.

"A fact I despise myself for, I assure you," she huffed as she examined herself in the mirror.

Although her gown was not as lavish as her friend's, it was pretty enough. She wouldn't look like anyone's poor relation, at least.

Not that it mattered. *She* wasn't here for courting.

"He was watching you at supper last night."

Lillian let her eyes squeeze shut. "At least we have not yet been seated beside each other. I cannot imagine what would happen then. But yes, I noticed he was watching me. And again at breakfast this morning."

Gabby got up from her seat and smiled. "I don't know, Lillian. I think it's rather romantic that he would so honestly declare his interest in you."

Lillian frowned. "I suppose under normal circumstances I might agree. I have always appreciated straightforward individuals. But these are not normal circumstances and Simon is not a 'normal' person. He is the son of a man I hate more than any other. And my father's dying wish was that our family have vengeance. I have no choice but to continue on that course. I certainly cannot cease simply because I find the man attractive. My mother deserves better. She deserves for the world to know that her attacker was not a good man."

"Yes," her friend said softly. "There is that."

Lillian stiffened as guilt bubbled up to the surface of her consciousness. She pushed it away by adding, "Besides, given his upbringing and his father, I rather doubt that he is being true."

"What do you mean?" Gabby's eyebrows knit together.

"His father was able to hide his real nature from the world. How can I take Simon at face value knowing that Roger Crathorne may have taught him some valuable lessons on the manipulation of women?"

"And you think he has been practicing those 'lessons' on you since your arrival? That nothing he has demonstrated or expressed has been genuine?"

Certainly the heated expression in Simon's eyes had seemed sincere and his words appeared earnest, but who knew?

"Perhaps he does *want* me, maybe because I am so very wrong for him. But does that mean he has any interest in me beyond getting me to his bed?" Lillian shrugged and tried to ignore the warmth that spread through her at the thought. "Well, that is another issue entirely."

Gabby blushed, and Lillian wished she could take back her blunt words. She sometimes forgot that aside from being younger, her friend was also far more innocent and sheltered.

"None of this really matters," Lillian said with a sigh. "For I have no interest in the man beyond what I can uncover about his father through him. Whatever the nature of his interest, I do not return it. I cannot even if I wished to. It would be a betrayal of my family."

Her friend looked at her as if she didn't quite believe it, but didn't argue. Instead, she glanced at the clock. "Oh my, it is time to assemble for the ball. Are you ready?"

Lillian took one last glance at herself in the mirror. She was presentable, but not flashy. Perfect to blend in, if Simon would simply allow her to do so.

And yet, as she followed Gabby from the room, she couldn't help but wish that she possessed a gown as pretty as her friend's. Something that would make her feel beautiful. Something that would erase, at least for a few hours, her true purpose in being here and allow her to pretend that she was just another girl spinning around the dance floor.

One who had caught the eye of the most eligible man in England, if only for a moment.

The ball was in full swing, and Lillian couldn't help but congratulate herself. In the past hour she had managed to avoid any direct contact with Simon. In fact, aside from a few pointed glances in her direction, he seemed to have forgotten her entirely. He was dancing with other women and chatting with his guests, utterly engrossed in his duties.

"You seem troubled," Gabby said, shooting a side glance toward her aunt Isabel. The older woman was standing just beside them, but she appeared completely oblivious to their conversation.

"Oh no, of course not," Lillian hastened to say. "I was actually musing on how lucky it is that Simon seems to have lost interest in me entirely. He has not so much as looked at me in over an hour."

Her friend's eyebrow arched. "I see."

Lillian's eyes narrowed. She didn't like her friend's tone and was about to say so when the dowager duchess approached from across the room and came to stop at their group.

"Good evening," Lady Billingham said, her voice as chilly as the brief glance she spared their group. "I trust you are all enjoying yourselves tonight."

Gabby nodded. "Oh yes, Your Grace. It is a lovely ball."

"Hmmm." Dismissing Gabby with a turn of her head, the duchess focused her attention on Lillian.

Normally she wasn't affected by the perusal of others. She had grown accustomed to the stares and shakes of the head that had followed her since her mother's death.

But Lady Billingham was a different beast entirely. When she looked at Lillian, a desire to turn away rose up in her. She wanted to run. Or at least hide from the dismissive glance of a woman who clearly had nothing for her but utter disdain.

"I would like a moment of your time, Miss Mayhew."

Lady Billingham's tone could be read as nothing but an order, and since Lillian had no good reason to refuse, she found herself nodding.

"Of course, my lady."

The duchess motioned her to follow and Lillian did, moving into a quiet corner of the room where no one stood. When the lady turned on Lillian slowly, she pierced her with another of those cold stares.

"Miss Mayhew, surely you understand that the only reason you were invited here is that Lord Watsenvale asked for that boon himself."

Lillian flinched. Her Ladyship was as direct as her son, although it did give her a small satisfaction that the duchess had no idea of Gabby's forgery of the letter from her father. It seemed her friend had been right to do so.

"Well, I thank you for including me, and I thank the earl for asking the favor," Lillian replied, drawing calming breaths before and after she spoke. If she behaved as if she was afraid, she had no doubt a woman like Lady Billingham would strike like a cobra.

A sniff was the other woman's reply. "Yes, well, I hope you don't take my charity for any other kind of acceptance. You are obviously well-aware that the new duke is looking for a bride, and that this gathering is a way to introduce him to *suitable* young ladies."

Lillian's heart throbbed. "Of which I am not."

"I see we understand each other." The duchess smiled, but it was very thin. "Miss Mayhew, I certainly understand your desire to elevate yourself. One could even admire your gall at making the attempt to snare a duke, if only it weren't such an appalling endeavor."

Lillian gasped, her hands coming up to clench in front of her chest. Her cheeks burned and her every limb trembled. "My lady, I assure you I am in no way trying to snare a duke."

"Are you not?" The duchess looked at her up and down. "If that is true, then you may forget what I have said. However, since it appears you are lying, I will reiterate. Simon *shall* marry someone appropriate, Miss Mayhew. I hope you won't forget yourself simply because you've shared some time with him. Or allow his charm to make you think he could truly overlook your more . . . *distasteful* qualities."

As Lillian stared, silenced by humiliation and anger, the duchess stepped back. "Now if you will excuse me, I have many *important* guests to attend to. Good evening."

Apparently she did not expect an answer, for she stalked away. Lillian was just as happy, for she could not have formulated a response if her life depended upon it.

It wasn't as if the woman had said anything that Lillian hadn't heard before. Her standing in Society had never been an exalted one. Her father had no title and a very small amount of money, but he did have a good family bloodline, so they had been included in many invitations. During her first few

Seasons, Lillian had even garnered some interest from men who did not need to marry for fortune. She had held out hope she might marry a man she liked and could love.

Those dreams had died five years ago when her mother took her own life. As hard as the family tried to cover up that fact, the truth had been impossible to keep hidden. Rumor and fact had leaked out, whispered in drawing rooms and back halls by servant and master alike.

Since then Lillian had seen Society change toward their family. They had still been invited, of course, but watched. Murmured about. The men who had once shown her interest slowly moved away.

Eventually Lillian had given up the hope of marrying someone within that circle. And she had told herself their words didn't hurt.

And yet tonight, standing in the corner of a crowded ballroom, Lady Billingham had managed to ferret out every wound Lillian had ever had, and she felt all the pain keenly, as if those past pains had just happened all over again.

What right did the woman have to tell Lillian that she wasn't worthy? Her own husband had been a monster masquerading as a paragon of virtue.

Lillian lifted her chin. When the truth came out about the late duke, then Lady Billingham would regret her words. She would feel their sting fall back on her and her family. For a moment, Lillian reveled in that thought, but then she sighed.

When the moment came, she knew it wouldn't erase this feeling of anger and sadness and humiliation. It wouldn't change what had happened to her mother, or bring her back to Lillian and Jack. But at least she could feel as though she had fulfilled her father's final wish. At least she would know that her mother's attacker would no longer be seen as a man to be honored and revered.

Suddenly the room felt too small, the people too loud, the dancing too wild. She was trapped by it all, including her own promises of vengeance, unable to escape this duty she had been forced to undertake by her father and her brother's irresponsibility.

She looked around. Across the room, the terrace doors all but beckoned. It was a bit chilly in the late spring air, and that would limit the people who would go out to escape the ballroom. Outside she could be alone.

And that was what she wanted. To be alone. And to forget the duchess and Simon. At least for a little while.

Simon watched Lillian edge around the ballroom to the terrace doors. There was something odd about the way she moved. She was stiff, her steps jerky in a way that was very unlike her normally graceful self.

He hadn't been able to talk to her all night. That had been orchestrated by Rhys and his mother, no doubt, for they were forever throwing people and responsibilities into his path so that he wouldn't seek out the only young woman whom he had any interest in at present.

But now, watching her practically run from the ballroom, he refused to be deterred any longer. He excused himself from the conversation he had been having and strode across the room. He saw Rhys moving to intervene once more, and pivoted to face his friend. The other man stopped and they locked gazes from halfway across the room.

Slowly, Simon shook his head. Rhys seemed to fight an internal war for a few charged moments, but finally he inclined his chin in surrender and returned to his fiancée. Simon pushed onto the terrace and snapped the doors shut behind him.

He didn't see Lillian. He had somehow expected her to be standing just outside the door, leaning on the gating that overlooked the garden where they had spoken earlier. But she wasn't there. Instead, the area was still and empty. The only sound was the occasional rustle of the leaves as a cool wind stirred them.

His brow wrinkled as he looked around through the darkness. "Miss Mayhew?"

There was no reply so he stepped farther into the shadows.

"Lillian?"

This time there was a response, but it wasn't an answer. Instead he heard a quiet sound coming from the side of the house, where a few chairs and a small table had been placed in anticipation of breakfasts and teas on the terrace when summer arrived. There were no lights from the ballroom on that side of the house, so no one would go there unless she wished to hide.

Which only increased Simon's concern about Lillian's well-being.

He made his way around the house and came to a stop as his eyes adjusted to the dark that was illuminated only by moonlight. Lillian sat on one of the cold metal chairs, her head in her hands.

To his utter surprise and dismay, her shoulders shook gently as she softly cried. He hesitated. She had obviously come outside to be alone with her distress, yet he couldn't leave her. Not like this.

He moved forward and placed a hand of comfort on her shoulder. She jumped at the contact and flew from the chair as she turned around. When she saw it was he who had intruded upon her, her face crumpled even further.

"Lillian," he whispered, feeling impotent and stupid in the face of her pain. But his instinct soon took over and he opened his arms to fold her into his embrace.

To his surprise, she allowed the intimacy of his

comfort. Though she made no attempt to put her own arms around him in return, she settled her head against his shoulder and did not fight to pull from his arms. They stood that way for a few moments before her crying subsided and she let out a great shiver.

Only then did she step from his grasp and turn her face away.

"My most sincere apologies, Your Grace," she whispered, her voice shaking ever so slightly. "You must think me very foolish."

He shook his head as he dug in his pocket for a clean handkerchief. He held it out to her and she took it with a wordless smile of thanks.

As she wiped her eyes, he said, "I don't think you foolish in the least. Obviously something or someone troubled you tonight. You are human, you deserve your feelings."

She shrugged one shoulder. "Still, one does not break down at a ball. It's just not done. And it only proves everyone right."

He wrinkled his brow. *"Everyone?"*

She pursed her lips. "I'm sorry, I should go inside."

She moved to leave, but he caught her elbow and held her steady. Looking down into her upturned face, he felt a strange and powerful swell of emotions move through him. Desire, yes. A lust more powerful than he had felt in a goodly long time.

But there was more there. Somewhere deep within him, there was a protectiveness that stirred. A desire to keep this woman safe from harm and free from the whispers that obviously hurt her, even if she was normally able to pretend otherwise.

"I saw you with my mother tonight," he said softly.

She turned her face, and Simon stifled a sigh. Apparently *everyone* included his mother.

"I can only imagine what she said to you," he said softly. "That her words caused you pain angers me more than I can express. Please know that she does not speak for me. In anything."

That statement, spoken more bitterly than he had intended, seemed to surprise Lillian, for she glanced back up at him sharply. Their gazes held for what seemed like a lifetime.

"She only said what a dozen others have repeated before," she finally answered, extracting her arm from his grip, though she did not step away. "And probably even more whisper the same condemnations behind my back. I should be accustomed to it by now."

He shook his head. "You should *never* grow accustomed to such flagrant disregard for your feelings. You should never accept it as a tolerable way of being treated. It does not matter the circumstances, *no one* deserves that."

She blinked up at him, her face reflecting surprise at both his words and the ardor with which he spoke them. He didn't blame her. Most men of his stature did not believe such things, but he did. He had fought for legislation to protect the poor and their children. He intended to fight for more. No one deserved to be treated as less than human simply because of the circumstances of his birth or life.

Especially the fetching creature standing before him, almost in his arms. This strange woman who pulled him in and pushed him away with equal strength. Whose lips were so full that he couldn't look away, and eyes were such an ever-changing hazel that he wanted to buy her gowns to match every color they reflected.

He wanted her. He just wanted to touch her. Feel her body against his. Feel it beneath his.

Somehow his hands moved, almost of their own accord. He clasped her shoulders and drew her forward. She didn't resist, only made a tiny gasp as her body molded against the hard planes of his. Her bottom lip trembled as he cupped her chin and tilted her face up, angling for the perfect kiss.

He couldn't have denied himself that kiss if his life depended on it. He lowered his mouth and brushed his lips to hers with every intention of pulling away after that chaste moment.

Instead, her arms came around his waist and

held there and she lifted up on her tiptoes, as if the space between them was too great. She returned the pressure of his lips, and when she shivered, a sigh parted her lips just a fraction. Feeling the heat of her breath on his mouth was too much for any man to resist.

He pulled her closer and tasted her flesh with just the tip of his tongue, probing her parted lips until she opened fully to him and allowed him entry.

Lillian couldn't have said how this moment, this kiss, happened, but now she was here and Simon was holding her so close that their breath was merging as one. In this space, she couldn't heed the fading voice inside her, telling her to pull away. She couldn't listen to the rational parts of her that were reminding her why she was here. She couldn't even comprehend that tiny bit of her that was saying Simon Crathorne was seducing her just as he had likely seduced a hundred women before.

No, all those things were blocked out by the powerful pounding of her heart as she surrendered to a desire so sudden and powerful that she felt she would do almost anything to make this moment last a little longer.

His tongue drove within her mouth with purpose now and rising desire. He tasted every inch of her, coaxing her to tangle her tongue with his.

He tasted of mint and a little hint of whiskey. But deeper than that, he tasted of desire and far more wicked pleasures to come.

Nothing had prepared her for this strange tingling sensation that seemed to originate in all the most unmentionable places and then spiral out to heat her entire body. She'd never wanted to rub herself against a man like some kind of cat in heat. Until now.

And it was that realization that finally forced her to step away from Simon, yanking herself from his embrace with enough force that she stumbled back against the terrace railing. They stood there in the cool night, staring at each other through the moonlight. Simon was short of breath, his mouth swollen and fists clenched at his sides like he was trying to regain control.

And Lillian could well imagine she looked much the same. Mouth pink and hot from kisses, eyes glazed and wild with confusion and desire and self-loathing.

She needed to say something. Or slap him. Or apologize. Something. *Anything.*

But in the end, all she did was gather up the hem of her skirt and bolt back inside. All she could do was run.

Chapter 7

❧

At three in the morning, even after a successful ball, the house was all but silent. Any servants who were still awake were on their way to bed, leaving the remaining tidying of the ballroom to be done in the morning before the guests arose and began demanding tea and biscuits and their eggs cooked in a certain fashion.

The partygoers had all danced themselves into exhaustion and were asleep or meeting for whatever assignations they had arranged during the gathering. No one lurked about to trouble Simon as he sat at the large cherrywood desk that had been in his father's office for as long as he could remember. Just looking at it brought back memories, most of them fond.

He had reported to his father on his marks in school here and received high praise that had warmed him to his very toes. Later, he and his father had debated politics, opening his eyes to a whole new world of responsibility. And finally, he had begun his education on the finer points of being a duke and all that came along with that exalted title.

He shook off the recollections with an affectionate smile. At present, he was supposed to be beginning the methodical search through his father's papers and personal effects. Instead, he stared out the window at the dark gardens outside and his mind wandered again. Only this time, he thought of soft lips and quiet sighs.

"There you are," Rhys said as he entered the room and shut the door behind him. His friend waited there, arms folded, as he stared across the chamber at Simon.

Simon sighed. He had guessed Rhys would find him. His friend had kept his questions to himself when Simon returned to the ballroom after his meeting with Lillian, but that had been a temporary respite only. Now it seemed to be time to pay the piper.

"Shouldn't you be in bed?" Simon asked. "Either by yourself . . . or down the hall with Anne?"

He said the last to raise Rhys's ire. His friend was so fastidious about propriety, Simon sometimes wondered if the "happy" couple had so much as kissed.

"You will not sway me, even by insulting my fiancée's honor," his friend said, though his jaw twitched as he came forward. "I want to know what happened on the terrace tonight when you pursued Miss Mayhew. You were alone for a while, and when you came back inside you were never quite the same. And the girl disappeared entirely."

Simon shrugged as he pushed out of the chair and paced the room. He raked a hand over his face before he responded.

"What do you want me to say, Waverly? That I find myself wildly attracted to a woman you think is entirely unsuitable for me? A woman my mother apparently abhors, not that I put much stock in her judgment. Do you want me to tell you that I found Lillian on the terrace and kissed her until I almost couldn't breathe? That I could think of nothing but putting her against the wall, hitching up her skirts, and rutting with her there and then? Would those things make you feel superior to me?"

Rhys moved closer and there was genuine concern on his friend's face. The sight of it made Simon regret his harsh, accusatory words. A snob Rhys might be, but he was an intensely loyal one. He had never once taken pleasure in Simon's pain, and it was unfair to think he ever would.

"You are truly enamored of this girl, aren't you? It is more than a way to upset your mother or thwart Society. You genuinely desire her." Rhys's tone was filled with shock.

Simon nodded once. He could deny none of those things.

Rhys pinched his temples with his fingertips. "So you are determined to ruin yourself?"

Simon shook his head. "I don't know that I'd go so far as to say I'm ruining myself. It isn't as if I'm in love with the girl. I feel a strange and powerful attraction to her. And I admit I am interested in her. By her."

Rhys looked at Simon, and there was a hint of relief to his friend's expression. "Then perhaps there is still hope. You have said that Miss Mayhew continues to be resistant to your attempts to court her."

Simon nodded. "She continually brings up her inappropriateness, rather like you and my mother do, actually."

His friend's brow wrinkled as if in surprise. "Perhaps the young lady is more honorable than I gave her credit for. Honestly, Simon, think of what you are doing. Let us say that you did pursue your interest and somehow ended up leg-shackled to this person."

Simon flinched. "I had not thought that far ahead, Waverly. I have an interest, but I'm not *marrying* the girl."

"Please." Rhys shook his head. "Since you have taken on the title, the urgency for you to wed has increased considerably. You know your duty. Therefore, any woman you have an 'interest' in must be considered as a potential bride."

"Then this is a hypothetical," Simon mused, though he found he could easily conjure an image of Lillian taking such a permanent role in his life. Strange, since he hadn't known her long and was merely compelled to determine more about her. And perhaps engage in a few more of those passionate kisses that so moved him.

Rhys shrugged, and the motion made Simon refocus on his friend. "Yes. I simply wish for you to see where this 'interest' could lead if you take it to its end."

"And that is marriage . . ." Simon tilted his head. "Or 'leg-shackling' as you so romantically put it."

His friend ignored his barb. "What if you *did* thwart all reason and marry Lillian Mayhew? If you won't take yourself into consideration, will you at least see what that would do to her?"

Simon tilted his head. "What do you mean? She would be a duchess, married into an important and respected family. It could only increase her standing."

Rhys laughed humorlessly. "As your wife, yes, Lillian would be invited, even 'accepted' by Society on the surface, but do you really think people would forget about her family?"

Simon thought briefly about the judgmental matrons of the *ton*. They could be sweet on the surface even as they drove a knife into another's back. He had certainly noticed their shunning of certain ladies and acceptance of others, sometimes on what seemed like a whim.

Rhys shook his head. "They would not. They would watch her constantly, judge her every mistake with a harshness that would be far worse than now. Perhaps *that* is the cause for Miss Mayhew's resistance. She might not wish to be exposed to such a future."

Simon paced away as he thought of Lillian's words to him in the garden earlier in the day. She had said something about not expecting marriage, perhaps ever. That memory lent credence to Rhys's words. She had been so upset by his mother's censure, and though she tried to hide it, the barbs of others obviously hurt her more than she showed.

If that were the case, if Rhys was correct that Lillian did not wish a marriage to a man whose elevated status would expose her to such pain and difficulty, that would explain Lillian's behavior toward him since her arrival. She was attracted to him, of that Simon was certain, but she pushed him away because she didn't want the disapproval that would surely come with courting him properly and eventually becoming his wife.

"And I know you think me an elitist, but you must consider the way a marriage to this woman would reflect on *you*, as well," Rhys continued, this time softer.

Simon spun on him. "You know I don't care about that."

"But you *do* care about how your father is remembered. I know you do. When they say 'Duke of Billingham,' do you not want them to think of his works in the House of Lords, of his goodness, of his honor?"

With a shake of his head, Simon said, "Nothing could change that!"

"A marriage to Lillian Mayhew might," Rhys insisted, like a dog with a bone he refused to release until he had sucked all the marrow from it. "If you marry this woman, when your name is spoken people will think of a duchess with no true connection and a potential suicide. You can shoot me every sour look you possess, but you know that to be true."

Simon flinched. There was no denying what Rhys said, even as he fought to find a way.

"Yes," he finally admitted softly. "I suppose all that could come to be. But what do you suggest, Waverly? She is the first woman I have been truly taken with in so long that I cannot recall the last. Do you suggest I throw that away just to protect my family's name? Or to keep her from an uncomfortable future? We are not at the point where I am asking for her hand, or even seriously considering such a thing. Should I ignore all attraction and interest just in case marriage *did* become the ultimate end to our affiliation?"

Rhys shifted, and his expression was suddenly pinched and ill at ease. "Neither of us is a rake, my friend. We do not brag on our conquests, nor have we ever talked coarsely about whatever pleasures we found with women. However, I've been thinking that perhaps the reason you are so drawn to this woman is that it has been a long time since you kept a mistress. The pain of your father's death, the pressure to marry well, the responsibilities you now shoulder . . . they could be eased by, well, an affair."

Simon could not help but stare at his friend in surprise. Rhys was right that they had not spoken so candidly about sex since they were green lads.

"And what do you suggest?"

"Miss Mayhew has long been on the shelf," his friend said with an uncomfortable sigh. "She must know that a good match at this late date and with her history is unlikely, especially if she is resistant to your formal attentions. But perhaps she would be less unwilling if you suggested she become . . . your mistress."

Simon backed away a step in utter shock. "You are saying I should ask a *lady*, an innocent, to come to my bed as my plaything?"

"It is not such a bad life, Billingham," Rhys said, raising his hands in a shrug. "Many a lady in her circumstance has chosen it and been content. You could provide her with a living, a small home in London, nice clothing. If you were discreet, it wouldn't damage her standing any more than her family connections already have. And when you were finished with her you would settle her well, ensuring her future in a way her father and brother did not."

Simon continued to stare, slack jawed, at Rhys. He never would have imagined his straitlaced friend suggesting such a shocking thing. But he could see Waverly did not mean it cruelly or coldly. He was truly trying to find a way that Simon could have what he desired without compromising himself. In some way, it was his friend's awkward attempt at a . . . *gift*.

"You say the girl responds to your touch," Rhys continued. "This seems like a way to have what you want without ruining your future, or making hers unbearable."

Simon moved to the window and stared out into the night. He wanted his friend's words to be distasteful, but in reality they made sense. It *was* one solution to his current problem. And perhaps Rhys was correct. Perhaps this was a better answer for both him and Lillian. Certainly the idea of having her, pleasing her, was far from distasteful. In fact, it made his cock ache.

But that wasn't the kind of gentleman he was.

In the end, he had been raised with too many scruples.

"She is a lady," he murmured. "No matter the other circumstances of her life. I cannot do such a thing, Rhys. Even if what you say is true, that we could not happily be together in any other way, I couldn't ask her to lower herself in such a fashion."

Rhys dipped his chin, but did not seem to be surprised. "If I overstepped with my suggestion, I apologize."

"No apologies," Simon said, still staring at the darkness outside and wishing he could stop thinking about Lillian Mayhew as his lover.

"You know I only have your best interests at heart." Rhys sighed. "I hate to see you pacing the boards long into the night, worrying yourself about a girl."

Simon turned and speared his friend with a look. He was just as happy to escape the awkward subject of his love life and move on to something he felt comfortable hearing Rhys's opinion about.

"Actually, it is more than the girl that has me pacing the boards."

His friend's eyebrows lifted, and there must have been something in Simon's expression that said this was a deeper conversation, for Rhys sank down into the chair across from Simon's desk. He dug around in the piles of paperwork for the cigar box Simon's father had buried there. He removed two and held one out to Simon.

With a sigh, Simon took it and returned to his place at the desk.

"So tell me what troubles you," Rhys asked as he lit the cigar.

Simon motioned around the room. "This duty, this place. This title and all that comes with it. Being here makes my father all the larger and his legacy all the greater."

Rhys nodded, and Simon knew his friend understood him perfectly. It had been only a few years since Rhys inherited his own dukedom. The transition hadn't been easy for him, either.

Simon sighed. "Not to mention the chore of going through my father's things. He kept such detailed and mishandled records that they overwhelm. I have much to sort through and collect before I leave here for London. And with this blasted house party, I must steal time when I can."

Rhys looked around the cluttered office with a wince. "Yes. It is quite a substantial undertaking. But if I can help, I'll do all I can. On either this score . . . or with Miss Mayhew."

Simon smiled at the honesty in his friend's tone. In the end, Rhys's pretentiousness only stretched so far. Simon had no doubt his friend would stand beside him, whatever he decided to do.

"Thank you, Rhys. I realize how much it pains you to make me that offer."

"Eh," his friend said as he ground out the stub of his cigar in an ashtray and moved it far from the old paperwork. "In the end, who you chase after is your business."

Simon nodded. His friend was being light-hearted about the subject now, but they both knew he had given Simon much to think about.

"What say you to a game of billiards before we turn in?"

Rhys shoved to his feet with a wide grin. "Now that is the best idea I think you've had yet."

But as Simon followed his friend from the room, he couldn't pretend that the image of Lillian in his bed, as his mistress, wasn't a powerful one. Even though he knew it was impossible, it was one that would keep him awake long after he finally returned to his chamber that night.

"But you have been kissed before!"

Lillian flinched as she sank into the soft upholstered cushion of the chair before the dressing table in the chamber she shared with Gabby. Her friend was only trying to help, but this conversation, which had started the night before and picked up immediately upon her friend's waking this morning, did nothing to ease Lillian's shaken nerves.

"I'm not sure that is the point," Lillian said as she let out a great yawn.

She couldn't help but steal a quick glance at herself in the mirror above the dressing table. She stifled a sigh at the sight. Her gown was perfectly fine, and the pretty way Maggie had arranged her hair earlier in the morning was more than acceptable. But if anyone looked at her, they would certainly see her exhaustion. The proof that she had not slept all night, simply tossed and turned as she relived that kiss over and over, was written in the shadows beneath her eyes.

As soon as Simon saw her, he would recognize that fact. More to the point, he would know *why* she lay in her bed without the pleasure of sleep. What a triumph that would be to him.

"What *is* the point?" Gabby said with a sigh. "If it isn't the kiss itself, tell me exactly what is troubling you."

Lillian covered her eyes briefly. "Of course the entire act of the kiss is troubling. After all, it would be terrible for my reputation had we been caught. Well-bred young ladies simply do not do such things."

Gabby rolled her eyes ever so slightly, but wisely chose not to interrupt.

"And yet the trouble is that I . . ." Lillian hesitated before she continued, for the confession she was about to make was a terrifying one. Once she spoke the words out loud, she could never take them back. "I shouldn't have *liked* it. It shouldn't have felt so good."

Gabby's expression softened as she crossed the room and laid a gentle hand of comfort on Lillian's shoulder. In the mirror, her friend smiled at her. "Because of who he is?"

Lillian nodded. "Because of who his father was, that is for certain. And because of what I am sworn to do by revealing the late duke for the charlatan he was. Not to mention the fact that I cannot truly be certain of Simon's intentions."

She said the last sentence slowly, hating the bitter taste it left in her mouth.

Gabby frowned. "You have said so before, but I don't know if that is fair, Lillian. So far Simon has given you no reason to believe he is a philanderer. What would he have to gain when there are other women here who would be far less resistant to his attentions?"

Lillian bit her lip, trying to push away the swell of hope that arose in her when she considered that Simon might truly like her as he claimed. She didn't *want* that, damn it!

"You're correct. But that doesn't change the fact that I shouldn't have wanted the kiss. I shouldn't have wanted Simon."

"And yet you do."

Lillian glared at Gabby as she rose from the

chair and paced away from her. "No, I *did*. Not anymore. Not again."

"Oh?" Gabby laughed, but there was no malice to the sound. "Then why do you keep touching your lips and blushing?"

Lillian swallowed hard. She hadn't realized she was doing such a thing. Those little nervous habits were telling. As was the fact that her heart rate rose whenever she pictured Simon's handsome face moving in closer in the seconds before the kiss. Even now, she let out a great shiver at the memory.

"Very well," she admitted. "Despite my best intentions, I-I am attracted to him, Gabby. I want him in a way I have never felt before with any other man in all the years I've been out in Society. But this is the one man I can never have."

Her friend looked at her, and the humor she had seemed to be having at Lillian's expense faded to a solemn frown.

Lillian sighed. "So explain to me what am I supposed to do now?"

"I don't know. I wish I did," Gabby whispered.

"So do I." Lillian moved for the door. "So do I."

The breakfast spread laid out by the staff at the Billingham country estate was legendary, with every delight one could imagine piled high in chafing dishes on the sideboard. And yet normally

Simon skipped the over abundance of food during these country events, opting instead for plainer fare taken in his rooms while he gathered himself for the day.

Only this particular morning he found himself in the thick of the milling guests, watching as they served themselves and gathered at tables scattered around the room to talk and stare at him. The attentions of the women reminded him why he normally skipped such events, and yet he forced a smile on his face.

It was all worth it because he was waiting. Waiting for Lillian. He hadn't stopped thinking about her since he last saw her, since that powerful kiss on the terrace. And despite the fact that it wasn't possible, he hadn't been able to stop thinking about Rhys's suggestion that Simon make her his lover.

In fact, he'd had some very detailed dreams about that subject in the few hours he had slept. Dreams where Lillian slipped between his sheets, her cool, naked skin pressed to his. Dreams where her honey blond hair wrapped around his fingers, tickled his chest, curled about the thick length of his cock just as her lips did.

He started as blood and heat rushed to the organ. That would not do in the slightest. He had to stop thinking about those sorts of things. Except at that very moment, Lillian stepped through the door on the arm of her friend Lady Gabriela.

Although the younger woman was dressed far more extravagantly, and might even be considered more traditionally pretty, Simon couldn't stop looking at Lillian. He memorized the lines of her face as she glanced about the room slowly.

Her stare finally fell on him and they merely looked at each other for a long, charged moment. Then her friend whispered something to her and Lillian blushed a deep, fetching pink as she turned away and made for the sideboard.

He watched as she put food on her plate in a haphazard fashion, hardly looking at what she chose. Once she had taken a place at the table farthest from his, he got up and moved toward her. He was painfully aware that every eye in the room followed him, and from the ramrod-straight position Lillian held herself in, she noticed that as well.

"Good morning, Miss Mayhew," he said as he stopped beside her. "May I join you?"

He watched as she scanned the room for her friend, but Lady Gabriela had not been as quick to get her food, and since she saw Simon standing with Lillian, the other girl had chosen a different table to sit at. Lillian scowled, and he thought he heard her mutter something akin to "traitor" under her breath before she nodded.

"Of course, Your Grace. This is your home, after all." She motioned to the chair across from her, but he took the one beside her instead.

"You seem uncomfortable," he said with a small smile.

She blushed deeply and his smile turned to a grin. It was actually fun to bait her a bit.

"Of course not," she said, but her words were belied by the way she squeezed them past clenched teeth.

He nodded and pretended to be thoughtful for a moment. "Good. I thought perhaps you would want to talk about what happened last night."

"Please mind your tone." Her gaze darted around the room briefly to see if anyone had heard his low statement. When it was apparent the others were watching, but unable to hear, she whispered, "It should not have happened."

He shrugged. She could say that all she liked, but he hadn't missed the fact that she kept glancing at his mouth. Whether she wished to admit it or not, she had wanted that kiss and she wanted another.

"Perhaps that is true," he said. "I suppose 'propriety' dictates that we should not have kissed."

"Quite so, Your Grace. I am happy you see it from that perspective." And yet she did not look particularly happy as she moved her food around her plate with her fork.

Simon leaned a touch closer. "But I would be lying if I did not admit that I wish it would happen a second time."

Lillian's fork clattered against the edge of her plate as she turned to face him full-on. Her eyes were wide and filled with disbelief that made Simon's heart ache a fraction. Had she been so shunned that she couldn't believe a man could find her attractive?

How he wished he could prove otherwise to her. Protect her, though that desire was so strange to him since he hardly knew her. But he wanted to know her. Even if it ended up coming to nothing at all, he still wanted that.

"Would you meet me later in the library?" he found himself whispering.

There was a long pause before she shook her head as if waking from a dream or a spell.

"No," she whispered, though there was little conviction to her refusal. "I-I cannot."

Despite her rejection, he smiled. It was evident she only said no because she felt it was her duty to do so. With a little work, he was certain she would eventually say yes.

"I certainly understand that you are *afraid*," he said as he got to his feet. He almost laughed when her lips parted in silent outrage at his accusation that she was a coward. "If you change your mind, I shall be there after tea. Good morning, Miss Mayhew."

Then he turned on his heel and left her gaping after him.

Chapter 8

Lillian stirred her tea absently as she stared at Gabby with what she knew were wild eyes. For the past few hours, she had gone through the motions of a polite guest. She had participated, rather poorly, in a game of whist. She had engaged in conversation with the Countess of Hephshire about the merits of silk versus satin and what colors would be the rage this Season.

She had even managed to endure a walk about the gardens with Ladies Portia and Penelope, the twin daughters of the Marquis Drisedale, who had been determined to talk about Simon as much as possible.

But none of those activities had kept her from constant thoughts of Simon's invitation to join him in the library after tea. The faster the tea and biscuits disappeared, the more nervous and uncertain Lillian became about her refusal to do just that.

"You must stop fidgeting, Lillian," Gabby said

softly. "You are drawing even more notice to yourself than Simon has with his attentions."

Lillian forced her foot to stop bouncing beneath her skirt and drew a long breath.

"You know, when I heard you had been invited to Simon's home, when I realized that by joining you I could possibly make a search of this place and find evidence regarding his late father, I thought I had planned for every contingency," she whispered. "But I was wrong, Gabby. I never thought Simon Crathorne would turn toward me in such an obvious fashion. Or that he would make overtures to court me!"

"I don't know why you doubt yourself," her friend said quietly. "You are a very pretty young woman, not to mention clever. Men *are* drawn to you."

"And most of them turn away the moment they hear the rumors surrounding my mother," she said with a bitter edge to her voice. "And yet Simon remains undeterred. His continued pursuit has stopped any chance I had at completing my purpose for coming here. What do I do?"

Gabby pursed her lips. "I suppose that depends on how far you're willing to go to prove the late duke was not what his public persona implied."

Lillian thought of that statement for a moment. Her father's dying words rang in her ears. Meant for her or not, they had been filled with such pain and regret that he had not avenged her mother's attack. He wanted retribution, but she couldn't trust Jack to do it. Her brother had already lost the chance to confront Roger Crathorne directly by waiting until the old man was dead. By the time Jack left the hazy numbness alcohol provided, it was likely there would be nothing of value he *could* do.

But Lillian was *here*. She could find the secrets and make them public. *Now* when it would still matter, before Crathorne became a distant memory and no one cared anymore.

Her mother's fragile spirit had been destroyed by the late duke. She deserved the revenge no one had given her.

"I have no choice. I must go as far as I can," she finally said, with a strange sense of dread filling her.

Gabby's face crumpled, but then she whispered, "Then you must go to him."

"What?" Lillian burst out, far louder than she had intended to speak. Instantly, a handful of heads swiveled in their direction. Some looked in interest, others with contempt. Flushing, Lillian corrected her tone. "Why do you say such a thing?"

Gabby covered her hand. "You shall not have a second chance to come to this place. Lady Billingham will never allow it if her discussion with you at the welcome ball is any indication."

Lillian clenched her fists at the memory, but

Gabby was right. Last night the dowager had made it clear she would do everything in her power to prevent Lillian from ever stepping foot in her home or near her son again.

Gabby continued, "If that is true you'll never again have the ability to search here after you are gone. As cold as it may seem and as much as I hate to encourage such behavior, using this situation, this attraction and interest Simon has in you, well, it could be the best way to get closer to the truth."

"Because of what we spoke of earlier," Lillian said, her voice dull and flat. "You continue to believe Simon might let something slip about his father. Or accidentally tell me where and how to best search for secrets."

Gabby nodded slowly. "Yes."

Lillian covered her eyes. Her stomach felt sick as she whispered, "I don't want to be that person. To be so cold as to use someone's affections against them."

"You are trying to prove that a man was the worst kind of predator and liar," Gabby said softly. "I'm not sure you can do that without losing part of your own soul, which was why I hesitated to help you with this in the first place."

Lillian looked at her friend evenly. Although Gabby was younger, she was wise. What she said made sense.

"Then I suppose I must truly dedicate myself

one way or another to a course of action," she said, straightening up. "No more dithering about right and wrong."

Gabby nodded. "You must. But do it quickly. I believe the duke is waiting."

Simon leaned against the cushioned leather seat with a sigh. The library normally gave him a sense of solace and peace, but today he'd made the mistake of bringing a pile of his father's paperwork along as he waited on the slim chance that Lillian would meet with him.

Now that he had spent the last half hour sorting through the items, he was ready to scream with frustration and boredom. The papers contained mundane rubbish including price listings for equipment that were at least two decades old, contact lists of local farmers who had worked for his grandfather, and references for servants who had *died* while Simon was still a boy.

Honestly, he would never understand how his father had been at once so disorganized and yet so capable. He made a mental note to create a pile for items to destroy. There was no reason to keep what he did not need or what did not track the history of his family's legacy.

The door to the library opened and Simon looked up. Instantly he forgot his frustration with his father. Lillian hovered in the doorway, as if she was not certain if she intended to come inside or not.

Setting the papers aside, he got to his feet.

"Hello, Lillian. I am glad you're here."

Actually he was shocked. Given her response that morning, he had been certain she wouldn't come. If he was a betting man, he would have wagered it would take a few more coaxing conversations to bring her to him.

Not that he was complaining when she stepped into the room and fidgeted her hands in front of her. She was remarkably lovely. Her plain yet pretty gown was a warm green, something that reminded him of the season. And it made her hazel eyes dance with green flecks. Her dark blond hair looked like spun honey in its plaited and curled style, and a few strands swung delicately around her cheeks. He couldn't help but recall that when he kissed her, her hair had smelled like lemons.

"I don't really know why I did," Lillian responded with a blush. When she glanced up, her gaze found the paperwork on the small table beside him. To his dismay she moved backward, raising her hands. "I can see I have intruded upon you."

He moved forward in a few long strides. "No. I asked you to come. Please, join me."

There was another long moment of hesitation before Lillian nodded her head and stepped into the room. She crossed the room in halting steps, as if with every movement toward him she questioned the prudence of coming here.

Simon frowned. "You hesitate. Is it because of the kiss?"

She stopped a few feet away and stared at him, apparently shocked he would be so bold. In truth, so was he. It was not his nature, but Lillian seemed to bring out the most powerful urges in him.

"We both wanted it, Lillian," he said when she didn't reply. "There is no shame in that."

She opened her mouth as if to refute his claim, but then she shut it again. He smiled. So she had no argument.

"Please sit."

Instead she stared at the chair beside him with wariness.

"I have no intention of ravishing you," he said. Then he winked. "Unless that is your desire."

Instead of laughing or feigning shock, Lillian flinched, and his smile immediately fell.

"I apologize. That was a bad joke."

She shook her head slowly and took the seat he offered beside him. "No, Your Grace. This is simply uncharted territory for me. Although I have been out in Society for a goodly long time, I do not think I have ever had a man pursue me so strenuously."

"Hmmm. And this troubles you?"

She shrugged one shoulder. "The fact that we kissed after so short an acquaintance . . . that I-I *liked* kissing you . . . yes, that troubles me."

He tilted his head. Normally a woman would be more coy, but Lillian's honesty was refreshing and arousing in equal measure. How he would love to kiss her again. But that was not the right course to take with her still so hesitant.

"We are two grown people who kissed because we both wished to do so," he said softly. "No laws were broken. Trust me. I am in Parliament, I would certainly be aware of them."

To his delight, Lillian looked at him, and this time it was with a smile. He realized it was the first time she had ever smiled at him beyond politeness, and his breath caught. The intelligence in her expression gave her eyes a twinkle, as if everything between them was a charming private joke.

"Perhaps you are correct that no laws were broken," she said, and her shoulders seemed to relax. "And I'll even go so far as to admit you may be correct that we both equally wanted the kiss. But I am left with a question."

He inclined his head slightly as silent permission to ask.

"What are we to do now, Simon?"

Again, her directness surprised him. And intrigued him all the more. Young debutantes with nothing in their heads but fashion and marriage rarely said anything but what they believed would garner them their prize. Lillian's candor was like a fresh spring breeze in the midst of cloying perfume.

"I have made it no secret that I find you interesting," he said, leaning across the arm of his chair to be closer. "And obviously desirable, as well."

Her pretty blush was his ultimate reward.

"I have no idea where that will lead, however I would like a chance to get to know each other a bit better. If this attraction grows, if you come to find me even remotely interesting, then perhaps there is a future for us."

His mind flashed once more to an image of her across his bed, but he pushed it away instantly.

Lillian shifted, the track of their conversation obviously making her uncomfortable. "Are you certain you wish to pursue even a friendship with me? It is evident there will be much disapproval of such a relationship, most especially from your mother, because of my family's past."

Simon frowned. By the pain that echoed faintly in her expression, she was thinking of her mother's death. Yet it was not yet time to broach the delicate subject of her mother's suicide. Lillian had little trust in him, and he feared he would chase her away by asking her for details of such a personal grief.

But he could open the door, even the tiniest bit, by trusting her with a little of his own life.

"My mother and I are not close, Lillian. Her disapproval has been my constant companion for so long, I fear I would not know what to do if she gifted me with approval."

Lillian's expression softened as she stared at him. If she was surprised by his confession, it did not reflect on her face. Only empathy existed there. Not pity, but a sense of understanding.

"I see," she whispered. "That must be difficult for you since it is clear you cherish both your bond with your sister and the one you shared with your late father."

He shrugged, dismissing with pretended ease a lifetime of confusion and pain. "Once it was. Now her feelings toward me simply . . . *are*."

There was a long silence, but it was not uncomfortable. Still, when Lillian spoke again, it was not on the subject of his mother, and for that Simon was pleased.

"So what are these papers, my lord?"

Simon smiled. "Does this mean you will forget my mother's approval or disapproval and take me up on my offer to spend a little more time together?"

Lillian hesitated before she finally jerked out a nod.

Simon grinned, then gathered up the items on the table beside him and held them out. As Lillian took them, he said, "These, I am afraid, are not particularly interesting. They are just some of my father's records."

To his surprise, Lillian let out a small gasp, and the items fluttered to the floor at her feet. They both dropped down to retrieve them.

"I do apologize," she said, but her voice shook as she handed him sheet after sheet. He noticed she looked at each one. "So you are organizing his estate?"

He nodded as he set the papers aside and helped her back into her chair. "Trying, at the very least. He was quite disordered. The state of his office is a bit embarrassing."

She swallowed hard. "I see. And what have you discovered about him so far?"

Simon frowned. That was a strange way to pose a question. He doubted he would *discover* anything of import about his father that he did not already know. The duke had been very much an open book, living his life in the public eye. It was why he garnered so much respect.

"So far I only know he decided not to keep sheep in the north fields and that he interviewed fourteen candidates for a role as butler in one of his favorite homes in London," he responded with a sigh.

Lillian leaned away, her brow wrinkling with confusion. "I beg your pardon?"

He smiled apologetically. "My father kept records on everything from the important to the mind-numbingly mundane."

She hesitated, and he thought he saw her throat

work as she swallowed. *"Everything?"*

"Yes. It is quite a task to sort through it all."

Her gaze flashed to him and held there briefly before it flitted away. "If you ever need any assistance . . ."

He tilted his head to look more closely at her. His stomach clenched as she tucked a loose lock of hair behind her ear. The slope of her neck was practically poetry, and he felt a powerful urge to explore it with his lips for a few hours.

Instead he reached out and ran a fingertip along her cheek. She jolted at the contact and snapped her gaze to him, but she didn't pull away as he traced the line of her jaw and finally trailed the digit along the throbbing pulse at her throat.

"Trust me, Lillian, if I ask you for anything, it won't be your services as my secretary," he whispered.

Her lips parted ever so slightly as the full meaning of his statement impacted her. She blinked a few times before she whispered, "Simon . . ."

He shut his eyes with pleasure. He did love the sound of his given name coming from her full lips.

"Say it again," he murmured as he slipped his fingers into her hair and tilted her face. Leaning across the space between them, he let his mouth come close to hers.

"What?" she asked, but she was so breathless that the word caught.

"My name," he murmured. "Say it, please."

"Simon," she indulged him after a moment had passed, but her voice cracked.

He let out a sigh of contentment and then pressed his mouth to hers. Just as she had on the terrace, Lillian melted against him. Her lips opened, inviting him deeper. He shifted out of the chair and without breaking the contact of the kiss, rose up on his knees before her.

He was slightly lower than she now, but she adjusted, changing the angle of her head so that he could continue his exploration of every part of her mouth. When he wrapped his arms around her and molded her body to his, she sighed. And when he gently sucked her tongue, she slithered to her own knees, her embrace tightening as she let out a soft, plaintive sound of desire and surrender.

Pleasure coiled within him. But although need thundered in his head like a thousand horses' hooves, Simon still had enough sense to know that this encounter, this kiss was rapidly spiraling out of control. The door to the library remained open, and unlike on the terrace, if someone caught them like this, it could spell utter disaster. Lillian was a lady and they would be forced to marry, which would take any other choice away from both of them. He did not desire that.

With difficulty, he pulled back. Lillian blinked as she looked up at him.

"God knows, I could do this all day," he said as he pushed a lock of hair away from her cheek. "But we're courting danger."

He rose to his feet and helped her up. She blushed as she smoothed her skirts mindlessly.

"I— This is not like me," she finally murmured.

"Nor is it like me," he said softly. "And that is part of why my reaction to you fascinates me. But for now, I don't think I can bear to be alone with you any longer."

She nodded as she backed away. "I should go anyway. The ladies expect me to join them on a jaunt to the village."

He smiled at her as reassurance. "Good afternoon, Lillian."

"Good afternoon, Your Grace . . . *Simon*," she whispered before she turned from the room and hurried away.

Simon stared after her. As he suspected, he was not alone in his desire for Lillian. It was a thrilling realization, but also a frustrating one. She denied him at every turn, and he wanted her so desperately that it was beginning to border on obsession. And the only way he would have her was if he offered a marriage she claimed she did not want, or if he took Rhys's advice and became her protector.

It was a very confusing situation. One that left him hard, aching, and utterly enchanted.

Chapter 9

How nice that you could join us this afternoon Miss Mayhew."

Lillian jolted as she was roused from her daydream by the shrill tones of Lady Evelyn, the daughter of one of the many gentlemen invited to Simon's soiree. Sadly, the group of them had all begun to blend together until she couldn't remember exactly who this girl's father was or even if they had spoken before. Lillian blinked at the young lady and tried to regain her bearings.

She was standing in the middle of a fabric shop in the village of Billingham with a dozen or so of the other women who were attending the country party. Inwardly she cursed herself for woolgathering and thinking of the passionate and unexpected kiss she had allowed Simon in the library that morning.

"Th-thank you, Lady Evelyn," she choked out

as she tried to banish the memories once again. "It has been a lovely day."

"Still," her companion said, picking up an extravagant bonnet and setting it on the crown of her brown hair as she preened in the mirror before her. "It must be so very awkward for you."

"Awkward?" Lillian repeated as she stifled a yawn.

"Yes."

The girl stole a side glance, and Lillian instantly recognized the malicious tilt to her companion's lips. She sighed, steeling herself for whatever the other woman was about to say.

"After all, I have heard much talk about how you have no money since your father's passing. How difficult it must be for you to spend any time in a shop with women of good company who do not share your . . . *limitations*."

When Lillian didn't respond, the woman continued with a sweet smile that was apparently meant to disguise the malice of her words. "I know it would be most cruel for *me* if I could not buy all the little things that make life worthwhile. And you can hardly afford a hat pin!"

Lillian pursed her lips as Lady Evelyn blinked at her innocently. "Indeed," she said softly. "Do excuse me."

She turned and made for the front door of the shop. Suddenly her surroundings were stifling. How she longed to breathe fresh air and be away from the jealous harpies who hated that their quarry, the exalted Duke of Billingham, had showered any attention on a woman they felt unworthy.

Lillian pushed the door open and stepped outside, letting it fall shut behind her. When she didn't hear the bell signaling that it had done so, she turned. A young woman stood in the doorway. Lillian stiffened as she recognized her as Lady Anne, the fiancée of Simon's disapproving friend, the Duke of Waverly.

Lillian could only guess at the sniping Lady Anne would make, but she still made an attempt at a smile. Unexpectedly, the one she got in return was wide and genuinely friendly. The lady stepped outside and let the door close behind her.

"Do ignore Evelyn," Anne said with a delicate roll of her eyes. "She has always been a shrew and she has *always* been interested in poor Simon, despite his best efforts to put her off kindly."

Lillian's eyes went wide as she stared at the other woman. Such frank talk was rarely displayed by a woman of such stature.

"I-I did not realize you were listening to our exchange, my lady," she finally stammered.

Anne shrugged. "I have been trying to find a moment alone with you since my arrival, but circumstances were forever preventing it. Today I merely saw my chance, I wasn't trying to eaves-drop."

Lillian found herself stepping forward. "I did not mean to imply—"

Anne waved off the remainder of her statement. "Of course you didn't, my dear. Now, will you walk back with me?"

Lillian cast a glance at the shop door. "But the others . . ."

"My chaperone is within and I told her the two of us were going to depart early. She'll make sure they do not wait or wonder about us."

There seemed to be no other argument, so Lillian nodded. "Very well."

To her surprise, Lady Anne linked her arm through Lillian's as they steered their way onto the cobblestone street and headed back toward the Billingham estate, which was a mile away.

"Had you ever visited Billingham before this gathering?" Lady Anne asked.

"No," Lillian said with a shake of her head. Truth be told, she had rarely been out of London at all, but she wasn't about to say that. It would only be a reminder of her place, and she found she didn't want Anne to think less of her.

"I think it is one of the prettiest shires in all the country," Anne said with a deep sigh of pleasure. Then she laughed as she shot Lillian a side glance. "But do not tell Waverly I said that. He would take issue since he believes his shire must be the best in all things."

Lillian found herself laughing along with the other woman. "I promise it will be our secret, my lady."

"Very good," the other woman said with a smile. "But I insist you call me Anne."

Lillian flushed, but it was out of pleasure. "Are you certain? I would not want to show any disrespect."

"I think addressing me more formally would show more disrespect since we are destined to be friends," Anne said with another light laugh. "After all, I'm marrying Waverly in no time at all. He is Simon's best friend, you know, and has been since they were boys in school. It is likely you and I will spend a great deal of time in each other's company in the future."

Lillian wrinkled her brow, uncertain as to what the other woman meant. And then understanding dawned. She drew up short, and since their arms were linked, it forced Anne to do the same.

"My lady . . . *Anne* . . . I think you misunderstand. His Grace has made no offer for me and I have accepted none."

Her cheeks burned as she thought of the infinitely passionate encounter she and Simon had shared in the library just a few hours ago, but she shoved that thought aside. "I wouldn't have you think that there was more between us than there is."

"I'm certain that is true," Anne said. "But Simon is actively searching for a bride now that he has taken the title of duke."

"I assure you, that has nothing to do with me!" Lillian insisted, her heart throbbing now.

Anne smiled, the expression indulgent. "Perhaps. But Waverly and I have been betrothed since we were children, so I've known Simon for many years. And I have never seen him take such a keen interest in a woman before."

Lillian blinked. Here she had all but convinced herself that she was just another conquest to Simon. "Certainly that cannot be true. And there are far better potential matches for him at this party and back in London."

Anne shrugged and began to walk again, this time forcing Lillian to move. "Unlike my fiancé, I think there are many qualities that make up a good match. Certainly there are those who can make a marriage for money or title alone work. But I believe the unions that seem happiest among our rank are those where the couple shares a common purpose, a similar sense of the world, and a parallel humor and intelligence. From all outward appearances, it seems you and Simon are well-matched in those things. At least the humor and intelligence part."

Against her will, Lillian's thoughts turned to Simon again. And not just his kiss. She thought of how often she wanted to laugh when she was with him. Or delve deeper into his thoughts. Was that what Lady Anne meant? That strange connection that went deeper than mere physical desire.

A shiver racked her as they crested a hill and came into sight of the manor house, rising like a beacon on the horizon. She kept her eyes on the home as they moved closer and it loomed bigger and bigger.

"Well, I've only known the man for a few days," Lillian finally whispered. "So I don't really know if we have much in common."

"Fair enough," Anne said, patting her hand. "Although I have always teased Simon that when he found his mate, it would be like lightning for him. A sudden burst that would make all others fade in his estimation. I'll be very interested to see if my prediction comes true."

Lillian shifted uncomfortably. "I don't know about that, but I hope you and I will be friends regardless."

Anne smiled as the butler opened the door for them and they stepped into the sunny foyer together.

"Of course, Lillian! I would be very pleased to call you a friend no matter what circumstances come in the future. Now why don't we go onto the back terrace and share some tea before the others return? I would dearly love to gossip shamelessly about that gown Lady Penelope was wearing last night. Have you ever seen such a terrible shade of green? I heard she was trying to match Simon's eyes, but if that is true, she failed miserably!"

Lillian laughed as she followed Anne to the back terrace. Even though she liked this woman a great deal, her words troubled Lillian. With every moment that passed, with every encounter, it seemed this situation was growing more and more complicated. And she feared in the end, no one would be happy with the outcome.

Especially her.

Simon read the ledger before him three times, but still the words and numbers didn't fully compute. What he saw could not be true. And yet there it was, in his father's own hand.

"You are troubled, what is it?"

Simon shook his head before he looked across the room to Rhys, who had been sorting through his own piles of correspondence and ledgers from over the decades. Now his friend was looking at him with concern.

Simon held up the ledger he had been examining. "I don't understand these notations."

"What are they?"

Simon returned his gaze to the line of names

and numbers. "Ten years ago my father put forth a piece of legislation in the House of Lords that would have helped ease the conditions for some of lower-class shipyard workers. There were men who opposed those laws, people who made their fortunes on the backs of the laborers."

Rhys nodded. "I vaguely recall that. There was some talk that bribery was involved in the stoppage of those laws."

Simon swallowed. He had a very sick feeling. "This ledger shows my father actually sent several payments to the very men who led the opposition. The ones he later accused of all manner of trickery in obtaining what they wanted."

He looked up to find Rhys still staring at him. "Why would my father do that?"

His friend looked away, but not before Simon saw a flash of suspicion in his expression. The same type of misgiving that turned his own stomach.

"I don't know, Billingham," Rhys said softly. "But I'm certain there is an explanation. Perhaps your father hoped to woo his opponents with money and convince them to your side later. Or maybe they made a false promise to him to stop their crusade if he paid them off."

Simon pursed his lips. "My father always claimed to abhor that kind of politicking. Plus there is another very large payment that went out *after* the entire situation was over and forgotten. If my father was trying to pay them out of opposition, why would he give them more money *after* they betrayed him?"

Rhys raised both eyebrows, and Simon's heart sank even further. There was one very obvious explanation, though he didn't wish to think on it. Not until he had more information, at the very least.

"Have you come across any other papers pertaining to a . . ." He looked down at his sheets again. ". . . Lord Kinston or Mr. Xavier Warren?"

"Not yet," Rhys said, flipping through the papers in his lap. "Why?"

"They are two of the men my father apparently gave money to who were involved on the other side of the bill. I would be curious if there is more correspondence or explanation on the matter."

"Wait," Rhys said, shuffling through the papers once before he held up an envelope. "There is this and it has Warren's name on the return address."

Simon crossed the room and took the letter from his friend. As he opened it, his hands shook slightly, though he wasn't certain why. There had to be a reasonable explanation for what his father had done. But what he found inside did nothing to relieve his worry and confusion.

"Your Grace, I received your payment dated July 13. You may consider this matter closed and my silence ensured. Xavier Warren," he read aloud before he looked at Rhys again. "Silence? What kind of si-

lence could my father have been buying?"

Rhys shrugged. "I have no idea. Your father seemed above any scandal. He was revered for his piety."

Simon nodded. "And yet there seems to be more to this matter."

Rhys looked around. "Well, I assume if there is a ledger and a letter referring to parts of the affair, there is probably more evidence scattered about this room. And now we know to be on the lookout for it."

As his friend returned to his own reading, Simon glanced around him with a deep sigh. There was so much material to go through, and now that he was looking for something specific, the entire search had taken on a deeper, not particularly pleasant meaning.

Truth be told, he wasn't certain if he *wanted* to find whatever it was he was looking for.

Lillian rested her head against the back of her chair and closed her eyes as the soothing sounds of the piano and the sweetness of Gabby's voice lilted through the air around her. For the first time since her arrival, she felt at peace.

The musicale had been the dowager duchess's idea, and she had invited all the ladies to regale the group with their talents. Lillian had been one of the few not anxious to share her "gifts." She had very little affinity in the area of music. Her voice was pitchy and she had never had the patience to become proficient in piano or harp or any of the other pretty instruments ladies were meant to play.

Of course, the dowager would probably be just as happy she did not rise. The older woman had been sitting behind her all night, and Lillian could veritably *feel* the contempt coming from her.

With a sigh, Lillian opened her eyes and smiled with encouragement at Gabby as her friend sang. Then she let her gaze wander the room.

It was a funny thing to look at a crowd when they didn't know they were being observed. Some of the women and men smiled, clearly enjoying the music. Others seemed jealous, especially the girls who had already performed and didn't have the vast talent of her friend.

A few in the crowd seemed bored, one gentleman even kept looking at his pocket watch, as if counting the moments until the entire experience was over.

Lillian smothered a smile until her gaze fell on Simon. He had taken a place by himself at the back of the room and there he stood, leaning against a wall. Separated from the crowd, he stared at the little elevated platform where Gabby played, but he did not seem to see or hear her.

In fact, he did not truly appear to be attending

to the music at all. His face was pinched, almost pained, and his brow wrinkled in a decidedly worried expression. Lillian caught her breath as she observed him.

Apparently their time spent together had taught her a great deal about the man, for she was able to detect a sadness to his eyes. And a faraway emptiness that told her he was thinking of troubling things.

He blinked suddenly as if he felt her stare on him, then his gaze found hers and focused. The corner of his lip lifted ever so slightly in a smile, and against her will, Lillian's heart leapt.

When he returned his attention to Gabby, Lillian let out her breath in a sigh. A stab of pain made itself known deep within her. And she knew the cause.

Guilt.

It had been so easy to plan the demise of the late Duke of Billingham's good name before she met his son. Before she spent time in Simon's company, she had been able to dismiss the man's family as conspirators, or at least as people who had known about Roger Crathorne's ways and ignored them for their own benefit. But now, knowing Simon a little better, feeling his kiss, hearing his honest and straightforward words . . .

Well, she was beginning to recognize just how much she would destroy his world if she followed through on the plans she had made when she came here to his home.

Perhaps they were a mistake. Perhaps she could stop this madness before it was too late. Perhaps . . .

Before she could finish her thought, she felt a sharp jab in her ribs. She turned with a gasp of shock and found the dowager duchess glaring at her, one long finger still pointing from where she had poked Lillian.

Their eyes met, and then the other woman slowly shook her head. "No, Miss Mayhew. *No*," she murmured, low enough that only Lillian heard her.

Lillian's lips parted in shock and anger as she spun back around and faced forward. Obviously the dowager had noticed Lillian's regard for her son.

How much had *she* known about her late husband's lies?

Lillian pursed her lips with renewed purpose. Tomorrow she *would* talk to Simon. She *would* find the justice her father had sought and her mother deserved.

She would complete the quest that had brought her here. One way or another.

Chapter 10

If Lillian's resolve to pursue the source of Simon's worry had faded by the time the sun rose, she ignored that. She roused herself early and readied for the day without ringing for Maggie, something she had begun to get quite good at since she lost her own maid.

Soon she found herself slipping through the quiet hallways of the Billingham estate, searching for Simon. She had a hunch that if he was so troubled and distracted last night, he might very well be awake as well, still worrying over whatever had caused him grief.

But where would he be?

Starting in the one place she knew he loved, she crept into the library. It was empty and quiet, without even a fire burning in the grate, but the large windows let in morning sunshine. She looked around with memories assaulting her. They had

kissed here. And it had awoken something so
primal in her.

Something she was willing to sacrifice for her
father's demand and her mother's revenge.

"Stop it," she murmured to herself as she left the
room and shut the door smartly behind her. She
had no time for regrets.

Thrusting back her shoulders with wavering resolve, she continued her search of the main rooms.
The parlors were just as empty as the library. Finally she came upon the door to what he had described as his office during their truncated tour a
few days earlier. She hesitated outside, heart throbbing, and finally found enough courage to knock.

"Enter," came Simon's voice from within, and
she noted that he sounded strained and tired.

Biting her lip, she stepped into the room. As her
eyes adjusted to the dimmer light, she gasped and
looked around in shock at the state of the chamber.
It was positively awash in paperwork. Disordered,
toppling, piled dangerously high, it seemed no
corner of the room was free of the stuff.

When Simon had mentioned his father kept
everything, she had never pictured such a mess
as this.

She found Simon amidst the chaos, sitting
behind a large desk . . . or at least she *assumed* it
was large, so buried was it. His head was bent
and he was reading, his eyebrows knit together as

he did so. A pot of tea was perched precariously beside him on one stack of papers.

She shivered. In this room was the late duke's past. His truth. Perhaps everything she had come here to find.

"You can take the old pot out and place the new one—" Simon broke off his direction as he glanced up. "Oh, Lillian."

He made his way to his feet carefully and came around the desk. "I apologize, I thought you were one of the maids, come to bring me fresh tea."

Lillian forced a smile, surprised yet again by the faint pleasure that lit behind his dark eyes. Here he was, pleased to see her, and she had been secretly plotting against him.

"Good morning, Simon," she managed to choke out.

He motioned to one of the few empty chairs in the room with a smile. "It is better now that I've seen you. What are you doing awake so early?"

She dipped her chin, but did not take the chair he had offered. "Unlike so many of the young ladies here, I've never been comfortable lollygagging in the bed until noon."

She thought she saw a light of something heated in Simon's stare, but then he smiled. "Well, I can understand that. It would take *quite* an inducement to keep me in bed after seven."

Blood rushed to her cheeks and she turned

away slightly. She could well imagine what kind of inducement he meant. In fact, she found herself imagining it a bit too much and cleared her throat loudly to snap herself away from the inappropriate daydream.

"Actually, I admit *you* are the reason I'm awake at such an early hour," she said, renewing her purpose.

He took a long step closer. "Me? How interesting. And what have I done to earn your attention?"

She looked up at him and her breath caught. When he focused his gaze on her, she was made even more aware of the beautiful color of his eyes. And how hot and focused that stare could be.

She swallowed hard before she whispered, "Last night at the musicale, I could not help but notice that you seemed . . . troubled."

He blinked and the seductive teasing in his stare faded, replaced by wariness. "I see."

"I thought—that is, I *hoped* I could be of some assistance to you."

He did not respond, but instead moved closer. She watched as he reached out, almost in half-motion time, and took her hand. He lifted it to his lips and then they were on her skin. Her eyes fluttered shut and her knees threatened to buckle at the harsh and hot sensations that rocketed through her every nerve ending from his lips. In that instant, she was on fire and she feared the man who had started it might be the only one who could put it out.

"Sweetest Lillian," he purred, and she opened her eyes as he tugged her closer. His arms came around her and she molded against his chest, leaning into him almost against her will.

She lifted her mouth in mute offering and he took it, gently pressing his lips to hers in such a sweet way that tears stung behind her eyelids at the warm pressure.

Lillian had been an average little girl, she had dreamed of a man who would kiss her just like this. And even though those dreams had faded due to circumstances far beyond her control, they hadn't died. And yet the one who fulfilled those fantasies so well was most certainly the very worst choice for the job.

But that didn't stop her from parting her lips, inviting him in with the slightest sweep of her tongue against his. And it didn't stop her from letting out a moan of pleasure when the thin wire of his control broke and the kiss went from gentle to passionate.

Suddenly she found herself moving as Simon spun her around so her back was to the desk. He urged her up into the edge of the table and leaned into her as he pulled her even closer. As in the library the afternoon before, Lillian felt the shift in their embrace as his ardor grew.

But this time she also sensed something else. A desperation. A driving need that sought to mask something unpleasant. She understood that need. How often had she wished to make the pain go away, in any fashion possible?

And strangely, she wanted to give him that gift. She wanted to make him forget whatever troubled him, to wash away his sorrow with the gift of her body. And perhaps wash away some of her own, as well.

Perhaps there was something about her that made him feel that surrender, for he let out a low, powerful groan of pleasure into her mouth. His body arched into hers, rattling the papers on the table behind her, sending a few fluttering off the edges. But she forgot all that, forgot everything when she felt the rigid edge of his erection press into her belly.

Although she had no firsthand knowledge of the pleasures of the flesh, she had heard of such things from married friends and seen illustrations in a few naughty books one of the servants had accidentally left lying around years ago. Unlike many of her contemporaries, Lillian had never felt fear at the idea of a man fitting his body into hers.

Excitement and nervousness, yes. But fear, no.

And those emotions increased as she experienced Simon's desire. She found herself lifting up, rocking in time to him as her fingers clenched against the back of his shirt collar. His hand cupped her rib cage and then it was sliding up, up until he covered one breast.

She gasped, tilting her head back momentarily as strange sensations overpowered her. This touch was so intimate, and she knew it would be called wrong by some, but to her it felt so right. Wonderful. Especially when he squeezed gently, massaging her delicate flesh with just the right pressure to make her lower belly quiver and heated wetness to rush to her sheath.

But just as her excitement mounted, Simon pulled back. He stepped away, his eyes wild and his breath coming in heaving pants.

"I'm sorry," he said, steadying her with a warm hand on her shoulder. "I assure you it is not a habit of mine to ravish my party guests on the edge of my desk."

She stared at him, unready to take to her feet again because she was not certain she could support her weight on her shaking knees.

"Is it not?" she whispered, trying to sound nonchalant even though her voice trembled. "And why am I so special?"

He looked at her for a long moment. "I have no idea, Lillian. But for some reason the moment I come near you I forget that I am a gentleman, I forget I have duties and responsibilities, I forget everything except for the fact that I want to touch you."

She blinked, totally taken aback by his words. It seemed he was, as well, for he backed away another step, as if he feared he would lose control if she stayed near.

"But you are a lady and I'm supposed to be a gentleman," he continued. "In our current circumstances, what I just did was very wrong. Even if it felt deliciously right."

She nodded, but it took tremendous effort. What she wanted to do was launch herself at him and demand he do those wicked, wrong things again and again, propriety and her own plans be damned.

"You came here with the best of intentions," he continued, looking around him with a sigh, as if he was remembering his difficult duty. "To inquire about my welfare."

She nodded, managing to get to her feet now without collapsing. If he had to remember himself, so did she.

"I-I did. And you never answered me. Is something troubling you?"

He squeezed his eyes shut for a moment and pressed his fingers against them. Finally, he choked out, "When we talked earlier about my desire to sort through my father's papers, you asked me if I had discovered anything yet. At the time, I thought it an odd question. I did not believe there would be anything to 'discover.' And yet . . ."

She moved forward a step, her heart lodged firmly in her throat. "And yet?"

He looked at her. "Well, I suppose there might have been things about my father that I didn't know. And it troubles me to uncover them and begin to see that he might have been human and imperfect."

Lillian's heart had raced when they kissed, but now the beat of it increased yet again. Only this time it wasn't with pleasure, but anticipation. She wanted to demand that Simon reveal all to her. She wanted to scream out that his father was a monster disguised as a saint and nothing would ever erase that.

But she couldn't do those things. Too much eagerness and this man would very rightly lock her out. Even a whiff of her true intentions would ruin everything, and now that she was so close to the revenge her father had demanded and her mother deserved, how could she go back? Even if she wanted to?

"What sorts of things have you found?" she asked, her throat desperately dry.

He shrugged as he glanced at the paperwork around them absently. "Mostly items related to his political stances."

Her stomach sank. Though she had no doubt Simon's father had been duplicitous in his political dealings, those weren't the secrets she wished to uncover. No, she wanted something dark and personal and devastating. Something no one could gloss over or excuse. She had to silence the voices of exaltation whenever Roger Crathorne was mentioned and replace them with whispers of scandal and vice.

But she couldn't give up. If there was one secret, there were more. She felt that as surely as she felt her own heartbeat.

"It seems like quite an undertaking," she said softly. "Perhaps I could help, Simon."

"I think you can," he whispered. He shook his head as if trying to shake a feeling away. "I want you to."

"Then tell me what to do," she said, unable to cover her eagerness. "I shall do whatever you need."

He shut his eyes with a low groan that seemed to fill the space between them and make the room shrink. She found she was holding her breath as he opened his eyes once more.

"I need a few more hours to search here and then I'm certain I shall need an escape." He held her gaze steady. "I will need to see you. I want to talk to you about a matter of great import."

As his words sank in, Lillian swallowed with

difficulty. For a man looking for a wife, there was likely only one thing he could wish to discuss. But could that be true? Could this man, a duke, someone who could have anyone, really want *her*? A woman with a checkered family past, with no money, a woman whom many in his circles would openly despise?

"Lillian?" he whispered. "You are staring. Will you meet with me?"

She should have said no. She should have said she didn't want to discuss anything with him, for in the end she could not have him. It was impossible for far too many reasons to count.

And yet she nodded. "Yes. I will meet with you. Where?"

"Behind the stables. We can walk to the lake together," he said. "In two hours."

She nodded as she backed toward the door. If she didn't leave, she could very well say or do something that could never be taken back. Like admit she was a liar. Or beg him to ask her whatever he wanted to ask now.

"I'll be there," she whispered, then fled.

Chapter 11

Simon shifted from foot to foot, restlessly watching up the winding path that led to the main estate. Any moment Lillian would crest over the low hill and they would be together.

The very thought of that gave him a shiver of pleasure and made his mind return to their passionate encounter in his office that morning. He had nearly lowered her to the floor and taken her then and there. A moment more and he would have done just that, his good intentions to treat her as the lady she was dashed.

He had never felt such a keen desire for a woman before. A need that seemed to transcend the physical; he actually *ached* for her touch, for her taste. He had realized, in that moment, that he had to have her.

And in that same moment he had decided to ask for her hand; the future, the consequences, and everything else be damned. As soon as she said yes, he could claim her and sate the desire for her that seemed to pound in his very blood. With such a powerful attraction between them, and with so many things that drew him to her, he was certain they could make a happy enough union, even if love never bloomed between them.

Undoubtedly it would be little worse than any other arranged marriage Society celebrated. At least it would be of his choosing, his design.

If only she would agree.

He caught his breath, his thoughts forgotten as Lillian appeared in the distance. She didn't seem to see him at first, for her gaze was focused on the ground in front of her. She walked with a stiff, purposeful gait, almost as if she were being led to a punishment, not a pleasure. Despite kisses and confidences, she remained wary of him. And that continued to be a fascination to him.

And a terror when he considered what he was about to ask.

But then her gaze lifted and as she came closer, he saw the light of desire and excitement in her eyes. His doubts fled. Lillian Mayhew wanted him. And he would find a way to ensure they would both get what they so craved.

He had to, for if he didn't feel her body beneath his soon, he feared he might explode from the tension of wanting.

"Good afternoon," he said with a smile that he forced as she stopped in front of him.

She nodded, and from the way she worried her fingers against each other, he could see she was as nervous about this meeting as he was.

"It—it is a lovely day," she stammered when he was quiet for a moment.

He couldn't help but smile. Always they returned to the benign topic of the weather, it seemed.

"Will you walk with me?" he asked, motioning farther down the path toward the little-used lake on the estate. His mother had abhorred the place when he was a child, as had his sister. Only his father would take him down to the water's edge in secret and stare at the lapping waves with a strange and sad expression Simon never understood and the duke did not explain.

He flinched and pushed thoughts of his father away. He didn't want to think about the series of lies he had uncovered in the last few days, nor did he wish to be plagued by fears about what more there was to find. No, he wanted Lillian to be a balm for all that.

She held out her arm and he took it, lacing it within the crook of his own. When they touched, his troubled thoughts faded and his smile became more natural as they began the short walk to the lakeside.

They made their way in companionable silence for a short while, but then Lillian huffed out her breath, almost in a sound of exasperation.

"Earlier today you said you wished to speak to me about a matter of great import," she said, sliding a side glance toward him. "I admit I have been trying to determine what in the world you could want to say ever since. May we discuss it before I make myself mad with pondering all the options?"

Simon chuckled at her candor. Surely there was no woman at the house who would broach the subject so directly. And he owed her no less than the same forthrightness in return.

"I'm sorry to make you wonder," he said, guiding her down the sloping curve of a hill as the lake came into sight. "I'll keep you in suspense no longer."

She leaned a little bit closer, just a subtle movement he might not have noticed had he not been so entirely attuned to everything from her tiniest breath to her smallest sigh.

"Lillian," he said, and cleared his throat uncomfortably. He still wasn't quite certain how to do this. "You—you must know why my mother arranged for this party at this time. My father's passing and my taking of the title has demanded that I wed."

She nodded, a jerky movement that revealed more of her discomfort and embarrassment with the subject than she probably would have said out loud.

"But I am not the proper woman for that, Your Grace. I think that topic has been more than exhausted by everyone involved."

He frowned at her continued refusal to consider any kind of connection to him, despite their obvious attraction. "Yes, you have said so and I know that others have *discouraged* you from any interest you might have in me. They continually harp on the circumstances that should keep us from any kind of true union."

Her face crumpled for just a fraction of a moment before she hardened her expression. "Are the 'circumstances' to which you are referring the suicide of my mother?"

Simon flinched. Her tone was so cold, and he hated himself for making her look and sound thus. "Whatever happened to your mother, Lillian, it was not your fault. It's unfair that it reflects upon you."

Her lips thinned and she looked away so that he could see her only in profile. She was so stiff he feared she might break and he dared not touch her.

"Nevertheless, it *does* reflect upon me. I'm not a child, I know how Society works."

Simon frowned. He wanted so desperately to make his offer and hear her answer, but in this moment she actually seemed willing to give him a little of the information of her past that he had been trying to pry away from her almost since the first moment they met. Perhaps if she shared some of that, if she felt his acceptance and his compassion, she would be more willing to accept *him*.

"Lillian, will you tell me about her? All I hear are rumors and whispers. I'd like to know the truth."

She jerked her chin toward him briefly, and there was a surprising heat of anger and even hatred in her stare before she dropped her gaze to her clenched fists.

"She was never very happy," she bit out through clenched teeth. "It seemed to be in her nature to be melancholy. But then something happened . . . *someone* hurt her very badly."

Simon frowned. He had never heard this detail. The fact that someone else had played party to her mother's untimely end made the outcome all the more tragic.

Lillian continued speaking, "It drove her to the brink and beyond. If you are trying to determine whether or not she truly took her life as the rumors say . . ." She drew a deep breath. "Then yes, Your Grace. My mother had been given laudanum to calm her troubled dreams. One night she took enough that she simply never woke up."

Simon leaned toward her and touched her hand. She didn't pull away, but remained stiff beneath his touch. "Could it have been an accident?"

She shook her head. "As much as I wish it was, there is no denying she meant to take her life that night. Her letters of good-bye and explanation to my father, my brother, and me proved it."

Pulling her hand away, she paced a few steps toward the edge of the lake and looked out over the still waters. For a long time she was silent, but then she cleared her throat.

"The family made every effort to cover up the truth, to protect her memory. We even managed to have her buried on sacred ground, though I think my father may have sold some of her jewelry to pay off the vicar for that 'honor.' And yet there was always talk. Perhaps a servant revealed too much, perhaps the vicar, or perhaps it was some other person entirely. One way or another, some details were put out into the public and the vultures of the *ton* have picked at them incessantly ever since."

She turned her face so he could see her and the sight of her broke his heart. Her jaw was stiff as she tried to hold back emotions.

Her lip wobbled, but her voice didn't tremble when she said, "You aren't the first man to want to end an affiliation with me because of what happened, Simon. I have no illusions that I shall ever marry within the circles I once debuted in. In fact, I think I would not wish to. The life that would bring would likely be very unpleasant."

Simon flinched. She was repeating almost verbatim the point Rhys had made to him days before. His friend had said Lillian might be reluctant to accept his attentions because she did not *wish* for the life of a duchess and all the consequences that would bring to her.

She faced him, lifting her chin in a falsely haughty and strong expression. "I shall go back to the house now. Please don't worry about me making a scene. I wouldn't do that."

He stared at her. If he asked her to marry him, he could see that she would refuse. But God, how he wanted her. To soothe her, to heal her, to heal himself. This exchange between them only strengthened his pulsing desire to mold his body to her and feel her surrender to him.

If Rhys had been right that she would not marry him, was it possible he was also correct she might instead accept an offer of protection from him? Would she become his mistress? Was her desire for him strong enough?

She began to move to pass him and return to the house. Desperate, he caught her hand and pulled her back toward him. He couldn't let her go, not like this. Not without even trying to find one last way to keep her.

"Lillian, I don't wish to break with you at all."

Her expression softened, although her eyes remained wary. "You . . . you don't?" she said in utter disbelief. "But I have told you I could never be—"

He shook his head to interrupt her. A last flash of chivalry, of gentlemanly behavior screamed at him not to do this, but it was overpowered by animal desires and a selfish need to bond himself to this woman in some kind of primal way.

"Lillian . . ." One last hesitation and then he blurted out the offer he had sworn he never would. "I want to offer you my protection."

"Your protection?" she repeated, her brow wrinkling as if she didn't understand. But then, perhaps she didn't. If she was an innocent, she likely didn't know much about the world outside of her own.

He cleared his throat. "Er, yes. You see, there are times when a man—"

She interrupted him by stepping back and staring up at him, lips slightly parted. She darted her tongue out to wet them and whispered, "Your Grace, are you asking me to become your mistress?"

He recoiled at the flat way she asked the question. This entire situation was not going according to plan in the slightest. He feared he couldn't salvage it at all, yet he was driven to try.

"Yes," he admitted. "That is what I am asking you, Lillian."

Her lip trembled as she turned away. "Why?"

That was the one question he hadn't expected. But it was easy enough to find an answer. "You've stated many times that you are not suitable for me, that you do not plan or wish to marry a man like me. Yet this tension and desire courses between us whenever we are near each other. I propose we allow it. Surrender to it."

"I see," she said so softly that he almost didn't hear it.

He moved forward, aching to touch her even though he could see that was not the proper response. Not until she understood.

"Please don't think I'm proposing we merely become temporary lovers. I do not mean to take your virtue and throw you away. I'd like something more permanent. As I've stated many times, I am fascinated by you. And I think we are well-suited."

She said nothing and didn't look at him, so he continued.

"Think of it, Lillian. I would provide you a living and a home in the city. I would escort you to wonderful places. You would host parties for my closest friends. Many would accept you, even if they knew of the nature of our relationship. You would no longer have to live on the kindness of friends."

She darted her eyes toward him. "Only on *your* kindness. And the fickle element of your affection and desire."

He pursed his lips at her implication. "If we came to a point when we parted company, I would provide handsomely for you. You would not be put out on the street."

She suddenly smiled, though it was a brittle expression. "So you are saying you would be doing this for my own good. For my well-being."

He threw up his hands in frustration. "You act as though I'm offering you charity."

"Are you not?" she snapped, and spun on him with sudden passion.

"No," he cried with equal vigor. "Great God, woman, have I not made it clear enough that I want you? This request is a selfish one. I make it because I ache to feel your body next to mine in my bed. If I cannot have it one way, I will beg for it another."

He caught her forearms and she gasped, but didn't pull away when he dragged her against him.

"I make this request because I want to taste you in every way, I want to fill your body with my own, I want to hear you sigh and moan when I claim you. *That* is why I ask you to be my mistress. Everything else is secondary."

Before she could answer, he dipped his lips to hers and kissed her. Despite her brittle posture and tart words, the moment their lips touched, Lillian's arms came around him, her fingers clawing into the back of his jacket as she maneuvered to get closer. He obliged, cupping her backside to fit her against him, letting her feel how much she could arouse him with just the slightest touch.

"You see," he murmured as he dragged his lips away from hers and to her throat. "We both want this, Lillian."

She stiffened at his words and struggled away, staggering back a few steps. He saw hurt in her eyes, anger, very proper reactions from a lady who had just been made what could be viewed as an insulting offer. But somewhere in those ever-changing hazel depths he also saw desire. A hint that his offer was tempting to her.

Even though she was hell-bent on refusing him.

"I've spent a lifetime living with disappointment, Your Grace," she panted as she smoothed her gown. "It is something you will learn to live with, as well."

He shook his head. "Lillian—"

"No." The word tore from her throat with a sharpness that silenced him. "No, Simon. I cannot do this. What you want is impossible, for so many reasons."

Then she turned away and started back up the hill toward the house, leaving him without another word, without further explanation and with no hope that he would ever hold her in his arms again.

He turned toward the water so he wouldn't see her disappear over the hill. When he was certain she was out of earshot, he fisted his hands at his sides and muttered, "Damn."

Lillian was so upset, she could hardly see as she stumbled away from Simon and back toward the protection of the manor house. What a fool she was! When she came to meet with him, she had thought the question he might ask was for her hand in marriage. The idea that she would have to reject him had haunted her all morning.

But that wasn't what he wanted at all. Just like everyone else around him, Simon didn't think her worthy of the title of wife or duchess. Whore was more suited.

Well, mistress, but what was the difference really? A dressed-up whore was still a whore.

The fact that she was actually *disappointed* that he hadn't asked her to wed was bad enough. After all, she didn't want to marry into this family. Even if she was inexplicably attracted to his son, she despised the late duke and remained bent on revenge. That did't exactly bode well for a happy marriage.

And yet the reaction that upset her more was the fact that some small part of her, a part she was trying desperately to crush with little luck, actually found Simon's insulting offer to be *tempting*.

When he said he wanted her in his bed and described so bluntly what that meant, she had found herself picturing how magnificent it could be. She had no doubt he would be a spectacular lover. His kisses made her melt, if he went further she just might combust.

"Stupid girl," she chastised herself as she turned away from the house and paced toward the gardens.

She wasn't ready to face the other guests, or worse, bump into Simon as he returned from their wicked little meeting. At present, she didn't think she could endure it.

Actually, she feared she might launch herself into his arms and take him up on his offer. After all, how many chances would she get at a great passion in her life? She was firmly on the shelf if just for the fact that she was more than twenty-five years old. Add to that equation her lack of funds, her wayward brother, and her scandalous mother, and there was no way she would ever marry well. She had meant it when she said she no longer even considered such a thing to be possible or acceptable.

In the past, she had to admit she had considered being a man's mistress. There was some security to the position. And yet no man had ever inspired her to take that thought beyond a passing fancy.

Until now. Despite everything, she could clearly picture what kind of life she would have as Simon's paramour. And it wasn't a bad one.

It didn't seem to matter that she could see Simon was truly his father's son. Despite his pretended honor, he was willing to take a lady into his bed as his mistress, driven to slake his desires no matter the consequences. And yet she was not repulsed. She still wanted him.

So was she any better than he?

She shook her head as she wandered the gardens, not even seeing the newly blooming flowers or fresh foliage around her. In her current situation, all she could think about, all she could concentrate on, was Simon. His handsome face. His devastating kiss. His remarkable offer that made her tingle all over when she considered it.

There was no question about it, she had to finish what she had come here to do. She owed it to her family to fulfill the promise her brother could not. But it was clear to her now that she had to do it sooner rather than later.

Before she fell too far under Simon's sway. Before she took him up on his tempting offer and found herself in his bed.

Chapter 12

Another afternoon had come and brought another gathering with it, yet Simon could hardly concentrate on taking his tea and chatting amiably with the ladies around him. There were too many distractions running a race in his mind.

First and foremost, there was Lillian.

Since she had run away after his offer the day before, she had been in hiding. Last night it was a "headache" that had kept her from joining the party for supper and cards afterward. He had been tempted to storm up to her room to see her just as he had the day of the picnic, but had managed to refrain. After all, she couldn't stay secluded in her room forever, could she?

Or perhaps she could.

Today she had taken a tray in her room for breakfast rather than join the others, and the same for luncheon. He'd been at the breaking point, ready to violate her privacy and demand they talk about what had transpired between them.

Luckily, he hadn't been forced to do so. Some-how she had been persuaded by Lady Gabriela to join their party for tea, but she kept herself as far away from him as humanly possible. She never looked in his direction, never acknowledged when he stared at her across the room, longing to talk to her. To touch her. To somehow explain himself to her and make her smile at him again. It was amaz-ing how much he had come to depend on that in such a short time.

Perhaps the entire situation was simply a lost cause. He sighed and stirred his tea absently. He had made his offer to her, however foolish it was that he had listened to Rhys's advice to make her a mistress. He had done it and he couldn't take it back. Nor could he change the fact that she had refused him.

A smart man would wash his hands of the matter and go back to the task of finding a suitable bride. A smart man would forget Lillian entirely.

Apparently he had grossly overestimated his own intelligence.

No, he had to think of other things. Get his mind off the troubling and temping Miss Mayhew. Un-fortunately, when it was not she who filled his mind, it was something else that was just as con-fusing and far more unpleasant.

His father.

He had always believed in the façade the late duke put on. They had been remarkably close, and Simon had never seen so much as a crack in the face his father put on for the world. But now, the deeper he searched, the more it seemed that it was, indeed, something the late duke had "put on." A lie.

At the very least, his father had allowed himself to be corrupted by politics a handful of times. While he crusaded for good, he had given money to and taken it from those who worked against the very causes he championed.

But Simon feared there was worse waiting for him in the tangle of paperwork and correspondence. Certainly there were hints of blackmail, lies, and dark secrets.

Pushing to his feet, Simon shot an apologetic smile at the ladies who had been surrounding him while he was lost in reverie. No doubt they had come here expecting an attentive host, and for that he was truly sorry.

But he had things to do. Inescapable duties that he now felt compelled to pursue.

"I do apologize, ladies," he announced to the room. "But as much as I have enjoyed your company this afternoon, there are a few things I must attend to before we reconvene for supper later on. I hope you'll understand and I bid you a good day."

Without waiting for a response, or even register-
ing the looks of shock, anger, or disappointment
on the varying faces around him, Simon turned
on his heel and departed the room in a few long
strides.

In the hallway, he felt slightly less stifled and
quickened his step toward his father's office. But
just as he stepped inside and began to close the
door behind him, a hand reached through the door
and shoved it back toward him.

He stepped back in surprise as his mother entered the room, her gaze flashing with emotions he
could clearly read as anger and frustration. With a
sigh, he nodded in acknowledgment.

"Madam," he said. "Is there something I can do
for you?"

Before she answered, his mother threw the
door shut behind her and then turned on him. He
almost drew away, for in that unguarded moment
he saw something else in her stare. Hatred. And it
was directed toward him.

"What you can do for me?" she raged, the hate
gone from her eyes but lingering in the tension
in her voice. "You can stop ruining everything I
have planned for you. Everything you have been
given!"

Simon turned away and paced around the
stacks of files toward the window. "I don't know
what you mean, Mother."

Instead of allowing him the space he had taken by walking away, his mother charged after him.

"You know very well what I mean. You were abominably rude by walking out in the middle of tea. Before you had even crossed the threshold of the chamber, several of the chaperones were talking about returning to London since it is clear that there is no point in them being here."

He faced her. What she was describing was indeed a problem, as he had to find a wife, and the last thing he needed was for rumors to spread and make that task difficult. But somehow he couldn't muster the ability to care.

"I am truly sorry to hear that the others feel I'm wasting their time—" he began, but she cut him off.

"You *are* wasting their time!" his mother snapped, throwing up her hands in disgust. "You ignore all your guests except for the least acceptable of them, you sneak off . . ."

Simon arched an eyebrow. She was trying his paper-thin patience now, and he had little positive emotion to buffer his response when he said, "Please do not dare to accuse me of such a thing. Not when *you* have been creeping away for hours, sometimes days at a time, for as long as I can recall."

To his surprise, his mother's anger and frustration seemed to bleed away, leaving behind a pan-icked fear that he had never seen before.

"That—that is my business, Simon," she said, quieter than before.

He shrugged, too exhausted to press her. "And this is mine, Mother. You must realize I have duties that stretch beyond this party. Beyond my eventual marriage. There are things I've found here that must be dealt with."

Now her eyes narrowed. "Things? What *things* are you talking about?"

Simon clenched his fists behind his back. His mother despised his father. Telling her about the old man's secrets felt like a betrayal, and he was reluctant to give her any more ammunition in her war against the man, even dead.

But he also knew his mother well enough to know she hated scandal more than she hated anyone else. Perhaps if she was aware of a little of what he was finding, she would retreat and allow him his duty.

"Father may not have been what he seemed," he admitted softly.

A little smile tilted her lips, but it was brittle and humorless. "Is that right?"

Simon ignored the sarcasm dripping from every syllable and continued, "There were discrepancies with his support in certain legislation. A difference between his public face and his private dealings."

One thin eyebrow arched as his mother said, "It does not surprise me. But Simon, these things can be ignored for now. No one knows this but you, apparently. Why stir up a controversy? Leave it be."

"But there might be more," he said, lifting his hands in a plea for understanding. "I am finding evidence that points to something deeper. Something more personal that Father may have been blackmailed over."

Her lips thinned. "Simon, it is *you* who doesn't understand." She stepped forward, one index finger extended until she pushed it into his chest. "Leave it alone. Put it away and forget it. For all of us, it is better left in the past."

Simon opened his mouth to answer, but she held up a palm to silence him. Slowly, she turned and stalked from the room, leaving him gaping after her in utter shock.

He had never known his mother to be so emotional. Normally she was reserved almost to the point of being icy. Yet when he accused her of running, he had actually seen her fear, and then again when he mentioned the blackmail he suspected.

Could it be that his mother had known about these things all along? That she also knew more about his father's secrets? Would she truly protect a man she had openly despised?

Simon frowned. If there was something nefarious in the late duke's past, that would certainly explain why his mother had hated the man.

But would it ultimately leave him hating his father as well?

"Thank you again for your assistance," Simon said without looking up from the items he was sorting.

Across the room, he heard Rhys's voice muffled by all the clutter between them. "You know I'll always do whatever I can to help you."

Simon nodded to himself. Yes, and beyond that he also knew that Rhys could be depended upon for discretion. He trusted the other man like a brother, which was why he had called him here hours ago to continue what seemed like a fruitless search for more information on Simon's father's past.

"This is utterly frustrating," he groaned, tossing a huge pile of useless paperwork in the rubbish bin to be burned later. "Perhaps there is nothing further to find, after all."

"Simon . . ." Rhys said, his voice strained and strange.

Simon stood up slowly to peer over the mess between them. His friend hadn't called him by his first name since he first took a lesser title years ago. That, coupled with Rhys's strange tone, made Simon's stomach clench.

"What is it?" he asked, coming around the desk toward his friend.

Rhys got up from his chair. He had a ledger in one hand and a yellowed, crumpled letter in another. He held out the envelope.

"I found something," he said softly.

Simon reached for the missive, his hands trembling ever so slightly.

"What is it?" he asked, suddenly loath to open it.

"I've noticed this in your father's ledgers before." His friend's voice remained strained. "If he bought a sheep, he often put the details of the transaction in the ledger along with the prices."

"The letter is about buying sheep?" Simon asked, his voice breaking as he met his friend's eyes.

Rhys's gaze flitted away. "No. But it *is* about a payment that was made to someone. You should look at it."

Simon stared at the letter. Yes, his friend was correct. He *should* open it and face whatever horrible thing his father had done. But he found it difficult to do so. Almost impossible.

But finally he opened the aging envelope and unfolded the brittle sheets within. After a few moments of reading, he glanced up.

"This is about his firstborn son," he whispered. "A boy who wasn't me."

Rhys nodded slowly. "From the date, it seems

as if the child was born only a few months before you were."

"A bastard," Simon repeated dully. "And then the duke was so vocal about the irresponsible nature of his colleagues. He preached so loudly about taking care not to create fatherless children that he shamed the entire *ton*."

Rhys looked at him with unmistakable pity. "To be fair to the duke, it seems he *did* make some arrangements for the child to be taken care of. That's why it was in this ledger. A large lump sum was paid out in the boy's name."

Simon scanned further. "Henry Ives."

"I've never heard of him," Rhys said. "So he's likely not of our social standing."

Simon could only stare at the name, written in his father's even, neat handwriting. Written so coldly, as if this was just another payment to another person. There was nothing in the letter that detailed the circumstances of the transaction. No indication whatsoever that his father cared about the baby son who could never carry his name. He never mentioned the mother's name at all.

Worst of all, his father made note that he considered the matter closed now that the money had been received. He clearly had no intention of ever thinking of the child or its mother again.

"Billingham, this ledger was from the year of your birth, over thirty years ago."

Simon forced some focus and looked up at his friend. "Yes?"

Rhys shifted uncomfortably. "Well, judging from the nonchalant way your father lays out the details, it leads me to believe it might not have been the first time he made such a payment. And . . ."

Simon sank into the closest chair. "And since he lived three decades afterward, it was likely not the last. You believe there are other children. Other bastards."

Reaching out, his friend briefly touched his shoulder in an awkward gesture of comfort. "I think it's safe to assume that is true."

Simon returned his gaze to the name on the sheet.

Henry Ives.

An abandoned brother who was living God only knew what kind of life. He could be in trade, or a parish priest, or a common thug.

Or dead.

Simon's chest hurt at the thought. His head spun when he considered the possibility of other brothers and sisters who very likely existed in the world. Children his father had created and then discarded with only a simple payment to make up for everything else they would lack.

"If she knew . . ." he mused, more to himself than to Rhys. "No wonder she hated him."

Rhys cocked his head. "I beg your pardon?"

"Nothing," Simon said, waving his friend off as he staggered to his feet. "I would like to be alone."

Inclining his head, Rhys backed toward the door. "I understand."

But as his friend departed, Simon looked around the room. It made him nauseous to be here. He wanted to scream. He wanted to shake his father. He wanted a drink.

And he wanted to erase what he now knew from his mind. Any way he could.

"Look at her pace," Lillian whispered, nudging Gabby with an elbow as she watched Simon's mother from across the room. "She is upset, for sure."

Gabby rubbed her side as she gave Lillian a glare. "Yes, dear. You've mentioned this several times. It's evident Lady Billingham is quite upset by her son's disappearance."

Lillian's stomach clenched.

"Don't say disappearance," she said, looking out over the group with worry. "It implies he might not return."

Her friend shot her a side glance. "Do you care so much?"

Lillian worried her hands in front of her. She wanted to say she didn't, but Gabby knew her too well to accept the lie. Of course Lillian cared. She had cared when Simon left the parlor today in the middle of tea, she had cared when his mother stalked after him with such furious intent in her cold stare, and she had cared when he had vanished from the group, appearing neither for supper nor for this gathering afterward.

In short, she was worried, no matter how much she tried not to be. Something was clearly troubling Simon. Something dark and deep that probably involved his father, if their earlier conversation was any indication. She tried to tell herself that was the only cause for her interest.

But that was a lie, too.

"I'm going to look for him," she murmured.

Gabby turned on her with a huff of breath. "Lillian!"

She shrugged. "I cannot miss this chance to uncover something about the late duke, can I?"

"That has nothing to do with your desire to find Simon and you know it," her friend hissed under her breath. "This has to do with your growing feelings for him. Admit it."

It seemed everything in Lillian's body froze at her friend's accusation. "F-feelings? For Simon? Don't be daft."

"I would be daft if I didn't see them." Gabby sipped her drink as she stared at Lillian evenly. "No matter your original motives for coming here or your misgivings about Simon's pursuit, the fact is that you have begun to care for this man. And your feeling for him seems to increase with each passing day."

Lillian shook her head. "His offer to make me his mistress made it clear he is no better than his father."

Her friend's snort interrupted her. "Please. You wish to be insulted, and perhaps some small part of you *is* hurt that he made such a shocking request. But your eyes also sparkle when you think of being in this man's life, even in such a scandalous manner."

Lillian's mouth dropped open, though she had to acknowledge to herself that every word her friend spoke was truth. But she wouldn't say it out loud. "I could never . . ."

She trailed off as Gabby's eyebrow arched incredulously.

"Well, believe what you wish, then," Lillian snapped, a bit louder than she had intended. She corrected her tone with a sigh. "Regardless, I'm going to look for him. Will you make my excuses if anyone asks?"

Her friend let out a long-suffering sigh. "You know I will. But don't think for a moment that you have me fooled."

Lillian ignored the parting shot and slipped from the room as surreptitiously as she could.

In the hallway, she drew a long breath. Now that

she was alone, Gabby's accusations rang with even more troubling clarity. Was her friend correct?

No, she refused to accept that she might have feelings for the man. Simon was a means to an end for her, she could not forget that.

Not ever.

Straightening her shoulders with this new resolve, she began wandering the quiet halls of his home, peeking in chambers and listening at doors in the hope she would find him. Once she did, she had no idea what she planned to do, but she would decide that once the time came.

She had all but given up on the main level of the house when she reached the final chamber on that floor. She pushed at the door and peered in. It was the billiard room Simon had shown her the day she arrived here. She thought it was empty as she looked around, but just as she was about to depart, she saw a twisting trail of smoke coming up from a high-backed chair with its back to the door.

Her heart jumped to her throat and Lillian almost bolted, but she forced herself to step inside.

"S-Simon?"

There was a long pause before a low, sensual chuckle came from the chair. The sound played along her spine and made her nerves jump and twitch.

"It *would* be you who found me," he murmured as he pushed to his feet and turned toward her.

She caught her breath. Every other time she had met with Simon, he'd been impeccably dressed and pulled together. Not tonight. Tonight his cravat was gone, leaving his shirt gaping at the neck to reveal a vee of smooth skin at his throat. He obviously hadn't shaved since that morning, and a dark hint of stubble had begun on his cheeks and chin. Actually, he looked quite like he had just stumbled out of bed.

The image was delicious.

"Why are you here, Lillian?" he asked, but despite his blunt question, his tone held no malice.

She glanced around before she answered. Her gaze slipped to the small table beside the chair he had occupied when she entered. The remains of a cigar smoldered in an ashtray there, along with an empty bottle of whiskey and a glass half full of the same.

Her stare returned to his face. His gaze was glassy and so sad and disenchanted that she nearly flinched at the powerful emotions he made no effort to hide.

"Are you drunk?" she whispered.

He shrugged one shoulder as he took a long step in her direction. "Not enough."

Her voice cracked as she asked, "And how much is enough?"

A bark of laughter escaped his lips. "I don't know yet. Ask again in a few hours."

"Simon—"

He reached out and caught a lock of her hair between his fingers. As he tugged it loose from her fancy style, her words cut off in her throat.

"You never answered my question," he said, his tone soft.

She swallowed hard. He'd moved closer again, and all she could see or feel at that moment was him. The rest of the room faded.

"Which question?" she asked.

He smiled. "You know which question, I think. Why are you here?"

"You—you disappeared," she explained, knowing she should move away, but somehow unable. Most definitely unwilling.

"And *you* have been designated as search party?" he asked solemnly. "Did you bring dogs to scent me out?"

"Simon—"

His eyes fluttered shut for a moment. "I do love it when you say my name."

He began to lean toward her, and she gasped. Somehow she found the ability to step away, though her pounding heart kept on beating like butterfly wings against her rib cage.

"There is clearly something wrong with you. Please tell me what it is."

"Why?" he asked, a hard edge to his voice as he grabbed the drink behind him and swigged the remaining liquid.

"Perhaps I could help," she whispered, hating herself for using him. And hating herself equally for the fact that she truly did wish to be of assistance.

He set the empty glass aside.

"How could you help me?"

She opened and shut her mouth a few times. In truth, she had no plan. Finding Simon was as far as she had gotten in her mind. She'd never thought she'd come upon him like this. Out of control. Needy and seductive in equal measure.

"I don't know," she admitted.

Once again, he moved on her, only stopping when he was just a fraction of an inch away. His heat suffused her gown, leaving her burning and branded. It made her ache. It made her *want*.

"I think you *do* know," he murmured. "I think you look at me and you know what I need. So tell me, Lillian, how will you help me?"

She shivered as his breath caressed her cheek. He was right. Deep inside her, in dark and hidden places, she knew how to make his hurt go away, if only temporarily. She knew how to erase the pain. To make them both forget.

And just as Gabby had accused her of earlier, that was exactly what she wanted. On her own terms. This moment was for her and no one else. She could return to duty later.

Her fingers trembled as she lifted them and threaded them through the crisp locks of his dark hair. He didn't resist her touch, only let his breath out in a ragged sigh, as if he had been waiting for this moment for an eternity and now he was ready to surrender to it. She trembled as she tugged gently and drew his lips to her own.

And then she kissed him.

Chapter 13

The moment Simon's lips met hers, Lillian realized that this encounter wouldn't stop until they had made love. But despite her innocence, despite her refusal of his offer the day before, despite all her duties when she came to this estate, she didn't feel afraid. And she didn't feel wrong.

No, the only emotion that roared through her as their mouths collided and tongues danced, was excitement. This was *her* choice and there was no doubt it had been made. There would be no going back.

She drank in every moment, memorizing the assault on her senses. He tasted of whiskey and sweet cigar smoke. But beneath it all was a sharp current of male desire. She smelled the same indefinable aspect on his skin, a heated, musky scent that called to her body and made a strange wetness rush between her legs.

His breathing echoed in her ears between kisses,

a panting drive of air that merged with her own as the only sound in the otherwise quiet room. But that shared breath was as beautiful as a symphony to her, inspiring feelings she wouldn't have been able to define even if someone offered her all the gold in the world to do so.

When his arms came around her to drag her against him, she felt the full power of his superior strength, as well as the insistent evidence of his desire. She shivered with the realization that she had done that to him. *She* had made his body hard and ready and edgy with need.

With a groan, he pushed her backward across the spacious chamber, devouring her lips all the way, until her backside touched the edge of the billiard table. Then he leaned into her, nudging a leg to tangle with her dress between her thighs. She found herself grinding down against him in some ancient give-and-take of pleasure. She reveled in the friction that wanton action created. It was something so focused and powerful, so wicked and yet so right.

The chamber seemed to get hotter, closer, as their lips and tongues merged. And Simon seemed to be getting closer, too, his body curling around her as they arched backward in tandem. Finally she was flat on her back against the top of the billiard table, with his hard body covering hers.

There had never been anything like this pleasure. She was on fire, her breasts tingled and ached most deliciously, her legs trembled as she crooked one knee around his calf, her sheath clenched in a rhythm she had never experienced before.

After what seemed like a sweet eternity, his hands moved. He flattened one palm to her collarbone, hesitating as her chest rose and fell on each fluttering breath. Then he stared down at her with an unflinching gaze. His green eyes were so intense at this short distance that she almost wanted to look away, but she couldn't, not even when his fingers slid down, dancing to rest between her breasts.

"Simon," she groaned, feeling she should be shocked by this intimacy, and yet not so.

It seemed natural that he would touch her in this way. That he would claim her in a fashion no other man had ever done before. Perhaps no man would ever do so again.

He smiled, but didn't respond verbally. Instead he moved his hand to cup her breast. She arched helplessly into the touch, shocked by how hot and needy he could make her. The delicate silk that comprised her gown was no match for the rough glide of his skin. She shivered when she imagined how right and powerful it would be when she wasn't covered by fabric. When his hand touched her bare body.

"Cold?" he murmured as he brought his lips to her neck and nuzzled.

Somehow she managed to shake her head. "Hot," she gasped as his tongue traced her throbbing pulse. "So hot."

His head lifted and there was a wicked intent that glittered in his stare. "I can fix that."

He drew back and pulled her gently to a seated position. She didn't resist. She couldn't, even as he popped one tiny button along the front of her simple gown. His gaze never left hers as he repeated the action all along the front of the dress. As she stared, he dropped his lips to the skin he had revealed and brushed them back and forth.

"Simon," she gasped, digging her fingers into his shoulders as his tongue played along the lacy edge of her chemise.

"Cooler?" he whispered, his breath burning against her skin.

"N-no," she said.

"Then I had best remove more."

He chuckled as he dragged her dress down around her waist, tugging it away from her arms. She lifted her backside up, and finally he tossed the gown aside and it landed with a swish of fabric on the floor.

"You are beautiful," he said, his tone reverent and low.

He looped his fingers beneath her thin chemise straps and glided them over her shoulders, down her arms. The fabric fell forward and she was bared from the waist up.

Modesty dictated embarrassment. That she cover herself. And yet she didn't. She didn't want to. She loved how he looked at her, how his eyes glazed with passion. How he seemed to see her as the most exquisite creature he had ever laid eyes upon.

She had never experienced such a thing.

"A-aren't *you* hot?" she stammered, untested in flirtation and seduction and feeling inadequate and silly as she tried to play a game in which he was master.

One corner of his lips tilted up in a sensual half smile. "Oh yes."

She reached out, trembling, and found the opening in his wrinkled shirt, gasping as her fingertips grazed his bare skin. She had never touched another person like that before. She had never felt the taut flesh of a man's body. She liked it. She wanted more. She wanted to see him and touch him and taste him as wantonly as he had done to her. In some small way, she wanted to claim him, no matter how temporary that owner-ship would be.

Her fingers felt thick and useless as she struggled

to unbutton his shirt. He made no attempt to help or hinder her progress, just watched her through a hooded, heated gaze as she finally pushed the shirt open and away from his shoulders.

Her breath caught. She had never seen a man like this, but she had a suspicion the one before her was quite a specimen. His broad shoulders were contoured, layered with lean cords of muscle that tapered into a chest sprinkled with just a dash of wiry hair.

She feasted on the look of him. Clearly he did not buy into the current fashion of lazy aristocracy, for his stomach was not just flat but rippled with the hint of muscles below the taut surface. And his chest hair continued in a thin line that disappeared into his waistband in the most interesting fashion.

"Lillian," he murmured.

She snapped her gaze to his with a gasp of embarrassment. "Yes?"

"Breathe, darling," he said as he cupped her neck and brought his lips toward hers.

She sucked in one gasping gulp of air before his mouth branded her yet again. Now that she was free from some of the heavier layers of gown, it was easier to be an active participant in this dance of desire. Her chemise only just skimmed her middle thighs, which meant she could actually part her legs when he nudged between them, she could wrap one around his thigh in an attempt to be even closer.

He groaned as they fell back against the table once more.

"The things you do to me," he whispered, though the comment seemed to be more to himself than her.

His mouth drifted down to cover her breast as his hand had moments before. She arched up with a helpless cry as he sucked her hard nipple between his lips. His mouth was so hot, so wet as he swirled his tongue around and around the sensitive peak, driving her wild as sensation after sensation exploded from the point of contact to flow through her entire body.

He switched to the other breast, repeating the action there. By that time, she was writhing, digging her fingers into his naked shoulders, pulling him closer with her legs and arching up into his tongue with wanton moans and cries.

"So deliciously responsive," he whispered, moving farther down her body. Her bunched and wrinkled chemise shifted against her skin as he kissed his way across her flat stomach, to her hip, and finally he parted her legs further and placed a kiss to her thigh.

She shivered, sitting up a bit to see what he would do next. She stared in wonder as he pushed her chemise up until it was a useless scrap of silk around her stomach. He spread her legs wide, his warm hands cupping her mound, then opening the tender flesh there.

Heat filled her cheeks as he looked up and met her gaze. Gone was the proper duke, gone was the polite gentleman. All that was left in Simon's eyes was an animal desire to have her. All of her. She thrilled at that fact.

"I'm going to give you such pleasure," he promised before he dropped his mouth to the already wet outer lips of her sheath.

When his tongue touched her so intimately, all she could do was cry out, her fists clenching against the velvety fabric of the billiard table. What was this sensation? Something so powerful, so pleasurable, so focused in that one place in her body, and yet whispers of it ricocheted to every other part of her, as if her entire being were now a sensual tool.

His tongue probed deeper, tasting her, lapping at her like she was some kind of sweet treat. She arched into him, demanding more without words, and when he chuckled against her, the vibrations made her cry out yet again.

He took advantage, suddenly sucking on the hardened pearl of nerves that was hidden with the folds of her flesh. She squeezed her eyes shut as a new pleasure rocked her. Something so powerful, so intense that she found herself shaking against her will as wave after wave of sensation rolled over her. It seemed to go on and on, and she cried out against it, surrendering to its power.

Finally it subsided and she opened her eyes to find Simon still stationed between her legs, watching her.

"Amazing," he whispered as he straightened up. He found his waistband and unfastened his trousers. They fell away and Lillian stared.

If she had been impressed by his upper body, she was mesmerized by the lower. Of course he had toned, narrow hips, powerful thighs and legs, and she was certain in the future she would marvel at the perfection of them.

But for now all she could stare at was the engorged, hard length of his sex, thrusting up proudly against his stomach. In another world, on another day, she might have been afraid. After all, she was an innocent, and by surrendering herself she was facing not only rumored pain, but also a loss of any chance at the future she had been taught to desire.

However, today, in this moment, there was no fear. No thought of those faraway consequences. There was only this man, and she wanted him. Wanted this.

So she reached for him and drew him closer, opening herself for him as she lay back until he covered her. His hard erection rubbed her swollen, tingling entrance, but he didn't drive forward.

"There's no going back once we start," he whispered.

She nodded. "I know. Please, Simon."

He shut his eyes at that low plea and then he was moving forward, fitting himself into her willing body with a gentleness that let her acclimate to the new sensations. None of which, to her surprise and delight, was pain. She had been told a few times that was what she was to expect in this moment, but instead she felt other things.

Yes, it was strange to be filled in such a way. And there was a tiny bit of discomfort as he stretched her untried channel. But mostly it was exciting and there was a great deal of pleasure as he thrust forward and claimed her in a way no other man would ever do.

Suddenly he stopped and that intense green gaze bore into hers. "It's going to hurt a bit now."

She clenched her teeth. "Don't stop."

"Relax," he soothed just before he drove forward and broke her maidenhead.

Whatever pain Lillian was waiting for, the twinge she felt was nothing whatsoever like it. It was a momentary burst of discomfort and then it was over.

She shifted a little and Simon's eyes closed with a harsh groan. "Just wait, sweet," he murmured, and it was clear his jaw was clenched. "You'll unman me yet if you do that."

Lillian's eyes widened. She'd never considered that she could control *him* with her body. A swell of heady power filled her at the thought, but before she could test that concept, Simon moved and she forgot everything except the exquisite sensation of his body sliding through hers.

What he had done to her with his mouth was one thing, and she had thoroughly enjoyed it, but this was something different. A deeper claiming, a different kind of intensity because they were face to face, looking at each other as he arched his hips deep into her and withdrew.

His mouth descended and she melted into the sensations as they kissed, just letting the desire, the pleasure, flow around her and sweep her away. It didn't take long for his slow, rhythmic thrusts to take her to the same place his skillful mouth had done. This time she knew what to expect as the tingling sensations of pleasure overtook her. She cried out against his lips as she lifted her hips and rode out the explosive vibrations that racked her body.

Her pleasure seemed to stoke his own, for as she quivered and sighed around him, his thrusts grew more erratic and his breathing labored. Finally his neck strained and at the last moment he pulled away from her, turning aside to spend his seed and leaving her curiously empty that they hadn't shared that moment together.

Not that she didn't understand his withdrawal. Simon had made it clear that all he wanted from her was an affair. A child would complicate things and utterly ruin her.

That reality brought her out of her pleasurable haze and she sat up slowly, fully realizing for the first time that she had just given up her maidenhead sprawled across a billiard table like a wanton. And with a man who probably thought her surrender meant she would become his mistress as he had asked.

With a blush, she righted her chemise and searched the floor for her wrinkled gown.

She felt Simon watching her before she actually looked up at him with a shy smile.

He reached for her and drew her against his still-naked body. When his arms came around her, she shivered with renewed desire and let her gown fall away.

"Come upstairs with me," he whispered against her hair "Stay with me tonight, Lillian."

She hesitated as she tilted her chin up to look at him. There was such an earnest desire in his face that she couldn't say no. And in truth, she didn't want to. What if when they parted the magic of this night faded? Certainly that was inevitable given what she was here to do, but she found herself reluctant for that future.

He must have read her hesitation for far different

reasons than were truth, for he cupped her chin. "I promise you, I'll make sure no one sees you. I will not let you be publicly ruined by this."

She hesitated. "This doesn't mean I'll be your mistress," she whispered, her voice shaking.

There was a moment's silence before he jerked out a nod. "Then just be my lover. Tonight."

Instead of answering, Lillian rose up on her tiptoes and pressed her lips to his. They kissed, just as passionate as they had been before they made love. It took a great deal of effort for her to part from him and nod shakily.

"Yes, Simon. Take me upstairs. I'm no more ready to end this than you are."

Chapter 14

Simon had had many intentions when it came to Lillian and their relationship. He wanted her in his life, so he'd certainly meant for them to make love. And somewhere deep within him, he'd guessed it would be as powerful and magnificent an experience as it had been.

However, he had *never* intended to take her innocence in a public room of his house with an entire party of guests just an unlocked door away. He should have protected her far more than that, and not only because if they were caught it would force a marriage between them that neither seemed to desire.

And he certainly hadn't meant to make her first time on a billiard table while he was still half drunk. She deserved better.

However, now, as they lay sprawled across his bed after making love a second time, with Lillian's naked body pressed to his and her head in the crook of his shoulder, he forgot those regrets. He forgot everything except how right it felt to be with her.

Lillian absently traced a light pattern on his bare chest with her fingertips, entirely unaware of how arousing that light, teasing touch was. And that innocence made it all the *more* powerful. In a few more moments he would be more than ready to show her yet again how much he wanted her.

She glanced up at him, hazel eyes hinting at gold in the fading firelight. "Do you want to tell me now what so troubled you when I found you in the billiard room?"

He tensed, immediately brought back to the problems he faced. To the fact that his father wasn't the man he believed him to be. To the realization that he had at least one unknown brother in the world and possibly more.

Looking down at her, he pondered the question. It was a risk to reveal anything to this woman. As close as he now felt to her, they hadn't met but a week prior. He liked to believe that she would never *purposefully* let his family's secrets out into the world, but even if she accidentally whispered the truth to the wrong person . . . well, it could very well bring the censure of the *ton* down upon them.

And while Simon hadn't yet ruled out letting the world see what his father truly was on his own terms, he didn't want an outsider taking that option away from him.

But still, he ached to share his pain. Especially with this woman who had given him such pleasure.

"I am beginning to think I didn't truly know my father at all," he finally said with a deep sigh as he gathered her even closer. Her warmth made some of the chilling facts he'd uncovered fade.

"How so?" she said softly, turning her gaze away.

He stared at the ceiling above them for a long time before he shook his head and continued.

"How much did you know about him?"

She hesitated before she shrugged one shoulder. "A little. Everyone knew *of* him, of course."

Simon frowned.

"Yes, my father had a very public reputation. He was highly respected for his support of sometimes controversial acts in Parliament and his passionate defense of those less fortunate. But beyond that, he had a personal reputation, as well. People saw him as decent, above reproach in every way. Pious even. Those things gave him power to fight the righteous battle. But now . . ."

He trailed off as bitterness tinged his mouth. What a lie those things had been.

Lillian propped herself up on one elbow and

stared down at him. Bright interest lit her eyes. "Now?"

He hesitated. Not only was it dangerous to reveal the truth, in some way it still felt like a betrayal of his father. He sighed. It seemed he was willing to protect the old man even now.

"Now"—he shrugged—"well, now I wonder if there was ever any truth to anything he taught me. And if I *had* known the real man, I wonder if I would have liked him."

She nodded slowly, and there was powerful emotion in her stare as she lay back down against him.

"When we are children, it seems our parents can do no wrong," she said after a long silence. "But as we get older, we recognize the complications, the humanity of them. It's not particularly comfortable, is it?"

He shook his head. "No. It is most definitely not."

Now it was she who stared straight overhead, her gaze unfocused as if she was lost in memory.

"I thought my mother was nothing short of perfection. My father sheltered my brother and me from many of her periods of sadness, so I didn't see how troubled she truly was. Not until she took her own life."

Simon flinched. It was hard for him to imagine what kind of loss this remarkable woman had suffered, both personally and then later as others began to suspect the truth and shunned her.

"The worst part of it," she continued softly, "was that at first I *hated* her for what she did. I felt betrayed that she would end her life rather than face her problems. I saw it as selfishness that she would leave her husband without a wife and her children motherless. For years I blamed *her*."

Simon rolled to his side and propped himself up to look at Lillian. Although she spoke with strength, tears sparkled in her eyes. Raw emotion lived there as well. Her vulnerability made her all the more beautiful to him, for he recognized it was a side she rarely shared with others. She put up a wall to protect herself, just as she had done with him when she first arrived here. Now he understood her reluctance to get to know him, to accept how attracted they were to each other.

Thank God she finally had.

"How did you overcome your anger?" he asked, taking her hand in his and looking at their interlaced fingers.

She glanced at him sharply. "What do you mean?"

"Well, it isn't as if either one of us can simply talk to our parents and work out the problem that brought us such pain. Because they're gone, it complicates things."

She nodded slowly. "Yes, I suppose that is true. The resolution has gone with them, leaving us with only the pain."

There was a long pause as she considered his question with a pondering frown.

Finally, she whispered, "It was only recently that I truly overcame my anger when I understood her real reasons for taking her life. I suppose I transferred my rage to—to someone else . . . someone I blamed for her death."

His brow wrinkled. There was something troubled and even guilty to her expression. Something he wished he could soothe away. And yet he couldn't, no more than he could end his own pain.

"I doubt that will help me in my situation," he said with another sigh. "I don't think anyone else is responsible for my father's actions. But perhaps I'll one day begin to understand them and that will ease the anger and betrayal I feel at present."

She turned her face and he couldn't read her tone when she whispered, "Perhaps that is true, Simon."

She pushed at the coverlet and moved to rise.

"It is very late. I must return to my chamber. Gabby will already have suspicions."

He realized what she said was true, but he found himself reaching for her arm and pulling her back to him, nonetheless. She didn't resist as he slid her beneath him and lowered his mouth to hers. In fact, with a sigh she instantly tilted her head to grant him greater access to her swollen lips.

"Don't go yet," he murmured as he moved to nuzzle the elegant curve of her throat. "Just stay another hour."

As his hand cupped her breast, she let out a low moan before she nodded. "O-one more hour."

Glancing around the quiet, empty hallway one more time, Lillian turned the door handle and pushed, wincing as it let out a great squeak before allowing her entry to the chamber she shared with Gabby. It was dark and quiet within, and Lillian let out a sigh of relief as she closed herself in and leaned back against the wall beside the door. She was safe and fairly certain no one had seen her. Now she could only pray she could convince Gabby that . . .

Before she could finish the thought, the harsh scrape of flint echoed from the corner of the chamber and suddenly a candle glowed to life. Holding it was Gabby, clad in her dressing gown and rising from a cushioned chair in the changing room.

"Lillian," she said, shaking her head as she made her way across the room. "Lillian!"

There didn't need to be much more said. There was enough censure in just her name to let Lillian know Gabby had been waiting for her for hours.

She winced as her friend lifted the candle and examined her in its glowing light. Slowly, her friend's mouth turned down and her eyes widened.

"Lillian . . . what did you do?" she whispered as she set the candle on the closest table.

All the emotion, all the guilt, all the confusion Lillian had felt in the past few days welled up in her and unexpected tears stung at her eyes as she fell into her friend's waiting embrace.

"We made love," she admitted, her voice muffled in Gabby's shoulder.

"Oh, Lillian," Gabby gasped as she guided her to the settee where they collapsed together. "You surrendered your body to him?"

She nodded, waiting for the heat of embarrassment to flood her cheeks. To her surprise, it didn't. Even when she thought of the passionate evening she had spent in Simon's arms, shame was not her reaction. In fact, she quivered with pleasure and renewed desire, instead.

Shaking off those troubling reactions, she forced herself to focus on Gabby.

"I think it might be worse than that," she said on a sigh. "I fear your earlier accusations are true. I've begun to involve my heart with this man."

Her friend drew in a sharp breath, but didn't interrupt.

"Tonight I forgot about his father, I forgot about my duty to my own father and my mother, I forgot everything but him. I lost myself in him. And it was . . . well, it was magnificent."

Gabby reached out to cover her hand gently. "Under any other circumstance, I would thrill over this news. But not this way. Lillian, you cannot go on like this. It's wrong to make love to the man, to have deeper feelings for him, if you still intend to betray him and his family."

Lillian yanked her hands free as more guilt threatened to overwhelm her. She knew her friend was right. She got to her feet and stalked away, her mind spinning on *all* the events of the night, not just the ones that involved her surrender or Simon's gentleness.

"I-I'm not sure if betraying him is possible anymore." She shook her head. "His father has done that already."

Gabby leaned away slightly. "I don't understand."

"I wasn't able to determine the specifics," Lillian whispered. "But Simon was so upset when I found him. I'm certain he has uncovered some secret about his father that goes far deeper than mere political intrigue."

"And somehow that changes things for you?" her friend asked.

Lillian squeezed her eyes shut, and an image of Simon's broken expression tormented her. She knew what he felt, she had felt it, too. That pain. That raw betrayal.

"It does. I came here because Simon's father destroyed my family with no thought to the consequences. I thought to reveal him for what he was and all the evil he had done. But if I do that, the only person it will destroy is Simon. If I do that, am I any better than his father was? Am I not involving innocents just as he did?"

Gabby shook her head. "Never compare yourself to that man!"

"I must. If I can be no better than my enemy, then he has won, hasn't he?"

A sigh was Gabby's response. "I've said from the beginning that I had my misgivings about your plans, so I don't wish to discourage this change of heart, but I must know, why does all this suddenly matter to you? Up until even a few hours ago you weren't certain that Simon wasn't as much of a liar as his father."

Lillian flinched. She had accused him of as much. Slowly she turned to Gabby and held her friend's gaze evenly.

"Tonight when I found him, there was no mistaking the authenticity of his pain. And when he spoke of his father . . . I-I *believe* him, Gabby. Perhaps that is foolish or wishful thinking, but I don't think he knew anything beyond what his father wanted him to believe. And now that the truth is coming out, it is breaking him."

Unexpectedly, tears stung behind her eyes at the thought that Simon had so much more information to find that could hurt him. Including the fact that she had come here with betrayal and vengeance on her mind.

"But can you truly forget why you came here?" Gabby asked softly. "Your father's deathbed request, your mother's sad end . . . *can* you release those things?"

Lillian covered her eyes. It was only those things that made her hesitate. For months she had been driven by them, her need to fulfill the duty her brother could not eating at her and keeping her moving forward even when she wanted to collapse.

"I don't know," she admitted. "I know my mother still deserves some kind of justice, but I just don't know how."

Gabby reached out and caught her hand. "You lost everything. It is understandable that you would want to steal some of it back."

"Tomorrow I'll go to Simon," Lillian finally said with a shiver. "In the light of day with a little distance from tonight, I think everything will be clearer for me."

"And what will you say to him? Admit why you came here?"

A shudder worked through Lillian. God, if he knew she had come here, she had made love to him, all while plotting to ruin his family name, well, she could guess he wouldn't have a positive reaction.

"No. Not yet." Lillian frowned. It was a coward's way, but so be it. "No, I want to see if I can find out a little bit more about why he was so upset. Perhaps if I know the truth, it will ease my mind. Perhaps knowing that Roger Crathorne's beloved son despises him will be enough vengeance, even if I didn't mete it out personally."

Gabby nodded, but Lillian could see the utter relief in her friend's eyes. Strangely she felt some of the same in her own heart. This drive for revenge had never been comfortable for her. Only necessary. A duty she had felt she had to take on since no one else would.

But the idea of letting it go made her lighter than she had been in ages.

"And what about Simon?"

A shiver worked through Lillian at Gabby's quiet question.

"What about him?" she asked, though she knew perfectly well what her friend meant.

"You two made love tonight and it is clear you have a bond that goes deeper than mere physical desire." Gabby tilted her head. "What do you intend to do about that?"

Lillian shook her head. "I don't know. I still think there is too much in the past to allow us to be together. Besides, if he discovered why I came here, what my connection to his father is . . . he would likely loathe me."

"And yet you still long to share more, don't you?" Gabby whispered.

Lillian turned her back on her friend and made for the bedroom. "I long for a great many things, Gabriela. But the majority of them I will *never* have."

Chapter 15

Two hours after she entered her chamber, Lillian found herself leaving it again. Dawn had come, and it was time to search out Simon. She wanted to speak to him at the earliest possible time, both to ensure they wouldn't be interrupted and also before she surrendered to more cowardly impulses.

Before she let go of her quest for vengeance entirely, she had to be certain it was the right decision. Somehow talking to Simon, finding out what had troubled him so, felt like it might be enough. She clung to the hope that it would free her of her father's dying wish.

She moved through quiet hallways carefully. The other houseguests wouldn't rise for hours, and though the servants might be waking, they would be too busy readying the house for the day to pay much heed to her if she was quiet and careful.

As she slipped down the winding stairs to the

foyer and the main area of the estate, Lillian stifled a yawn. She hadn't slept last night. Even after she climbed between the sheets, she had tossed and turned, remembering Simon's touch. She would likely never feel it again. There was so much to keep them apart, both the obvious and the things he didn't even suspect.

With a sigh, she reached for the handle of Simon's office door. After a brief prayer for strength, she pushed and entered the chamber.

To her dismay, the room was dark. Simon wasn't there. Apparently he had better been able to sleep than she after their night together. Perhaps he wouldn't rise until the others in their party had.

And she would have to wait to discuss these very private issues with him. She turned to go, but a thought stopped her. She wouldn't have to wait if she was able to determine what had troubled him herself.

Slowly she faced the messy room. If Simon wasn't awake yet, she could have hours to look through the office. Certainly he would have separated out the items he had already uncovered, if she could find that information, then she could read through it at her leisure.

Heat filled her cheeks at the thought of searching this chamber. It was ironic that she finally had the freedom to do so and yet she was no longer certain she wished to do it.

"Don't you want to know the truth?" she murmured to herself. "Don't you want to end this one way or another?"

Somehow hearing that question out loud helped. Just because she might find the evidence she had sought for months didn't mean she would use it. But she needed to *see* it. Somehow she felt it would end the hunger she had to avenge her mother. Even if she never followed through, the fact that she *could* had to help.

Didn't it?

She moved forward. She came around the desk, and after opening the curtains to let the morning light flood the room, she sat down to examine the overwhelming number of piles before her. There was a stack set off to the side that she turned to first. From the way they were placed, it appeared as though they had already been sorted, which meant they might be the items that had so upset Simon.

Pulling the first sheet from the stack, she began to read. She wasn't certain how much time passed as she went over document after document. Many had to do with legislation, and as Simon had confessed to her before, his father's public support of laws had often been belied by his private acceptance and conveyance of money from parties opposed to the same ideals.

She sniffed her disgust. That showed the late

duke hadn't been honorable, but it wasn't the devastating, overpowering secret she had set out to find. Even now when she wavered on the edge of giving up revenge forever, she wanted to discover something personal and humiliating.

She flipped forward, scanning more ledgers and letters and making mental notes about what she saw. She was nearly halfway through the piles and starting to get interested in a thread that seemed to imply the late duke had some kind of secret when the door to the chamber suddenly opened.

Reflexively, Lillian dropped the paperwork to the desk and staggered to her feet as the intruder stepped within. She sucked in a harsh breath when she saw it was Simon himself who came into the room.

It took a moment for him to notice her standing there, guilt-stricken and terrified, and she took that reprieve to drink in the sight of him. He looked as exhausted as she felt, and she guessed he hadn't slept any more than she had. Both of them had been troubled, despite the pleasure they found together.

Finally, he actually looked at her and lurched back in surprise before his face softened.

"Lillian," he said, moving toward her almost as if he couldn't control the action.

She longed to fly into his arms and comfort him

with kisses, but she refrained. "G-good morning, Simon."

He looked around, as if remembering where they were. "Wait, what . . . what are you doing here, Lillian?"

Utterly unprepared, she closed and opened her mouth a few times as her mind raced for the right answer. He was staring at her, his expression filled with tired confusion.

For a brief moment, she considered telling him everything. She thought about confessing what exactly had happened to her mother, about her father's deathbed desire for revenge and her decision to take it when her brother wouldn't. She thought about revealing all and facing the consequences, whatever they were.

But then he met her eyes with such warmth and sweetness, and her throat closed. If she told him, he would never look at her like that again. He would stop thinking of her as an interesting riddle and see her for what she was. An enemy.

Since they had no future together, why did he need to know? Why did she need to change what they had for a few more fleeting days?

"I couldn't sleep for thinking about our shared problem."

She drew a deep breath. There, that wasn't a direct lie.

"Shared problem?" he repeated with a cock of his head.

She nodded, her stomach churning. "Y-yes. Last night we spoke of our parents and trying to find some kind of peace with who they were and what they did. I cannot ever have a true resolution to my own issues with my mother, but I—"

She hesitated. It wasn't too late to stop. To forget about finding the truth, to stop lying and just leave.

But she couldn't.

"I hoped I could perhaps help you," she whispered. Her voice cracked when she said it and her hands shook at her sides.

He moved forward, closing the door behind him. "You came here to search in order to help me?"

"You were never clear on what it was your father did to disappoint you so greatly. I hoped I could understand if I found more information."

The self-loathing she had felt when she began speaking doubled when Simon's expression softened and he moved across the cluttered room on her.

Gathering her up, he held her against his chest, breathing in the scent of her hair as he whispered, "Thank you, Lillian. Thank you for that."

She blinked furiously to prevent tears from falling and nodded as she pulled away. "I shouldn't have intruded without your permission. I apologize. It was my—my worry that drove me. I only want to help you. Will you allow that?"

After a long pause, he nodded. "Yes."

Lillian waited for relief to flood her. For there to be a thrill in her belly that she was about to uncover a dark truth about a man she had considered her mortal enemy, even if she never used it.

Neither materialized. There was only more of that nausea. That knowledge that in her use of the past to make him share his secrets, she was as manipulative as Simon's father had been.

Simon took her hand and led her across the room to two chairs beside the sunny window. He pursed his lips in frustration as he cleared away the piles of paperwork on the chair seats, and then offered her a place.

They sat together, their knees close and Simon's hand upon hers as he stared at her with an intensity that seemed to bore into her.

"I mentioned that my father was not as honest in some of his support of legislation as he led the world to believe."

She nodded, remembering well the pain on his face the day he had confessed that fact. It had been the first time she'd truly felt empathy for him.

"Yes," she whispered when he was silent for more than a moment. "I know that felt like a betrayal to you."

He nodded. "It was. I was raised to worship him for his honesty and his goodness and suddenly I was faced with the fact that he possessed very little of either quality. But it has gotten worse. What I am about to tell you is something that could easily destroy his reputation . . . and perhaps my own, if you chose to share it, so I hope I can count on your discretion."

Lillian swallowed. After months of hoping and searching, here was the moment of truth. She was about to be given what she had so yearned to find.

Her silence seemed to appease him, for he continued, "I've found evidence that my father not only had at least one bastard child, but that he made a payment to the mother and then utterly abandoned them both."

She drew in a breath, recognizing instantly the importance of this information. Many men of the *ton* had bastard children, but few of them had the exalted reputation of the late duke, a man who had once railed publicly against the lack of care among his peers. A man who had once said that all bastard children deserved support and consideration.

It had outraged and shamed the peerage when he stated it. If there was proof he had been an utter hypocrite, that he had deserted his own bastard son . . . well, that would certainly be a huge step in utterly ruining the name he had created for himself. Who would build a statue then? Or murmur platitudes at gatherings?

"The worst part is that I think there may be more children just like the one I've found information about," Simon said, covering his eyes with his hand.

Lillian stared at the man before her. He was slouched down in the chair, rubbing his temples with a look of disillusioned pain on his face so powerful that it made her heart hurt. This information had already broken a part of the man before her. Simon could never go back to his idealized view of his father. He could never forget what he knew and suspected.

In that moment, Lillian knew she had to let the past go. Even if she managed to convince the *ton* that Roger Crathorne had been the biggest hypocrite ever to walk the earth or an evil monster masquerading as a crusader . . . it wouldn't bring her mother back. It wouldn't change the pain the man had brought to her family.

The victory would be hollow. And with it, she would only succeed in breaking up another family. Hurting Simon and his sister whom she had never met, but who had seemed kind enough from a distance.

She thought of her mother. Not of what had happened to her all those years ago, not of her suicide, but of the woman Lillian remembered. She had been kind, she had been good. If Lillian broke another person in her mother's name, it would not be something her mother would have liked.

She blinked at tears. It was over.

"Have I offended you?" Simon asked, lowering his hand. "If I have, I apologize."

Shaking her head, she reached for him, covering his knee with her hand.

"No, of course you haven't. I know this was something difficult for you to share with me. I can see your pain. But—" She stopped. Perhaps comfort was all she could offer this man. A last moment of atonement, for herself . . . and for his father. "At least the late duke provided some kind of payment for the child. That's better than some men do."

She pursed her lips, hating to defend the man, but knowing it was what Simon needed to hear.

Simon shook his head. "It was sizable enough, but there were no stipulations tied to it, nor any oversight over it that I could see. Lord knows if the boy ever saw a farthing, let alone if it lasted into his adulthood. He could have ended up on the street, Lillian. Or dead. And my father neither knew nor seemed to care about it."

She reached for straws to comfort him. "But the child's mother might very well have been reasonable and frugal. She could have easily set aside a healthy amount for his future. He could be doing well for himself."

After a long moment, Simon shrugged. "I suppose that is true. I have no idea what his mother was like. There may be more notes about her here, but I've yet to find her."

"Well, there you are," she insisted.

"Still, I wish I knew what happened to him," he said, his voice wistful and faraway.

She hesitated. "Th-there is one way you could find out, you know."

He tilted his head. "How?"

"You could find him."

Simon's eyes widened. Slowly, he shook his head. "No, there were no further facts beyond his name and the amount of payment to the mother. I have no idea in what town she lived or any other information."

She looked around. "Your father kept such voluminous records, I have no doubt there is a ledger or piece of correspondence here that gives a clearer accounting of what happened. I could help you look if you'd like."

She couldn't believe the words had left her mouth. But once they were out, she felt no desire to take them back. In some way, if she could help Simon find his missing sibling, that would thwart Crathorne, who had tried so desperately to keep the children apart. And even more, it would give Simon a way to heal.

"Find my brother," he said, rising and turning to look outside at the sparkling, cloudless day that was blooming as they talked. "I admit I hadn't thought of it."

She tilted her head. "Because he might not be of your class and rank?"

He waved that comment off. "That is Rhys's mindset, not my own. Unlike my father, I actually believed in the ideals we fight for. I could not care less if my brother was a pauper or a politician."

Lillian turned her face away. It seemed Simon's feelings on class only applied to marriage. Not that it mattered. He didn't know the entire connection they shared, but she did. There could be no future for them, despite her desire to comfort him and despite the passion they had shared last night.

"No, I didn't consider it because I suppose it would complicate things a great deal," he murmured.

"It would risk more people finding out about your father's true colors," she murmured, watching his every reaction carefully.

He turned on her, nostrils flaring slightly. "At this moment, I don't care about that. I deserve to know my brother if he still exists. And he deserves to know me and our sister, Naomi."

"Are you saying you wouldn't care if your father's treachery were revealed to the world?" she asked, shocked.

He hesitated and then he shook his head. "I am angry at him for his duplicity, but I don't want the world to see it, at least not yet. Perhaps someday . . ."

Lillian blinked. That meant he might one day allow the truth to come out, only on his own terms. And that made Lillian even more certain about her decision to release her own drive for revenge.

"I think of Naomi and her children when I think of the truth coming out. And my mother. I suppose I think of myself as well, though perhaps that is selfish."

"It isn't selfish, Simon," she whispered as she looked down at her feet. "You have done nothing wrong. You shouldn't have to suffer for what your father did. It isn't fair."

Simon frowned. "Well, so much in this life isn't fair. I think of all the people he hurt . . . Don't they deserve retribution?"

Her stare jerked up. Yet again he was offering her the perfect opportunity to reveal the truth about herself, her mother. She could confess why she had come here and what she wanted from him when she began. Maybe, in this charged moment, he would understand.

Or perhaps he wouldn't. And now that she had

allowed him to tell her this, his greatest secret, he would hate her all the more.

Could she take that risk?

Before she could decide, he let out a great sigh.

"You see why I am twisted inside about it. But I must face one thing at a time. If I *do* look for this man, this brother I never knew I had, I'll have to use great care so as not to reveal my true purposes."

He looked at her. Framed by the sunny window, he looked like a dark, fallen angel. Sensual and beautiful and tempting. Despite all her misgivings, she wanted him more than ever.

And yet she had promised to avoid temptation. Especially considering their conversation this morning, touching him, kissing him, making love to him . . . it was wrong. She couldn't do it again, no matter how much she wanted to.

Staggering to her feet, she turned away. "I should leave you. You obviously have much to consider and plan."

He caught her hand. "Please don't go, Lillian."

Gently he tugged and she moved toward him with little resistance. It seemed she could summon none when he was tempting her.

"Simon," she whispered, helpless.

He tilted his head, and suddenly his lips were on hers. She couldn't resist him. Her arms came around his neck, her body molded to his. The needs she had been trying to fight overtook her and she forgot everything else.

"Thank you," he whispered as he moved her flat against the wall. He braced a hand on either side of her head, and those intense green eyes snared her. "Thank you for hearing me, and for your lack of censure."

Moisture filled her eyes and Lillian turned away in the hope he wouldn't see the tear that trickled down her cheek. Of course he did and swiped it away with his fingertip.

"Don't cry, Lillian," he murmured, burying his lips into her neck. "No tears. Just pleasure and laughter and everything good. I want to give you that. I want you to give that to me."

She shut her eyes as he kissed the column of her throat. If there was something *good* in this situation, it was Simon. Him with his warm eyes and warmer hands. Him with that strange ability to make her feel right and comfortable even though she really didn't fit into his world.

And he didn't know it, but he had somehow given her permission to forget the past, forget her anger.

She wanted the strength to resist that temptation, to do the right thing, but she couldn't find it. She surrendered. And she told herself it was the last time.

She arched into him as he slid his hands to her backside and cupped her harder against him. She moaned against his shoulder, massaging the heavy fabric of his jacket as she breathed in the masculine scent that was so uniquely *him*.

If this was to be the end between them, if she was to find the strength to let him go, she wanted this last encounter to be memorable. Perfect. Later she wanted to be able to remember it in full detail and have no regrets.

She leaned back against the wall and went to work on his jacket, yanking the heavier fabric aside until she freed him of the vestment and tossed it away.

"Here?" he panted even as he lifted her, grinding against her in a way that made her catch her breath.

"Yes," she moaned, as both commentary to his actions and answer to his question.

He didn't ask again. Instead, as she tore at his shirt, he began to hike her skirts up, balling them in one fist as he slipped the other hand beneath them to stroke warm fingers against her thigh.

When he moved higher, finding the damp entrance to her body, she shut her eyes and let out a long, ragged sigh. She was still tender from the previous night's activities, but that only served to make her exquisitely sensitive to his gentle touch. Almost immediately, her body twitched and grew hot and wet in anticipation of the invasion to come.

She spread her legs wider, a wanton invitation, before she finished removing his shirt. She couldn't help but smile as she looked at the broad expanse of his bare chest again. Great God, but he was beautiful. Perfect.

She pressed her lips to his shoulder, tasting him, tormenting him with the tip of her tongue. When she dipped her mouth lower, it was his turn to groan in pleasure.

"Careful now," he whispered, his tone rough and seductive. "Don't play with fire."

"I like fire," she said, moving all the lower to suckle one nipple between her lips.

"Enough," he growled, and suddenly she was off her feet, lifted against the wall and utterly helpless as he fitted himself between her legs.

He kissed her, flattening her back against the wall with his body, arching into her so she felt the hard length of his erection. And suddenly it was free, though she hadn't seen him unfasten his trousers. He arched again and the tip of his hard length breached just the outer folds of her body.

She found herself holding her breath, waiting for more. Waiting for the utter pleasure and possession that was to come. When he maneuvered her just slightly and thrust forward, everything she had been anticipating came to be. He slid into her body with no resistance and was fully seated in a heartbeat.

They moaned in unison and she clung even tighter as he began a grinding, pleasurable rhythm that took her to the brink so quickly she could hardly breathe. She tilted her head back, gasping as pleasure overwhelmed her, overtook her, owned her, just as he did. She lost all control, clinging to him and groaning out his name as wave after wave washed over her.

He was quick behind, his thrusts driving harder, faster. His neck strained as he neared the point of no return, and then he moaned deep within his chest, and for the first time she felt his essence fill her. She wrapped her legs about him tighter and reveled in the feeling of them joined, their breathing in unison, bodies still quivering.

It was a perfect moment.

One that was utterly ruined, just as she was, when the door to Simon's office flew open and three of Society's pushiest, gossipy ladies stepped inside with Simon's butler close behind.

Chapter 16

To say that all hell broke loose would have been an understatement. And yet Simon felt remarkably calm as the three intruding women commenced shrieking, his butler began calling for them to leave, and Lillian wrenched away from him and turned to smooth her skirts over herself.

While all this should have felt like an utter disaster to Simon, and he kept waiting for that realization to hit him and send him in a tailspin, it simply never happened. Instead he merely lifted his trousers up over his waist, fastened them, and turned to face the trespassers.

"Has no one ever heard of knocking?" he asked, tilting his head in question at his butler, Vale. He bent to retrieve his shirt from the floor and calmly put it on.

"My apologies, Your Grace. The ladies were quite insistent upon seeing you," the butler said, beginning to collect himself now that Lillian was properly covered, though she had not yet turned to face the group. She continued to stare straight out the window, as though if she remained still long enough, everyone would forget her.

Her obvious humiliation was the only thing that truly troubled Simon in that moment, which was still quite amazing.

"I understand, Vale. You may go."

He turned on the three women, recognizing them as the Marchioness Piddleford, the Countess of Covington, and the Viscountess Rogers. All three were vicious gossips and had come here with obvious designs that he marry one of their daughters.

"As you can see, ladies, you have interrupted me in a private moment with my fiancée."

When he said that, it forced Lillian to spin around. She faced him with wide and wild eyes, and her mouth opened but she didn't seem capable of making coherent sounds. He met her stare briefly, but then turned back to matters at hand.

Strangely, the three women before him had identical expressions to Lillian. Shocked, somewhat horrified . . . utterly speechless. And that was so rare that he took a moment to enjoy it.

Only a moment, though, for Marchioness Piddleford recovered first.

"You are *marrying* that little mouse?" she repeated, shaking her head.

He nodded. "Indeed I am, my lady. I assume you'd like to give congratulations on the happy news."

The two held stares for a long moment, but then the marchioness eased out a slight nod. "Congratulations, Your Grace," she managed through clenched teeth. "And to you, Miss Mayhew."

The Countess of Covington followed her friend's lead, but Viscountess Rogers was beside herself. She flew forward.

"And just why did you waste our time in coming here? We could have accepted invitations to any number of house parties. Instead you toyed with our daughters, Your Grace!" she snapped, ignoring her friends as they made lame attempts to silence her with fluttering hands and murmured pleas.

Simon arched a brow. "I brought a large group of ladies here to see if any of us were compatible enough for a marriage. While all the women in attendance were more than charming, Miss Mayhew captured my interest. There was no deception in my actions, nor any intent to toy with those I invited, my lady. I had never met Miss Mayhew before she arrived here, if *that* is your implication."

"My implication is that you have chosen a women far beneath you, and why?" The viscountess's face was bright red now. "Because she was willing to spread her legs for you?"

Simon moved forward one long step, extending

a finger toward the woman in warning. "Have a care, Lady Rogers. That is my future wife you are maligning. I doubt you will want to isolate yourself from her or from me in the future."

Lady Rogers pressed her lips together, and for a long moment not a sound filled the room. Then she turned on her heel and marched out with the other two women trailing behind her.

Drawing a deep breath, he looked at Lillian. She was staring at him, hands raised at her sides and shaking wildly. Her eyes were wide and stormy, her mouth still open, and yet no words were forthcoming.

"Well, this news will certainly be around to all ears in the party before twenty minutes have passed," he mused, tilting his head to look at Lillian more closely. He was rather concerned by the expression on her face. "Why in the world were those biddies awake at this hour anyway?"

Instead of answering, Lillian took a step forward.

"Why? Why did you *do* that?" she asked past pale and trembling lips.

"Defend you?" he responded. "Because no one will speak of you that way. Ever. I won't allow it."

"No," she said, and there was a hint of hysteria to her voice now. "Not that. Why did you say we were getting married?"

He moved forward and took her bloodless

hands. They were cold as he placed them between his own. He smiled at her, hoping to reassure her. To calm her.

"Because, my dear, you and I were just caught in the worst of compromising positions by three of the most notorious gossips in London Society. Marriage is our only option, and I thought it would reduce the damage if I implied we had already come to that agreement."

Lillian whipped her hands from his and stared at him. Then her gaze slowly took in the room around him, the piles of paperwork, the mess of files. She shook her head.

"I cannot marry you. I can't."

His brow wrinkled. "Because of my father's actions?"

She let out a bark of laughter that was anything but humorous. It was harsh and frantic. "Simon, you said yourself you only wanted me as your mistress."

He shook his head. "That arrangement would have been different. If you had come to London and I had put you up and we carried on an affair, it would have been discreet. A group of gossips wouldn't have walked in on us. When you and I were finished, you still might have been able to marry another, or at least to have a life of your own choosing. Now . . ."

She stared at him, and the full ramifications of

what had happened seemed to be hitting her. She blinked a few times. "Now that cannot happen."

"No."

She cocked her head. "So you are trying to save me. As a consequence, you're being forced into a marriage far below you in order to make *me* whole."

He reached for her hand, clasping it in his own and pulling her a fraction closer. "That isn't why I'm marrying you."

The moment he said it, he knew it to be true.

"I think . . ." He paused, pondering his words carefully. "I think in some way I *wanted* to force my own hand. I wanted to be put into a position where I couldn't talk myself out of a union. Today I wasn't careful when we made love."

Her eyes widened. "You did that on purpose?"

He shrugged. "No, but I think some part of me allowed it to happen. If there could be a child, that changes everything. Even if we hadn't been disturbed, I would have asked for your hand."

She shook her head. "But you wouldn't have had to, Simon, you could have—"

"Been just like my father?" he interrupted, hating the bitterness in his tone.

She stared up at him for a long moment before she shook her head. "You are *nothing* like him."

"Then you know I couldn't have abandoned a

child, even the hint of a child." He drew in a deep breath. "And there is more to it than that, even."

She blinked, and the terror that had streaked her face since they'd been intruded upon was beginning to fade just a fraction. "More?"

He nodded. "Lillian . . . from the first moment we met, we felt a pull toward each other."

She hesitated, but then inclined her head as agreement.

A smile he couldn't help tilted his lips. "How very enthusiastic of you," he teased, and was pleased when she smothered a laugh. In that moment, he knew everything would be well, even if it took a while. "I really *did* look around at the other women here. I tried to find an interest in them, but in my mind they were empty. And all I could picture when I thought of myself shackled to one of them was a life just as empty. But when I was with you, it was different."

She blinked again, and this time there were tears sparkling in the ever-changing depths of her eyes. Right now they were dark, almost brown, and seemed to go on forever.

"With you there was, there *is* a connection. And that changed everything for me. I tried to make it less than it was, tried to say that if you were in my bed, my mistress, it would be enough, but I don't think it would have been."

"There will be so many obstacles, Simon," she whispered. "Perhaps more than you even know."

He frowned. "You mean the gossip our being caught will cause? Well, we won't read the banns. I'll arrange for a special license so we may marry the moment we return to London."

"It won't be just that," she began, but he interrupted her with a raised hand.

"Are you referring to your past? People can hang. If this situation with my father has taught me anything, it is that even the most 'perfect' citizen has secrets. Those who talk about you are likely trying to cover their own."

"What you are saying means more to me than you know." She shook her head. "But I need to say that—"

He lifted his fingers to cover her lips. "There is nothing more to say. This is what we shall do. I make you no false promises, I think neither of us feel love for each other, but in time that may come. I do think we could be happy."

Leaning down, he took her in his arms and pressed his lips to hers. He felt her stiffness, her resistance for only a moment, and then she softened. Her arms came around his neck, her lips parted. She was saying yes with her body when she couldn't with words.

And Simon felt a peace that was deeper than any he had ever known.

* * *

Simon let out a moan as he slipped into the hall-way and quietly shut the door behind him. Since that morning, he had endured visits from virtu-ally every angry mama and chaperone who had descended upon his home a week before. He had been screamed at, cried to, and narrowly avoided two duels. Now his head ached and his jaw hurt from clenching it.

What he wanted was a large tumbler of brandy and a warm bath. More to the point, he wanted Lillian if only he could manage to convince her to join him in those other pleasures.

He opened the door to the library, intent on call-ing for her. But he came to a stop when he stepped inside and spied Rhys and Anne sitting together beside the fire. His best friend's face was pinched, but Anne lifted her chin with a genuine smile as he entered.

"Hello," he said, closing the door behind him. "I wasn't informed you were waiting for me."

When the pair did not reply, he tilted his head and speared Rhys with a stare. "You *are* waiting for me, aren't you?"

Anne pushed to her feet and crossed the room with both hands held out. As she reached Simon, she pressed a kiss to each cheek.

"Of course we are, dearest Simon. We wanted to congratulate you on your engagement."

"Anne," Rhys said, his sharp tone making Anne wince before she turned on her fiancé.

"Don't make this more difficult," she said softly. "Simon is your best friend."

Suddenly Rhys was on his feet. "And that is why I won't stand by and let this travesty happen. Not without offering my assistance."

He moved toward Simon with an intense focus in his eyes.

"You do not have to do this," Rhys said softly.

Simon smiled. "But I will." He clapped a hand on Rhys's shoulder. "And I do not desire an escape, though I appreciate your offer of one. I know it is kindly meant. But I hope you'll never make it again."

Rhys's eyebrows arched. "Truly?"

Anne moved closer now. "Look at him, Waverly. I don't think he is saying this out of duty. Let it go."

Rhys pursed his lips, and Simon could actually see the capitulation on his friend's face.

"Thank you," he said softly.

Rhys shook his head in disbelief before he said, "You realize Anne and I are leaving this afternoon, just as we originally planned."

"Ah, yes," Simon said, grateful for the reminder, for he had forgotten that fact. "The wedding is so close now. Who would have thought I might beat you to the altar?"

Anne smiled. "You'll marry upon your return, then?"

He nodded. "As soon as the special license is procured we will take our vows."

Rhys shifted. "We could delay our departure if you require my assistance."

"Great God, no!" Simon laughed. "I wouldn't dream of keeping you here when you have so much to do. I will send word when we arrive in London. Perhaps you'll stand up for me, just as I hope to still stand up for you."

Rhys tilted his head, as if the idea that there was any other choice was foreign to him. "You know I will."

Simon smiled. So much for utter snobbery.

"We must hurry along, then, if we hope to depart amidst the crush of upset debutantes." Rhys sighed. He moved toward the door, but Anne held back a moment.

She took Simon's hands and squeezed them.

"Be happy," she whispered, being sure that Rhys could not hear her. "We have so few chances at love. You deserve it if you can find it."

She released him and turned, but not before Simon saw a look of sadness on her face when she moved toward her fiancé. It was then Simon recognized that Anne was in love with his friend, a man bent on marrying for position, not passion.

He frowned as the two departed. He hadn't expected to be so troubled by Rhys and Anne's farewell, but he was left feeling sad. And resolved to do as Anne had suggested. Try to be happy with the future that had been laid out before him.

Lillian watched from the window as carriage after carriage pulled away from the drive. In stunning form, she had not only brought Simon's party to a screeching halt, but ruined his reputation. Not to mention her own, which had really only been holding on by a slender thread.

And yet, when she thought of marrying the man, it wasn't terror that filled her. It wasn't guilt, although that emotion waited just below the surface since he did not yet know the truth of why she had come here.

No, when she pictured being by Simon's side forever . . . it was pleasure that came to the front of her mind. A peaceful happiness that she shoved aside with all her might.

There was nothing to be happy about!

"This is a colossal mess," Gabby said as she stomped into the room.

Lillian turned on her friend and just barely resisted the urge to hug Gabby for reminding her of the bare facts of this situation. She could not be joyful. She had to see the truth.

"Yes," she agreed far too slowly. "It is not the way I planned."

Gabby's eyes went wide. "Well, I should hope not, Lillian! I would hope you would not be capable of such treachery, such *duplicity* as to seduce a man you are bound to destroy. To marry him so you could further access secrets which aren't even his."

Lillian's lips parted as she realized Gabby wasn't actually defending her. She was asking her a question. Her friend was wondering if that, indeed, was what she had done.

"Do not think so low of me," she pleaded as she lurched forward and caught Gabby's hands. "Please, you are one of the few friends I have and I cannot have you think such of me. Today I decided . . . there will be no revenge."

Gabby stopped and stared at her. "Because you will wed him?"

She shook her head. "No. I decided before that. You were right all along, my dearest friend. I should have listened to you."

Her friend's smile was brief but soundly triumphant.

Lillian did not return it. "We talked today and I understand more about what Simon is facing. I realized I cannot make him suffer for something someone else did. At least, no more than he already is. It would do neither of us any good, nor would it change either of our circumstances."

"I'm so glad." Gabby grabbed for her hand.

"But Lillian . . . do you—do you think you'll be happy?"

She froze. "I don't know. I have such hope that I could be, but I fear the future still. It was one thing to keep the truth about my motives a secret when we were surely to part in a few days and never meet again. But now I'll be his wife. I must tell Simon what my true intentions were when I arrived here. I must reveal all to him. If I don't it will hang over us like a guillotine, coloring everything we do and say. And when the truth comes out, it will only be worse."

Gabby's face softened and she wrapped her arms around Lillian. They stood that way for a long moment before Lillian sighed.

"What will I do, Gabby?"

Her friend pulled away and paced the floor to the window. "I overheard the dowager duchess speaking to my aunt when I was downstairs."

Lillian winced. "She must be murderous."

"She didn't sound pleased, I can tell you that much," her friend said with a grim nod. "But there is little she can do after such a public display. Apparently we're to stay here until Simon obtains the special license, which shall take a few days. Then we will all travel to London as a group and you shall be married there. It seems all the Billingham brides are married in the same church, and Lady

Billingham doesn't want that changed for fear of even more talk."

A shudder worked its way through Lillian and she sank into the closest chair. "While that is all very good information to have, it isn't exactly what I meant when I asked what I shall do."

Gabby smiled sadly. "I know. But since the wedding is in such short order, perhaps there is no hurry in telling Simon the truth. You imply he already has much to consider, and now there is the scandal of your engagement on top of it. In time, you'll find the right words to say."

Lillian considered her friend's statement. It offered her a lifeline. She could wait just a short while to reveal the truth, perhaps she could find a way to do it and cause the least amount of hurt.

"Perhaps you are right. A few more weeks can't really make things worse, can they?"

Gabby nodded, but Lillian could see the hesitation in her eyes. It reflected her own and she turned away from it.

"Well, I should return downstairs. My poor aunt is mightily confused by all these happenings and I'd like to reassure her."

With a nod, Lillian stared as her friend stepped outside and left her alone in the chamber. She turned to look at her reflection in the mirror and gave a long sigh. She looked as haggard as she felt.

"There are so many lies," she whispered. "So many secrets, both mine and his father's. Could a marriage built on those things really stand the test of time?"

She didn't know the answer, but for the first time she acknowledged, if only to herself, that she wanted that to be true. Desperately and with enough passion that it frightened her.

Chapter 17

I f Lillian had thought the dowager duchess cold before, now that she and her party were Her Ladyship's sole guests, the strain between them had grown even worse. Simon's mother had been absent from luncheon and all day after the engagement "announcement," leaving her remaining guests to fend for themselves. When she finally resurfaced at supper the night before, she had hardly said two words and only picked at her food.

Lillian had held on to some hope that a new day would perhaps improve the duchess's mood. After all, the engagement was unavoidable now, at some point she had to accept it.

But a new day had dawned with only a slight improvement in the dowager's mood. Lillian thought perhaps Simon had said something to his mother, for at least now she occasionally engaged with Gabby's aunt, but as for Lillian . . . well, the lady was behaving as if she wasn't in the room at all.

Except to send her dark and hateful looks from time to time.

Of course, she sent an equal number of looks toward the door and they were far less cruel and more anticipatory. Today Simon's sister and the dowager's only other child, Lady Westford, was to arrive, and it seemed Her Grace was actually excited to see her.

That fact surprised Lillian. When she looked at Lady Billingham, all she saw was a frigid woman, so embittered by life that she couldn't even summon love or friendliness to her own son. But here she was, practically bouncing with delight every time she so much as looked at the door through which her daughter would enter in a short time.

Suddenly the butler appeared in the entryway. Before he had even spoken, the duchess was on her feet, hands clasped in front of her.

"Lady Westford has arrived," he intoned, then stepped aside to allow a very pretty woman to move into the room.

Lillian rose to her feet and watched as the newcomer crossed to her mother and embraced her.

"Mama!" she said, her voice filled with joy.

The dowager was completely transformed, her smile wide and genuine and her hands trembling as she returned her daughter's hug with a heartfelt one of her own.

"Dearest," she breathed as she clung to her child.

"How glad I am that you are finally here."

Lillian's stomach clenched at the scene before her and she found herself turning her face away, an unwanted outsider to the love of mother and daughter.

God, how she wished she could have that kind of reunion. How she hated that she never could.

As if he sensed her longing, suddenly Simon was beside her. She jumped as he rested a comforting hand on the small of her back while they waited for the two women to part. It seemed he could read her body language. Thankfully, he couldn't read her thoughts, or else he would be privy to the intense hatred she felt for his father at present.

She forced a smile for him.

"Don't be nervous," Simon whispered as his sister broke away from their mother and turned toward the two of them. "She is as kind as she is beautiful."

Shaking away her dark thoughts, Lillian stared at the lady who was now walking toward them. If Simon's statement was true, then Naomi would be the depth of compassion, for she was as lovely a woman as any Lillian had seen.

Despite the fact that she was six years older than her brother and had borne two children of her own, Lady Westford could have easily been mistaken for a woman in her debut year. Her brown hair had not a streak of gray in it and was full and lustrous. Her eyes, a warm brown more like her mother's than Simon's remarkable jade, were bright and filled with good humor and intelligence. And her skin . . . well, Lillian knew of women in their circles who would quite possibly kill for such flawless perfection.

She looked everything a lady should, and Lillian couldn't help but tense as she stopped before the two of them. Would Naomi hate Lillian as her mother did? Would she blame Lillian for "entrapping" her brother into such a poor match?

But she seemed to do neither. After an appraising moment, Naomi launched herself at her brother, giving him a loving hug that Lillian couldn't help but smile over. There was some relief in seeing that Simon hadn't been ostracized by everyone in his family.

"My dearest," Naomi said as she pulled back to look at him again. "Oh, you do look well. Happier than I have seen you in an age."

Then the other woman turned on her and Lillian held out a trembling hand. Naomi ignored it and instead she hugged Lillian just as tightly and warmly as she had her own brother. Lillian hesitated a moment in shock, but then put her arms around her future sister.

"I assume his happiness has to do with you. Mother sent word along the road that you two were to marry. A most felicitous union to you both. I'm very happy for you."

She withdrew, and there wasn't a hint of censure or sarcasm in Naomi's eyes as she looked from one to the other, though Lillian had little doubt as to how the dowager had stated their engagement in her missive. And yet Lady Westford was like Simon. She hadn't taken her mother's side immediately, but was willing to give Lillian a chance to prove herself.

Shame filled her at the thought.

"Thank you, my lady," Lillian managed.

"Posh," Lady Westford said as she briefly touched her cheek. "We are to be sisters. You shall call me Naomi and I shall call you Lillian. My husband has no sisters of his own so you are my first and I am quite thrilled at the prospect. I'm convinced we will cause all kinds of trouble together."

Lillian couldn't help but join in Naomi's laugher.

"I think for now we shall avoid trouble. I don't think I could bear any more surprises at present," Simon said with a wink in Lillian's direction that made her stomach clench with nerves and just a hint of desire. Then he took his sister's arm. "Now let me introduce you to our other guests."

Naomi let out a small sound of distress and clasped Lillian's hand. Simon's response was a laugh.

"You will have plenty of time to acquaint yourself with my fiancée later. Come."

Naomi gave her hand a quick squeeze and then she allowed her brother to lead her away. Lillian watched, her heart growing heavier with each of her future sister-in-law's warm smiles for Gabby and her aunt.

Gabby caught Lillian's eye. For a moment, concern darkened her face. She quietly excused herself and made her way across the room. When she reached Lillian, Gabby slipped an arm through hers.

"You seem out of sorts. But Lady Westford likes you, she is nothing like her mother."

Lillian nodded, the action jerky. "Yes. She's more like Simon, and I admit that my first reaction is to adore her. However, I am increasingly troubled by my lack of honesty with this family. Here she is welcoming me into her life and I—"

She cut herself off as she found the dowager duchess watching her through narrowed eyes. Almost *knowing* eyes, as if she recognized Lillian for a fraud and was just waiting for the right moment to prove it.

With a shiver she turned away. Gabby shot a glance at Lady Billingham and then slipped an arm around her shoulders.

"Simon is already beginning to understand

more and more about his father. What you tell him later won't be a total shock to him."

"But the lie will," Lillian murmured.

"It may take time, but I think they will all come to understand your motives eventually," Gabby whispered.

"I hope so," Lillian replied as she felt Lady Billingham's stare still burning at her back. "Either way, at least his mother will be pleased. I shall prove her right that I was unworthy all along. How she will crow at that."

She could only pray that Simon would understand as Gabby had said he might. The idea of facing his reaction was becoming harder to take.

As soon as Simon closed the door to the parlor and he and Naomi were alone, she spun on him with a wicked smile.

"Great God, Simon, you do know how to make a visit exciting!" she said with a musical lilt of laughter that had always brought a smile to his face even in the most trying of times.

"I cannot believe Mother sent word to you along the road," he groaned. "And I can only imagine what she said in her missive."

"Well, there was little good to the note, I admit," Naomi said as she took a seat. When he held up a bottle of sherry, she nodded. "But I must say I like

Lillian from what little I have seen. She looks terrified as a mouse facing a cat whenever I look at her, but I think once she gets past that little issue, she'll fit in quite well."

Simon pursed his lips as he handed a glass to his sister. He had noticed Lillian's discomfort earlier, as well. Even though Naomi had been kind, Lillian still shifted and shook whenever she thought no one was looking.

"If she appears terrified, it is likely because Mother despises her," he said with a deep sigh.

Naomi gave an audacious wink. "Well, that is one more mark in Lillian's favor."

They shared a brief laugh, but Simon's soon faded. He and his mother had never had a close relationship, which had been a point of great pain to him as a child. A pain sharpened by the fact that their mother had interacted very differently with Naomi. In fact, she had doted on her daughter, while almost entirely ignoring her son. Other girls might have taken her cue and treated him badly.

Naomi never had. She had always been loving toward him, protecting him from the worst of their mother's moods and sometimes even attempting to mother him, though she was a child herself. Often he had caught her looking at him, guilty and sad. Those were the worst times.

"Really, Simon," his sister said, interrupting his thoughts. She was all seriousness now. "I could never find fault with a person you chose to love. After all, you have impeccable taste."

Simon set his drink down. "I don't think I ever said love," he said, suddenly uneasy. "This union is one that was somewhat forced upon us."

Naomi shut her eyes and held up both hands like a shield. "Yes, I know, Mother said something about father's office and you being caught there. But *do* spare me the details. I still imagine you in short pants when I don't see you before me. I do not want to ruin that image by replacing it with another more unsavory one."

Simon laughed despite himself. "My apologies. I am as innocent as a lamb, if it will help you sleep at night."

She opened one eye and stuck her tongue out at him playfully. "It does a little."

Then she set her drink aside. "Truly, Simon, so you do not love her. You have really just met the girl, I don't think that is such a bad thing. But I wonder, do you think you *could*? Because a lifetime is a long while to share with someone who you do not love."

He pondered that question for a long moment, thinking of Lillian. He had desired her from the moment she stepped from her carriage and that desire had been returned, though somewhat reluctantly. Still, that feeling alone was not likely to have held his interest. He was not a profligate led by his cock, as some of his contemporaries were. He had desired many an inappropriate woman and never pursued that craving.

No, something else had kept his interest in Lillian alive, beyond the fact that he longed for her physically.

"From almost the first moment," he mused, "she has been a riddle to me. A puzzle that is not immediately solved. In one moment, she was open and friendly, the next she shut me out like she couldn't bear to look at me. But in all the times we talked, I was always struck not just by her beauty but by her intelligence. She is quick-witted and well able to hold her own in a verbal sparring match."

His sister's eyebrows lifted slightly. "I can see how that would be interesting. Many of the current day's debutantes seem dull as plain toast. A girl with a tongue and a mind behind it would certainly stand out. But that does not answer the question, Simon. Do you think you could love her?"

He shut his eyes, running over their short time together in his mind. Lillian had been standoffish at times, but there had also been moments when she had been kind. When he confessed the secret of his bastard brother, she seemed to understand the pain that discovery had caused him. She had supported him, comforted him, and once he'd begun, his hesitation in revealing that secret to her had faded almost instantly, replaced with relief at having someone with whom to share his pain.

"Yes," he finally said softly, his eyes coming open. "I think perhaps, with time, I *could* love her."

It was a stunning revelation, but he found himself smiling at it. The idea of falling in love with his future wife was actually a very pleasant one. They had years to court while being able to share a bed. It was bound to be an interesting proposition.

Naomi smiled at him. "Good. That makes me happy. At least it is better than Mama and Papa."

All the pleasant thoughts Simon had been having of Lillian suddenly faded at the mention of his parents and their very unhappy union. He understood the cause better now. The truth had a funny way of clarifying the unfathomable.

"Yes, Father," he murmured, looking at his sister from the corner of his eye.

Should he tell her what he knew? Conventional wisdom said that as a woman she had to be protected from such indelicate subjects. And yet it didn't feel right to keep such a secret. If he was entitled to know their father's true colors, wasn't she? They had both loved and looked up to him.

"Why do you look at me so?" she asked, and she shifted in her chair nervously. "Simon, what is going on?"

"You know that part of the reason I came here was for the party Mother was so insistent upon.

However, there was something else that drew me to the estate," he said slowly, still uncertain how much he wanted to reveal.

She nodded. "I assumed as much. Father was an important man, and with the new Season starting in such a short time, I thought you probably came here to take care of some of his affairs."

"Yes, that is exactly why. Do you remember how messy his office always was?"

Naomi's smile was instant and wide. "Heavens yes. Both here and in the other homes. In London Mother forced him to have a second one where he could meet with people because she was so embarrassed by his disorganization."

Simon got to his feet and paced to the window. As he looked down at the gardens below, he said, "Well, part of what I must do is put his papers in order. I thought to go through his paperwork myself before I had the staff do the rest. In fact I thought I might have a memoir written about him."

His sister straightened up a fraction. "I-I see. Yet from your expression, it appears you aren't happy with what you have found while sorting through the receipts and letters."

He turned on her. "How much did you know about Father beyond the face he showed the public?"

Naomi shrugged, but she didn't seem comfortable. "I'm not certain what you mean by his 'face,' Simon."

He sighed. "I-I mean what did you know about the real man? The one who wasn't always good or decent or fair."

Now it was Naomi who was on her feet. "What do you mean? Are you accusing Father of something?"

Simon drew back. His sister's wild expression and her trembling hands were not common. Normally Naomi was cool and collected, her high emotions happy ones, not ones of fear or upset. And yet at the mere mention of their father and the potential for secrets, she was in a panic.

Was it possible she already knew something?

"Naomi—" he began, moving toward her. "I was only asking—"

"You were *implying*," she corrected, backing up. "Implying that he did something wrong. I do not wish to hear it, Simon. The past is best left there. Leave it alone."

With that she spun away and virtually sprinted from the room, leaving Simon staring at her retreating back and wondering what his sister knew that made her so afraid.

And if it could possibly be something even worse than what he himself had already uncovered.

Chapter 18

In the library, Lillian sat in a chair close to the fire with a book in hand. Her legs were tucked beneath her and a steaming cup of tea was at her side. It was heaven.

The chamber was quickly becoming a favorite retreat of hers, for it held not only books to feed her enthusiasm for the written word, but there were also memories here. Memories of Simon. Of passion.

When she was in this room, she could almost forget the true mission that had brought her to this estate and to the man she would now marry. She could almost forget she had lied to him and misled him in the name of revenge. That she had yet to be fully honest with him.

Almost.

She was about to shake away her troubling thoughts and return to her book when the library door swung open and Lady Westford hurried into the room. Lillian got to her feet, but Naomi didn't seem to notice her at first. She turned to close the door and lifted a hand to her lips, her breath coming in heaving sighs, as if she was fighting tears.

Immediately Lillian moved forward. "My lady, are you quite all right?"

Naomi jumped as she turned on Lillian. For a moment, Lillian saw a world of hurt and upset and even fear in her companion's eyes, but then it faded, pushed away. Hidden.

"Oh, I didn't see you there, you gave me a fright." Naomi laughed, but it was a mere false echo of the earlier pleasant sound.

"You seemed quite preoccupied when you entered," Lillian said, setting her book down and coming closer. "Is anything amiss?"

"No, of course not," Naomi said as she patently avoided Lillian's gaze by staring up at the high shelves that rose above them. Her expression relaxed. "My, I do love this room."

Lillian looked at her for a long moment. It was clear her future sister-in-law had no desire to speak to her about whatever was upsetting her, but since Naomi had been spending a few private moments with Simon, Lillian felt an uncommon interest.

Still, she set it aside as she joined Naomi in looking up at the shelves. "It is wonderful. I believe it may be my favorite room on the entire estate."

That and the billiard room, which she didn't

mention to Naomi even as her cheeks burned hot at the thought.

"Yes, I feel the same. And it's Simon's favorite as well." Naomi's face dulled and her voice grew distant. "He would hide here when he was a boy, sometimes for hours."

Lillian tilted her head. "What about you? Would you hide here?"

Naomi looked at her sharply. "I had less to hide from. I suppose it isn't a secret to you how strained my brother's relationship with our mother is?"

Lillian shifted, suddenly uncomfortable. "It hasn't escaped my notice that they do not have the bond that you and the dowager have."

Naomi's face softened. "Mother has her reasons for that. But Simon suffered for them."

With a frown, Lillian said, "But it seems clear you two are as close as a brother and sister can be. So her disregard didn't affect you as it might have done others."

Naomi nodded. "No, I did my best to give him what my mother couldn't. Love and affection. And protection."

"Protection?" Lillian asked, wondering to what Naomi referred. Only their mother's wrath, or something else? Her gaze was so faraway and sad that it seemed she meant something deeper.

Naomi nodded. "Yes. There are some things it is better to leave buried. Some truths that will only hurt if they are revealed. Simon has had a difficult enough life, why should his burden be made heavier?"

Lillian stepped back. So Naomi *was* talking about more than a mere rift with his mother. She sounded like she knew secrets, perhaps the very ones that Simon had begun to uncover about their father.

"But Simon doesn't have to be protected any longer," Lillian said softly, though she flinched because she was doing that exact thing by keeping her own secrets from him. "He is a man and he deserves to know the truth. He longs for that truth, even if it hurts him."

Now Naomi turned on her, face pale and tense. "He said he's been searching through our father's things."

Lillian nodded slowly.

"What does he know?"

She hesitated. It seemed wrong to insert herself in the private pains of the siblings. If Naomi knew something new about their father's past, it wasn't fair that Lillian would hear it before Simon. Even if her curiosity was at its peak.

With a sigh, she said, "I think it's best if you speak to Simon about what he knows."

Naomi shivered as she sank into the nearest chair. "Yes, I suppose I owe him that. It is simply difficult for me not to think of him as the child

I vowed to protect, to never let anything bad happen to."

Brow wrinkling, Lillian tried to picture that. Somehow a Simon who couldn't take care of himself, a child Simon who needed a guardian . . . that was difficult to picture. All she could see was the capable, strong Simon who intrigued her despite herself.

"But surely you can see he isn't that child anymore," Lillian pressed.

"No," Naomi said as she rose to her feet and smiled. "He isn't that child. I only forget sometimes. You are good to remind me. I shall speak to him again, perhaps after supper."

Lillian nodded; she remained strangely unappeased. Despite the fact that Simon wanted to know the truth, she felt as though she had wronged him in some way.

"Now," Naomi said with a devilish look in her direction. "Let us not speak of my brother any longer, but let us talk about *you*."

Lillian stiffened as she faced Naomi with discomfort filling her. "Me?"

"Yes." Naomi motioned around the room. "Which is your favorite? And be mindful I shall be judging you based solely on your choice of reading material."

"Then I shall be careful." Lillian laughed as she moved toward the shelves and the wide array of choices to impress and amuse her future sister-in-law.

But even as they laughed, Lillian couldn't shake her sense of unease. Every moment that she kept her own secrets from Simon, she kept a piece of the puzzle he longed to solve from his hands. And whether that was for his protection or her own, in some way it made her no better than his father.

Despite the events of earlier in the day, supper was a lively affair. Lillian was placed on Simon's right with Naomi across from her. Gabby was beside her and her deaf aunt beside Naomi. At the opposite end of the table from Simon was his mother. She was the only one not laughing, joining in stories, and generally having a good time. Even Aunt Isabel shared a few stories of her own days as a debutante.

But Lillian sensed a continued tension between brother and sister. Occasionally Naomi and Simon locked eyes and an unspoken battle raged between them. And though Lillian realized there was nothing she could do beyond the brief talk she'd had earlier with Naomi, she still wondered what the outcome of their war would be.

As if Naomi had read her thoughts, she suddenly leaned over, and Lillian heard her murmur, "After supper tonight, I'd like a moment with you."

Simon arched a brow. "Would you?"

She nodded, and there was a pain on her face that made Lillian ache for her. She recognized Naomi's look as one of staunch resignation. As if Simon's sister knew nothing would be the same once she spoke to him and yet she was willing to face that future.

"We began a conversation earlier," Naomi said with a shuddering sigh, "which I was too tired to finish. But I'm ready to do so now."

Simon was quiet for a long moment before he nodded. "Very well. Might I ask what changed your mind on this score?"

Without speaking, Naomi turned her gaze firmly on Lillian. Simon followed her stare and suddenly the world faded away. All that was left was him. No lies, no decisions, no pains.

Just him.

And it was utterly terrifying. Lillian was about to turn away from it when the dowager duchess rose suddenly from her place and snapped out, "We shall retire to the west drawing room."

As the others at the table rose and made their way from the room, Simon stood and carefully helped Lillian from her chair. As he offered her an arm, she shivered. It had been only a day since the last time they were together, but at that moment it felt like an eternity. She was starved for him, for his touch, for his breath on her skin.

It seemed he felt the same, for he leaned in and

subtly breathed in her scent before he whispered, "I don't know what you said to my sister, but I thank you for it."

Lillian squeezed her eyes shut. "Wait until you have spoken to her before you thank me. Perhaps you won't like the outcome of the conversation."

He shrugged one shoulder. "It doesn't matter. I'm beginning to appreciate the truth more than I appreciate the protection of lies."

Lillian jerked her gaze to his face. He almost looked peaceful, even though he had to know his sister might tell him something he would hate. Something that would hurt and change him forever. Yet he *wanted* it.

He sighed. "Tonight I'll tell her what I know and perhaps I will hear something new from her, as well. And we shall move on from there. It is all we can do in the end."

Lillian nodded, ignoring the sting of tears behind her eyes. The realization that she had to tell him the truth and tell him before they married hit her so hard she almost felt it physically. He deserved that. *She* deserved it.

"I would like to move on to you," he murmured, a bit lower as they walked down the hallway. "I *need* to be with you."

She shivered at the hint of desire laced through his tone and present in every word he spoke. That feeling was mirrored in her heart, in her body.

"I want that, too," she admitted, glancing up into his face and marveling at the perfect beauty of his every feature.

He smiled, and the expression softened some of the hard angles of his face. "Then meet me in my chamber at midnight."

She swallowed hard. That would be the perfect time and place to confess everything to him. Tonight, when they were alone, with no interruptions, she could finally give him the truth he deserved. The consequences would come, she was certain of it, but as he had said, they would move on from there. It was all they could do.

"Lillian?" he said softly. "Will you meet me?"

She jerked out a nod before they entered the room and couldn't speak of such indelicate topics any longer. But as she parted from him and crossed the room to speak to Gabby, Lillian couldn't help but shiver as she thought of what would happen once they were alone again.

Simon couldn't account for the nervousness he felt as he awaited his sister in their father's office an hour later. When she stormed out of the room that afternoon, he'd suspected she knew something about the late duke's behavior, but now he questioned that belief. Why would Naomi have knowledge of something he didn't?

It was foolish, just his tired and disillusioned

mind playing tricks on him, looking for shadows where there was none to find.

He heard his sister approaching in the hallway and straightened up as she entered the room. Her cheeks were pale as she looked around at the disarray. Finally she shook her head.

"Oh, Papa," she murmured, more to herself, it seemed, than to him. Then she looked at him with a sad smile. "You've been forced to go through these things all alone?"

"Not alone," Simon admitted as he motioned to two chairs he had cleared for them. As they sat, he continued, "Rhys was in attendance at the party earlier."

Naomi's smile fell a fraction. She had never been close to his friend.

"Yes, Rhys. It has been a long time since I saw him. How is he?"

"About to be married. Even if my own sudden engagement hadn't sent the party running back to London, he never intended to stay the entire fortnight." He shook his head. "He's back in Town, making final arrangements for the wedding to Anne. When I return, Lillian and I will have our own quick service and then I intend to stand up for him a few days later."

His sister nodded. "I certainly wish him much happiness. And you say he helped you file through Father's papers?"

Her worried tone made Simon frown. "He may be many things, but he *is* trustworthy, Naomi."

"I'm sure." She nodded slowly.

"And—and Lillian helped me somewhat, as well," he admitted after a moment's hesitation.

At that, both his sister's eyebrows rose. "You must have stronger feelings than you let on, to have trusted her with such a delicate task."

He stared at his sister for a long moment, all his suspicions rushing back as he watched her pale face and listened to her cryptic words. Leaning forward, he held her stare evenly.

"What do you know, Naomi?" he whispered, his voice rough.

She flinched, and his stomach turned.

"Oh, Simon. Why don't you start with what you know and I shall fill in the gaps," she finally said, her voice filled with pity and pain that twisted the knife already in his heart.

Quietly he told her of the evidence he had found about their father's duplicity in politics. His back-alley dealings and secret money exchanges didn't seem to surprise his sister in the least.

And then he reached the part about the abandoned son.

"Henry Ives," his sister said quietly.

He tensed. "You know his name?"

She shut her eyes. "Like my own." When they

came back open, they were filled with tears. "And do you know about the others?"

Simon flopped back against his chair as his breath left his lungs in a great gasping whoosh. This was his greatest suspicion, his deepest fear, come true. "There were others?"

She nodded slowly.

"How long have you known?" he asked, his tone sharp.

At that, she got to her feet and paced away through the mass of paperwork. She hardly seemed to see where she was going, but somehow managed to avoid dumping the piles over as she stepped around them.

"You don't understand what it was like," she murmured. "You thought your relationship with Mama was strained, but there were disadvantages to being her favorite, too."

When she looked at him, his heart swelled in pain for her.

"She told you her secrets, *his* secrets," he finished for her when it seemed she was unable to do so herself.

A nod was her only reply for a long while, then she sighed.

"I was her confidante, her partner in poison, sometimes I felt like a prisoner to her hate. How I despised hearing her go on and on about our father's sins. But if I turned away, she would have no one to share her pain with. I feared it would drive her mad, and then who knew what she might do."

"What she did was unfair to you," he cried, lurching to his feet.

She held up her hands in entreaty. "You don't know the life she has led, Simon. What she has endured!"

"Then tell me," he said, running a hand through his hair. "Tell me how much more I have left to find. Tell me the secrets that are still out there. How many children did our father abandon? How many lies have I been told?"

His sister looked up at the ceiling with a groan. "I have kept their secrets for so long. I know you deserve the truth, I've known that all my life, and yet the idea of being the one to tell you . . . to hurt you . . ."

She trailed off as she lifted her hands to her face and began to cry softly. Simon watched her, awash in a combination of anger and pity. Finally he crossed the room and wrapped his arms around his sister. She wept into his shoulder for a few moments more, and he brushed her hair as comfort.

"She put you in the middle," he soothed. "And now I'm doing the same. It isn't fair, I know."

She looked up at him, hiccupping back a final sob. "Nothing about this is fair."

"Can you at least point me in the right direction?" he whispered, wiping away one of her tears with the back of his hand. "If it pains you too much to tell me yourself, could you at least give me that?"

She nodded. "I can give you two clues which will surely end your search," she whispered. "First, look to where Mother vanishes. That is one place you'll find the truth."

"That is a riddle more than a clue," Simon said, just biting back a curse of frustration.

"And this is a direct fact," his sister said softly. "Father had a secret stash of papers he thought no one knew about. They are hidden beneath the floorboard under his desk. Once you've read them, you'll understand the riddle."

Simon spun to face the desk and then back to his sister. "How do you know that?"

She frowned, and a ghost of pain moved over her face. "Because I was hiding in this room one day when he placed papers there. Years later, as I understood more, longed to know more, I came and read them all." She reached out and touched his arm. "They contain the answers you seek. I only hope you'll be able to stand them once they are yours to bear."

She gave him one last touch on his cheek and then silently left the room. Left him alone with the knowledge that everything he wanted to know had literally been beneath his feet all along.

Simon turned and paced the floor to the desk. Pushing the chair aside, he got to his knees and began to slide his hands over the gleaming wood. Back and forth he moved, searching for a loose board or something to indicate that this was the place his father had put all his secrets.

And then, he found it.

A rough piece of panel clearly different from all the others, with a notch in the corner to allow a person to slip a finger beneath its edge. With a firm tug, the plank pulled away. In the dim light, he saw a box tucked into the cubbyhole. His hands shook as he withdrew it and got to his feet.

He took the box to the lamplight beside the fire and sank into a chair there. There was nothing ornate or interesting about the container, just a plain pine box, rather like a tiny coffin. He shivered as he considered that. His father had all but buried his secrets.

And now Simon was about to raise them from the dead. All he had to do was lift the lid and see what was waiting for him there.

Chapter 19

Lillian lay on her side across Simon's bed, staring at the door as she awaited his return to his room. He'd said he'd meet her at midnight, but it was already a quarter past that hour. She glanced at the clock nervously and then back to the door.

Where could he be?

Getting to her feet, she moved across the room restlessly, fiddling with a book on his end table, absently touching an arrangement of spring flowers on the mantel.

The longer she waited, the more she believed his talk with Naomi hadn't gone well. Lillian suspected his sister might have new information about their father. If that was true, she shuddered to think of what it was, for nothing that had been uncovered so far was good.

She pictured how tormented Simon had been when he found out he had a brother who had been abandoned. If Naomi's information was worse than that . . .

Pivoting, Lillian made for the door. She had to find him and verify that he was well. She had almost reached the chamber entrance when the door opened of its own accord. She stepped back with a gasp, expecting Simon to come inside.

Instead, Naomi was revealed when the door swung away.

Lillian froze in her spot. Although she had already been ruined, it was still a humiliation to be caught waiting for Simon in his bedchamber.

But if Naomi thought ill of her, it did not show on her pale, worry-lined face.

"Good, I have found you," she said, breathless as if she had been running.

Lillian stepped forward, her embarrassment forgotten in the face of Naomi's obvious distress. "What is it?"

"My brother—" She cut herself off and clenched her fists at her sides as she drew a few long breaths.

"What about Simon?" Lillian cried, grabbing for the other woman's arms and squeezing. "Is he hurt?"

"No," Naomi burst out. "Not in the sense you mean. But—but he *will* need you tonight. He'll need *someone* and I'm not the one who can help him now."

Lillian stepped away, confused and unwilling to go without more information, though her heart ached to simply run to Simon's side. "What do you mean? What has happened?"

Naomi shook her head. "I know you have been privy to some of Simon's investigation into our father's less savory dealings. He told me you assisted him."

"Y-yes," Lillian stammered, shame flooding her at the true reason behind her "helpfulness."

"Well, there is far more to discover and I've set him on the path of it. What he learns tonight will—" She broke off again and let out a heaving breath that bordered on a sob. "He will need you, that's all. Please, go to him. He's in the office our father used."

Lillian didn't need further encouragement, without a word or a look behind her, she hurried from the room and rushed down the stairs. For the first time, she didn't care who saw her streaking through the halls in the middle of the night. She didn't care about judgments.

She only cared about finding the man she was to marry. She only cared about helping him in whatever lame, useless way she could.

Within moments, she had reached the office. Her hand trembled as she reached for the door. Whatever happened, she was about to face a man who needed her. And she wouldn't let him down.

The chamber was cold and dark except for a few eerie shadows cast by the faint light from the low lanterns and the nearly extinguished fire. She scanned around, but didn't see Simon.

"Simon?" she said softly.

There was such a sense of sadness to the room that she dared not call out too loudly. It seemed irreverent to do so.

There was no answer and she stepped deeper into the room. "Simon?"

Still nothing. Had Naomi been wrong? Had her brother left this chamber? And if so, where had he gone, for Lillian hadn't passed him in the hallways when she rushed downstairs.

She clenched her fists at her sides and finally forced herself to speak louder. "Simon!"

"That isn't my name."

The slurred, pained voice came from a darkened corner of the chamber, and Lillian didn't hesitate to rush toward it and him. As her eyes fully adjusted she finally saw him, sitting on the floor almost beneath his father's desk. All around him were letters, ledgers, paperwork.

He looked up at her, and his beautiful jade eyes glittered in the low light. His expression was the most heartbreaking she had ever seen. It put her to mind of her father the day her mother died.

"Oh, dearest," she breathed as she reached for him, then pulled her hand away. He seemed so stiff she feared he would shatter if she touched him. "Let me raise the light."

After a few moments of fumbling with the lantern on his desk, the light in the room lifted, and it took everything in Lillian not to stagger back at Simon's face. He was . . . broken.

And all she wanted to do was fix it. Fix him.

Setting the lantern aside, she got to her knees and moved toward him slowly.

"What is it, Simon?" she whispered, using the same tone she would have with a skittish colt.

"I told you, that isn't my name," he said as he pushed to his feet and turned away.

"I don't understand," she whispered, watching his stiff posture with tears stinging her eyes.

"You do not wish to marry me, Lillian."

She struggled to get up and moved on him. "What are you talking about, Simon. What do you mean?"

Turning, he speared her with a sharp, clear stare. He wasn't drunk, that was something. Regardless, he seemed to be impaired, if only by a pain so deep that it radiated from him.

"I'm not the man you think I am. I don't even know what or who I am."

She reached for him then, determined not to be lost in his riddles. Clutching his forearm, she whispered, "Tell me what has happened. Explain why you are in this state."

"Yes," he mused absently as he stared at her gripping fingers like they were a foreign object he didn't recognize. "You deserve to know. After everything, you shouldn't be lied to like I was."

She forced herself to remain silent as he extracted himself from her grip and gathered up a few of the items at his feet.

"My sister came to me tonight and told me about hidden papers in this office. Something that would explain more about my past, my father's past."

He clutched the items to his chest as he stared at her evenly. "I never thought they would tell me this."

"What?" she asked, covering his clenched fingers with her hand. "What is it, Simon?"

He flinched. "That is exactly it, my dear. I'm not Simon Crathorne. I am not the Duke of Billingham at all. My real name is Henry Ives, and I am the eldest bastard son of the biggest liar in all of England."

Simon watched as Lillian read over everything he had found in the hidden cubby beneath his father's desk. She was sitting in a chair by the fire he had stoked an hour before, but despite her position, she seemed unsteady. Off kilter.

Just as he was. In such a short span of time, his entire world had changed. Nothing would ever be the same.

She finished the last item and set the pile aside gingerly, as if she feared the words she had read might bite her.

"Let me see if I understand this," she said softly, steepling her fingers on her lap.

When she lifted her gaze and looked at him evenly, he felt relieved she didn't shy away. God, she was strong. Stronger than he was at the moment.

"The real Simon Crathorne was permanently injured in an accident at the lake here on the estate thirty years ago, when the boy was just two."

He nodded. That certainly explained why his mother and father hated the place and were so protective about him going there.

"Apparently he nearly drowned. He was revived, but his mind was never the same," he choked out.

"Your father, not wanting to lose the chance to have the next Duke of Billingham come from his own blood, came to London, found your real mother, and essentially bought you and her silence. You and the real heir were almost the same age and looked similar enough that after a few months your father and the duchess felt comfortable enough to bring you out in front of guests as the real Simon. No one was the wiser, including you, because you were so young."

He nearly choked as he heard the words out loud. It sickened him to think of the lie his life had been. And all for what? For his father's vanity?

"But why did your father not simply have another child with your mother?" Lillian asked. "Why instigate such a ruse?"

He shook his head. "She has always said that my . . ." He hesitated. "*Simon's* birth did some damage to her body. She was told she could bear no more children."

Lillian shut her eyes. "And so he simply replaced one for another. Without thought to you or to anyone else around him."

He nodded. "Yes. They raised me as if I was their legitimate son. And apparently believed I'd never know. Never question."

Lillian frowned. "But the items you found earlier that explained your father had an illegitimate son . . . *you* . . . why would he leave those for you to find?"

"I don't think he intended to," Simon said with a sigh. "All other references to the bastard children were hidden in the cubby below the desk, never to be found. I think the first information I found about . . . well, myself, I suppose, was left in the ledger accidentally. He fell victim to his own disorganization."

Which would be ironic if it wasn't so bloody sad and pathetic.

"Even if he *did* know there was evidence for me

to find," he finished quietly, "he died suddenly of an apoplexy. There was no warning or way for him to organize his affairs first."

Slowly, Lillian stood and moved toward him. Part of him wanted to back away, but a greater part wanted her comfort. Especially since he saw no pity or disgust in her stare when she reached for him. If there had been that, he couldn't have borne it.

She reached up to touch his face, and the sadness in her expression made his own eyes sting with tears.

"Simon—"

"No. That isn't my name," he snapped, pulling away.

She grabbed for him and clung surprisingly tight for such a small woman. "It *is* your name. This information, it changes what you know, it doesn't change who you are."

"Of course it fucking does, Lillian," he cried out, pulling away from her and making his way across the room.

"No!" She followed him, tenacious as a bulldog. "A life is made of experiences, choices, friendships . . . your father and mother—" She stopped and then corrected herself. "Your father and the duchess might have taken away your name, they might have slipped you into their son's life, but they didn't take away those experiences or choices or friendships. Since you were two, you have *been* Simon Crathorne."

"But there is a real Simon Crathorne still out there somewhere," he argued, fisting his hands at his sides in pure frustration. "He didn't die in that accident, his mind was just maimed. I'm living his life, Lillian. I *stole* his life. And this title, if the real Simon is not capable of serving with it, then it should go to our cousin, whether he wants it or not. I have *stolen* that man's title."

"You stole nothing!" Lillian cried out, and there was such passion in her voice that it silenced him.

He stared at her as she came toward him, a passionate Valkyrie, ready to fight for him, whether that meant she dueled with him or the world.

"You had something thrust upon you that you did not choose," she said, her voice much softer. She looked as if she understood, even though that was impossible. How could she?

"And now what do I do with it?" he asked, sinking into the nearest chair. "What do I do, Lillian?"

She knelt down on the floor before him so they were at eye level. Taking his hands, she let out a long sigh as she pondered that question.

"When you gave me those things you found, you told me your sister said if you discovered where your mother went, it would reveal all. What did she mean?"

He blinked, trying to clear his mind.

"For as long as I can recall, my mother . . ." He caught himself. "The *duchess* disappeared for long periods of time when we came to this estate. Sometimes hours, once for a few days. Father never commented on it. Once when I was eight, I tried to follow her, but when she caught me she beat me with a switch and was more careful after that."

Lillian flinched, but made no comment. "And your sister said once you read the facts, you would understand the riddle."

Simon nodded. At present his mind was so tangled he couldn't *understand* anything except pain. So much pain. So many lies.

Lillian thought for a moment, pondering what Naomi had said. Then her eyes widened and she let out a gasp.

"What is it?"

She stared at him. "Simon, if the duchess went someplace she didn't want you to know about . . . could it be your brother, the real heir, is somewhere on the estate? Could she be visiting her child?"

He blinked down at her. He had been so wrapped up in the shocking realization that he wasn't the man he thought he was . . . he hadn't even considered that. But it made sense. Hiding the injured boy on the property reduced the chance of being caught in their deception.

As he stared at her, Lillian grabbed for the discarded things she had read through a few moments before. She flipped through them, pausing to read from time to time. Finally, she held out a ledger.

"Here."

He took what she offered. It was a line of figures and a crudely drawn map Simon had dismissed when he read through the other more damning items in his father's hidden cubby.

"It says the year you would have been brought to the estate, a small cottage was built in a remote corner of this wooded area. There isn't even a road to get there." Lillian tilted her head. "Perhaps that is where they keep . . . *him*."

"Simon," he said dully as he stared. The place was about five miles from the house and hidden among brambles and heavy woods. It would be the perfect location to hide something.

Or someone.

Lillian rose up on her knees and cupped his face gently. "Yes. And I think we should go there."

Simon flinched, but Lillian held fast.

"We must go, if only to see if he's there."

He drew in a harsh breath. The very idea of it made him queasy. If Lillian was right and Simon . . . the *real* Simon . . . was there, how could he face the man whose life he had taken? How could he look at the brother he had never known?

"I don't know . . ." He moved to turn his face, but she didn't allow it.

"Simon," she whispered. "You *need* to do this. Only by seeing him will you know what road to take. And I'll be with you. I won't leave your side unless you ask me to do so."

She was right, of course. He had come so far in uncovering his father's lies, he had to see the task through. And if Lillian would be with him, the duty seemed slightly less daunting.

He found himself jerking out a nod. "Yes. We shall go tomorrow."

"Now come upstairs with me," she whispered. "I'll stay with you tonight."

He tilted his head to stare at her. She was offering him comfort, not sex. And he needed it as he needed air. So he got up and silently followed her to his chamber and what he knew would be a sleepless night.

Lillian looked down at Simon. He had fallen into a fitful, restless sleep after hours of tossing and turning. His head rested in the crook of her shoulder and his mouth was turned down into a deep, troubled frown. Occasionally he let out a groan and shifted against her.

She smoothed his hair gently, and the motion seemed to calm him, for his mouth relaxed and his breathing became heavier. She sighed. At least she could grant him that fleeting peace.

There was little else she could give.

Staring up through the darkness of his chamber, Lillian blinked back tears. The events of the night played over and over in her head.

Simon had laid out at her feet the darkest, deepest, most devastating secret she ever could have hoped for when she came here. If the world found out that the supposedly good Duke of Billingham had in fact replaced his injured son with a bastard . . . if they knew he had lied about everything in his life and the boy's life . . . well, there would be a scandal unlike any other. It would be splashed across every paper in London and throughout the countryside. It would be on every lip at every party for the next ten years.

And yet, she felt no pleasure in that fact. She had given up her decision to reveal the duke for what he was, so knowing he could be so cruel gave her nothing but a sick sensation in her stomach. All she could think about was how much the man had hurt Simon.

Somehow in the time she had known him, Simon's pains had become her own, his disappointments cut her, his future was hers. And now, lying beside him in the dark, she knew she loved him.

She hadn't even been stunned to realize it. And

she still wasn't. Loving him seemed natural. True. Right.

Even though he didn't know who she was, why she had come here. She had planned to tell him tonight, but she couldn't. He was bearing the weight of far too much already. Later, *later* she would confess. For now she had to concentrate on helping him.

And so tomorrow she would go with him to face the most difficult challenge he would likely ever encounter. And she would stand by his side, supporting him with all her love and strength.

And then she would marry him.

She could only hope that in the lifetime she had to build with him, she would find a way to make up for her original intentions. That she would find a way to be worthy of the man who had washed away her anger and replaced it with a love so powerful that it mattered more than anything.

Chapter 20

The day dawned cold with a faint drizzle that made fog rise from the rolling hillsides. As Simon helped Lillian into the carriage that would take them as close to the hidden cottage as possible, he mused on the perfection of the dreary surroundings. They certainly reflected his present state of mind.

It was slow going down long-neglected pathways until finally the carriage rolled to a stop. It shook as the driver climbed off and opened the door. While Simon helped Lillian down, the servant looked around them quizzically.

"I can't go no further and there ain't nothin' 'round here, Your Grace," he said. "Are you sure this is where you want to be dropped off?"

Simon nodded. "I am. Please wait here while my fiancée and I take a walk. We shall return, though I don't know how long we'll be."

The man looked around him once more and

then shrugged as he pulled his hat down lower as protection against the rain. "Whatever Your Lordship wishes."

Lillian looked at Simon, and her expression was as grim as his own felt. He took her arm, and the two of them made off away from the path.

After they were far enough from the carriage so the driver wouldn't see, Lillian withdrew from her reticule the makeshift map his father had sketched out nearly three decades before. The ink was fading and the paper was yellowed but most of the landmarks within remained.

And in some way, Simon didn't need the map. Something was calling him, guiding him to the place where they might very well find his brother. Where his past, which was now so shadowy, might become clearer. Perhaps seeing this man whose life he had been living would give it all some kind of purpose.

They had walked nearly two miles through untamed fields and into a copse of trees when suddenly the cottage came into view over a low hill. Simon stopped. It was a pretty little place. Cheery, with bright white walls and plenty of colorful flowers around the front door.

He didn't realize how long he had been standing there until Lillian gently tugged him forward.

"Come, love. Let us finish this. We've come all this way."

He drew in a long breath as he looked down at her upturned face. Although he was uncertain of his past, when he looked at her the future didn't seem so bleak.

"I'm glad you are here," he murmured as they approached the door.

Then he lifted his hand and rapped smartly on the face. There were sounds of movement from within and then the door opened to reveal a round-faced, merry servant woman. The moment she saw Simon, her smile fell and her eyes widened.

"Why . . . Y-Your Grace," she stammered, moving subtly to block the door. "What are you doing here?"

His eyes narrowed. "I've come to see *him*."

"No," the woman cried, and she shook her head wildly. "The duchess said we weren't to let anyone see. She said he was to be protected. She said never—"

"Her Grace has no authority over those who live on *my* lands," he said, using that "lord of the manor" tone he had always loathed. Still, it had its purposes, for the woman ceased her listing of all the reasons why she couldn't allow him entry.

"She will be very angry," she finally whispered, her eyes welling with fearful tears.

Softening his stance, Simon touched her arm. "I will take full responsibility . . . What is your name?"

"I'm the housekeeper, Mrs. White," the woman said as she curtsied first to him and then to Lillian.

"Mrs. White, I promise you Her Ladyship will spend any anger on me, not you," he said. "Now please, where is he?"

The woman stepped aside and granted them entry. She was silent as she closed the door behind them and then moved down a narrow but brightly lit hallway. She stopped at a door and hesitated.

"He is within," she whispered.

Simon nodded. "Is he alone?"

"No, he has a companion who takes care of him and keeps him company. She's been with him all these years, since the accident," the housekeeper said. "Her name is Miss Lewiston."

"Thank you." Simon turned his attention back to the closed door. "You may go."

The servant nodded and then all but fled, leaving Simon and Lillian alone before the chamber. For a long time, he merely stared at the door.

"What if I cannot do this?" he finally said through clenched teeth.

Lillian rubbed his upper arm gently, and somehow the action soothed him. "You can."

He nodded and then pushed the door open. The chamber was a big, airy room, brightly lit by a roaring fire. When it was sunny out, the many windows would have brightened it even more. The walls were painted in pale, friendly colors and the furniture was comfortable and large, though somewhat worn.

Simon stepped inside, almost unable to breathe as he looked around. He saw the woman first. Miss Lewiston, the housekeeper had called her. She was older, thin and tall, but not severe in the slightest. When she noticed his presence, she rushed across the room, her hands up.

"Who are you, what are you doing here?" she snapped.

Simon looked her up and down. "I'm Simon Crathorne, Duke of Billingham. I am here to see my brother."

Before the pale woman could respond, a deep voice echoed from behind a couch. "Simon? My name is Simon, too!"

Simon watched, utterly mesmerized, as a tall, heavyset man stood up from his hiding place behind the settee. He looked utterly normal, like any man of two and thirty would, only his hair was tousled and his eyes flitted almost as an excitable child's would.

He lumbered across the room and smiled shyly at Simon and Lillian. "Miss Lewiston, he has my name."

The servant looked at her charge with a soft smile. "Indeed, he does." She cast her glance at Simon with a frown, her nervousness making her fidget her hands at her sides. "Isn't it nice to have visitors?"

As his brother nodded, Miss Lewiston looked to Lillian and Simon.

"Do you intend to do him any harm?" she asked through gritted teeth.

Simon drew back. "Of course not. I'm here only to meet him. To try to understand . . . well, *this.*"

After a few moments of observation, Miss Lewiston nodded and stepped back, allowing Simon and Lillian full access into the room.

"This man is very important," she said to her charge. "He is a duke. How does one address a duke?"

"Your Grace," his brother said as proudly as a child in school would do when quizzed.

Simon shut his eyes. His brother was clearly a boy trapped in a man's body, his mind cut off by the accident that had happened all those years ago. He might look like an adult, but in reality, he was probably no more than five or six years old in his mind.

"You may just call me . . ." Simon hesitated. "Henry, if you like."

The other man shrugged. "Yes, Henry. Did you come to play?"

"Play?" Simon repeated.

He moved forward and Lillian released his arm.

He looked back at her over his shoulder but she only smiled in encouragement, letting him go, letting him interact with his brother, but never inserting herself into the situation.

"Simon loves to play," the nurse said quietly, also standing back to allow him access. "When it is cold or rainy, like it is today, we play inside games. His favorite is 'find me.' We were playing when you came in, which is why he was hidden behind the couch."

"It sounds like you are quite fine at the game," Simon said as he came forward. "I didn't know you were there when I entered."

His brother grinned, a crooked smile that made him seem almost as young as he behaved. "Very fine. Mama comes and she can never find me."

Simon bit back a groan of pain. God, his mother . . . or the woman who had posed as his mother. She had been coming here for three decades, looking in on and loving this boy even while she hated *him*. And now it all made sense.

"I have soldiers, want to see?" the other man said, pulling Simon from his reverie.

He looked over his shoulder. Lillian was wiping tears from her eyes, but she managed another encouraging smile. Her presence bolstered him and he stepped closer.

"Yes," he said softly. "I would very much like to see your soldiers."

His brother led him to a tidy corner with tray after tray of children's things stacked neatly. "We can play together. We could be friends."

Simon stared as his brother got to the floor and began yanking items from the shelves.

"I promise you, Simon," he said as he reached down to tousle his brother's already messy hair, "I will be the best friend I can be to you. I'll protect you. No matter what it takes."

Then Simon Crathorne, formerly Henry Ives, sat down on the floor with his brother and played soldiers.

Lillian slipped her fingers into Simon's hand as they walked down the tidy path away from the cottage where they had just spent the last three hours. She was wrung out, emotionally exhausted, so she could only imagine what Simon was enduring. He had been perfect with his brother, playing games with him and asking about his life. After a while, when the nurse realized he had no intention of harming her charge, she had become more and more open. They had learned about Simon's life and routine, as well as what the doctors said about his capabilities and limitations.

Lillian looked over at him. He was staring straight ahead, lost in a haze as they slowly made their way back to the carriage and then the place he had called home all his life.

"Simon, do you want to talk about this?" she asked softly.

That brought him to a halt. He looked down at her, then back over his shoulder at the cottage. Only the roof was visible now, for they had crested the low hill. In a few more steps it would be entirely gone, almost as if it didn't exist.

Except that it did and it was time to deal with that fact, at last.

"Simon," he repeated, then he laughed, though the sound was humorless and tired. "Simon is *his* name. Should I even be called that?"

She lifted his hand to her heart and held it there, aching for his pain and realizing from bitter experience that there was nothing she could do to take it away. Nothing but support him, hear him, *love* him.

"Yes, you should. *Simon*, the circumstances that brought you to this place, this family, this life were not of your making. They weren't your fault. You cannot blame yourself for what was done to you . . . or what happened to him."

"I took his life!" he burst out, shaking off her hand and pacing away restlessly. His tone was so raw that it brought tears to her eyes for what seemed the hundredth time that day.

"No," she insisted, grabbing his shoulder and pulling him around to look at her. "You were *given* his life. And it is a gift. Moreover, you have lived

that life with honor and dignity. You have represented him and his name and all he should have
been because he couldn't do that himself. I'm sure
if he understood the circumstances, he would be
pleased. He would love you for all you've done and
who you are."

He seemed to ponder that for a long time, then
he let out a long, heavy sigh.

"He does seem content here," he whispered.

She nodded, thinking of the happy home that
had been built for the child, and she could think of
him as nothing else but a child, despite his tall stature and heavyset build. The longer they stayed, the
more this man-child Simon had told them about
the fun he had and how much he loved his mama's
visits and how he even had a dog to play with.

"He is happy, Simon. Your brother may be
more . . . *simple* than others around him, but it's
clear he has a great capacity for love. His housekeeper and nurse adore him, he evidently has a
strong bond with your mother, and now . . ." She
reached up to touch his face. "He has you. And me."

Simon nodded, but she saw the sparkle of tears
in his eyes. "Yes, he does, indeed. And I intend
to come here, to see him, whenever I can. When
I arrived, I wasn't sure what I would find, what I
would feel."

"I know," she said softly.

"But the moment I saw him . . ." He trailed off,

and suddenly his smile became warm and genuine. "I loved him. I knew I could never let anyone hurt him. I would do *anything* to prevent that. Anything."

Lillian flinched ever so slightly. There was so much passion in his words. If he ever knew that her purpose when she first came here was to do just that, to uncover the kind of secret she now knew and then spread it to every corner of the *ton*, consequences be damned . . .

Well, he wouldn't be reaching for her hand again, that was for certain. He would despise her. He would rightly see her as a threat to his brother, a threat to his own future.

He threaded his fingers through hers, and her worries faded at his touch.

"There are more brothers, you know," Simon said finally. "I found the evidence of it in the same hiding hole where my father put the information about me. Mine was the only actual name listed, but there is a solicitor named there who took care of at least one of the payouts to the mother of another of his sons."

Lillian shook her head in disgust at what Simon's father had caused. Now Simon would have to tidy up all the messes the duke had left behind out of selfishness and greed.

"How many?" she asked softly.

He shrugged. "Two others. At least that's how

many were detailed here at this estate. But my father had more estates all over the countryside, who knows what he hid in those places."

The carriage was in the distance now and both of them hesitated. It seemed he had the same feeling as she did, not ready to return to the estate, not ready to face the consequences of what they had discovered and experienced today.

"I want to find them, Lillian," he said, turning to face her. "Everything I've ever known is a lie, but there is a true family out there for me. Fractured, but real. I deserve to know them and they deserve to know the truth."

Her brow wrinkled. There was so much potential for pain in Simon's plan. "Even if the truth hurts them? You have no idea who those men could be."

He considered that for a moment, but then he nodded. "Everyone deserves to know who they are, even if it hurts. No one deserves a life of lies."

Lillian shut her eyes briefly. Once they married, would that be what she doomed him to, another life filled with lies because he didn't yet know the truth of her family's link to his father?

But that wasn't a problem for this moment. Simon needed her, and she was determined to help in the best way she could. Reaching up, she cupped his cheeks and drew him down to her. Pressing her mouth to his, she kissed him. She felt the tension leave his shoulders as his arms came around her and the kiss deepened to a much more pleasurable one.

When they parted, she smiled at him. "You're right, Simon. Everyone deserves the truth. And we will find your brothers. When we return to London, we go directly to this solicitor and get the names of the other sons."

"After we wed, of course," Simon said with the first smile in a while that hadn't contained a healthy dose of pain. "And with you by my side, I'm certain we will do whatever we decide is best."

They joined hands again and made for the carriage. As the driver opened the door with a quiet acknowledgment, Simon helped her in. She settled back against the comfortable leather seat and sighed. It had been a trying day, and what she wanted more than anything was a hot bath and a long nap.

Except when Simon got in, she could see that wasn't what was on his mind. His earlier smile had vanished and he was grim again.

"What is it?" she asked, reaching across the carriage seat to cover his knee with her hand. "You're thinking of something troubling, I can tell."

"It has been a trying day," he said softly. "But there is one thing I have left to do."

Lillian looked at him for a long moment. She understood. There was one person left alive in this world who had perpetrated this lie, one person who could answer at least some of Simon's questions.

"You wish to confront your mother," she whispered.

"My mother." He said the word slowly, as if it felt foreign on his tongue. "Do you know I have dreamed of the real woman who was my mother all my life? I never knew it was her, but now it seems so obvious that my dream specter was her."

She frowned. "And now you could find her." His face twisted, and in that moment she saw the bitter truth. "Oh, Simon. Is she . . ."

He nodded. "This morning I went into my father's office. I found a notation in a ledger about her. Apparently she died four years after he took me. She's gone. I shall never know her."

Lillian squeezed her eyes shut as pain washed over her. She missed her mother terribly, but she had good and happy memories to sustain her. Simon . . . Simon had nothing but questions.

"I'm so sorry, my love," she whispered. "Why didn't you tell me?"

He shrugged. "I suppose in part it was too raw. And there was so much more to think about coming here to find . . . *him*. My brother. I didn't want to pass along one more sorrow for you to bear."

She shook her head. His justifications were so like her own. To protect him, she kept the truth from him. To protect her, he did the same.

"At any rate, it seems the duchess is all I have left." He cleared his throat, and she could tell he wished to move away from the painful topic, at least for a while. "And it is high time we handled this for once and for all." He touched the hand still resting against his leg. "Will you be at my side as I do that?"

Lillian drew back, surprised at his request.

"Is this not a private matter between the two of you?" she asked.

He shook his head. "You are to be my wife, and unfortunately you will inherit a world of problems and issues along with that title."

"But she hates me, Simon. With me in the room, she might not tell you anything," she said with a shiver as she thought of the duchess's glares and nasty comments over the short time of their acquaintance.

Simon folded his arms, and in his expression was every inch the lordly duke. A man not to be trifled with. And born into it or raised into it, she had to admit the look was quite intimidating.

"She can rot with her opinions of you after all she's done." Then his anger was gone. "And I'd like you to be there."

At that, Lillian shoved aside her misgivings and nodded. "Then I shall be at your side, Simon. For whatever you need."

Chapter 21

Simon stepped into the private parlor in his mother's chamber and looked around. The duchess was sitting by the fire with a steaming cup of tea by her side, reading a book. The regal quality that had always hung around her was present in the way she sat ramrod straight and delicately held her cup.

But for the first time, he saw other things. Signs he had missed as a child. She appeared tired. There was a sadness around her eyes that never quite faded. Now he knew why.

"Are you going to speak your purpose, Simon, or just stand there gaping at me?" she asked, not even bothering to spare him a glance.

He moved farther into the room with Lillian at his side. There was no use dancing around the topic, especially as his mother . . . no, the *duchess* . . . seemed peevish.

"You didn't come to tea earlier this afternoon,"

she snapped before he could speak. "I was forced to entertain Miss Mayhew's guests alone."

She shot Lillian a glare that spoke volumes about how beneath her that task had been, how beneath her *Lillian* was. Her superior attitude erased Simon's hesitation in an instant.

He arched a brow. "I was out for a visit, Your Grace."

"A visit to whom?" she snapped as she tossed her book on the side table and glared in his direction, though he noticed she didn't actually meet his eyes. "I wasn't informed. You might have had the courtesy to—"

"I made a trek out to that little cottage that stands in the middle of Flicket Orchard," he said, keeping his tone utterly cool.

His mother's head jerked higher as she staggered from the chair and stepped away from him. "What?"

"You heard me," he said, keeping his tone low and measured. "And I think you know very well what I saw there."

All the color left her cheeks, and her hands shook like fall leaves. He had never seen her like this before, so frail and frightened. So human.

"You saw him?" she asked, and her voice was almost nonexistent. She shot a glance over his shoulder at Lillian. "*She* saw him?"

He nodded wordlessly.

"What did you do?" his mother practically screeched as she came toward him in a few long steps. Her hands were raised like useless weapons and her eyes were wide and wild. "What did you do to my baby?"

Simon's mouth dropped open in shock at her reaction, and he stared at the woman he had called his mother for his entire life. For the first time, he felt her desperation, her fear, and the pain that seemed to throb in the room around them like a broken heartbeat. How could he not have noticed those things before?

Before he could answer, Lillian came forward. "Your Grace, you should know Simon better than that. All he and your son did was talk. He would never harm or confuse that boy. I don't think he could."

The duchess blinked as if Lillian's admonishment was sinking in. Slowly, the terror in her stare faded. After a few long moments she grasped for the chair she had evacuated when he told her he saw his brother and sank back into its cushions with a shuddering sigh.

"No, perhaps you wouldn't," she breathed.

Simon stared at her. She seemed so small, so weak now. As if the air and hatred had been let out of her, leaving only a shell of her former self. He almost pitied her.

"I deserve to know the truth," he said softly.

She looked up at him, her hands shaking as she fussed with the hem of her sleeve restlessly. "Yes, I suppose you do. And it seems it's too late to keep the truth from you at any rate."

Simon motioned for Lillian, and she took a place beside him on the settee across from his mother. The dowager stared at her, but she seemed too exhausted to have her usual disdain for his future bride.

"Is *she* going to stay for this?" she asked.

Simon squeezed Lillian's fingers as he nodded. "She is my future wife. She deserves to hear this as much as I do, I think. To know exactly what she is entering into."

If his mother had an argument, for once she kept it to herself. Instead, she let out a long sigh and murmured, "Very well."

"Tell me," he said softly. "Tell me everything from the beginning."

She nodded. "The family was beside the lake for a picnic. Your sister was eight and your brother had just turned two. He loved the water, and we used to spend many a day there in the sun while he played around the edge of the lake."

Simon couldn't help a small smile. He had always loved the water as well, despite being kept from it by his parents.

The dowager continued, but her voice had begun to tremble. "Your father and I had been arguing. I had just discovered he had another child, *you*, born a few months before Simon. Our latest exchange on the subject grew heated, so we went just up the hill so the children wouldn't hear our voices. And that was when *it* happened."

Simon tensed and Lillian squeezed his hand in reassurance. "He fell in."

The duchess nodded, but didn't continue for a few long moments as she struggled to compose herself.

"It took a moment for anyone to notice," she finally whispered. "When she saw him floating there, Naomi began screaming, which alerted us. She waded into the water, trying to pull him out. But she was so small and he was too heavy for her. By the time we got down to the edge of the lake, he wasn't breathing. Your father managed to revive him, but it was instantly recognizable that he was terribly injured."

Simon shook his head. "You brought in doctors?"

"The best in the countryside, one after another, for weeks. But they all said the same thing. My child had been . . ." Her breath caught on the edge of a sob. ". . . *damaged*, broken beyond repair. They told us he would likely never fully recover in mind, even if he survived in body."

Lillian let out a shiver beside him, but remained quiet, her gaze fully fixed on his mother. Simon knew what she was thinking of, for he couldn't put it out of his mind, either. He was thinking of his brother, a child trapped in a man's body, incapable of taking care of himself, incapable of fully living any kind of life outside of the small one he had been provided in the hidden cottage.

"Some of the doctors told us to have him put away, locked up in an asylum. They told us to have another child." His mother laughed but it was empty. "But I couldn't. My son's birth was a terrible one, I nearly died. We had tried for children again since him, but never successfully. It was clear we couldn't have another baby, so I wasn't able to provide your father with an heir."

"But why not just let the others in the family know?" Simon asked. "My uncle Charles would have made a fine duke, and my cousin Andrew is as good a man as any I've ever known."

His mother rolled her eyes. "I would have done, but your father insisted we keep what had happened a secret."

"But why?" Simon insisted.

She shook her head. "He was the duke and, by God, his son would be, too. It didn't matter to him that he was thwarting birthright or law, he wanted *his* blood to carry on his title, and he was willing to lie and cheat to ensure that would happen. We argued, but I was too weak and devastated to put up much of a fight. Afterward, your father disappeared for a few days and when he returned . . ."

She trailed off, and Lillian lifted her hand to cover her mouth. "He brought Simon . . . *this* Simon, back with him to replace your son."

His mother's eyes grew sharp as she glared at Lillian. "Yes." Her voice cracked and was filled with the bitterness of years of lies and heartbreak. "He brought this *boy* into my home, this child with my son's eyes and hair, and told me I would have to behave as if he were my Simon. That if we waited a few months no one would be the wiser, children changed so fast and the two boys looked somewhat alike."

"I'm so sorry, Your Grace," Lillian whispered.

Simon saw she wanted to reach for his mother, to comfort her, although the dowager had never been kind to Lillian. As if his mother sensed that, too, she turned away slightly.

"It was horrible," she hissed. "To have to pretend my husband's bastard son was my precious Simon." Her gaze shifted to him. "To see *you* whole and alive while my boy languished in a broken hell, not even allowed to live in the house with me where I could see him and hold him whenever I wished to do so."

Simon shook his head, overwhelmed by the cruelty of his father's actions. He could hardly imagine how horrific that time must have been for his mother.

"That was why you hated me so," he said without censure, without judgment.

"Yes," she said, her voice cold as steel, but her strength lasted only a moment.

As soon as the affirmation was from her lips, she sank her head into her hands and began to cry in a way he had never seen or heard before, great wailing sobs that echoed in the room for several hellish moments.

Finally, she pulled herself together and continued, "I did hate you. But I hated myself more. You see, there were moments when I . . . I loved you. And every time I felt like it was a betrayal. Like I was forgetting my son, allowing him to be replaced as my husband wished him to be. So I pulled away from you, putting as much distance between us as I could."

He nodded. In some way, this confession was a relief. He had spent so long wondering why she didn't care. Now that he knew, it helped somehow.

"But why didn't you just reveal his secret?" he asked. "You could have ended this years ago."

"Your father never struck me," his mother said softly. "However, he made it clear that there would be swift and terrible retribution if I ever revealed the truth. I feared the consequences, not just to myself, but to our children. Your father could have had our son committed, or even hurt him if I told anyone what we had done. He could have taken my daughter away and made sure I never saw her again. I'd lost so much already, I wasn't strong enough to risk more. So I remained silent. I allowed him do as he wished."

"What about when the duke was dead?" Lillian asked, her voice gentle. "You could have told the secret then with no reprisals."

"Could I?" his mother asked, her voice dripping with sarcasm. "You saw my child, Miss Mayhew. He is alive, yes, but completely incompetent. If I told the secret, if I revealed the truth now, so many years later, there would surely be an inquest to determine the facts of the situation. All the parties involved would go before panels and hearings, including my son. There would be tests for his fitness to serve as duke, as well. Do you think he could stand that?"

Simon shook his head as he thought of his brother, so simple. He had been kept in that cottage, isolated and utterly protected for his entire life. Simon couldn't imagine how he would react to the loud and busy streets of London, let alone being grilled by people whom he had never met before, ones who might not treat him with delicacy and kindness.

"He couldn't take it," he said softly. "Worse, there would be ridicule and laughter. Some would treat him like a circus sideshow."

The dowager nodded, tears streaming down her

face. "And for what? Your uncle Charles has been dead for a decade and your cousin Andrew long ago chose the life of a clergyman over the life of a peer. You know as well as I do that he would *hate* being dragged into the light, especially with so many whispers about the circumstances of his taking over."

Simon considered that. She was correct, of course. Every time he saw his cousin, Andrew made a joke thanking him for taking the worst job in the family. He would wither as duke, losing all his zest for life, not to mention the occupation he had come to adore.

Simon let out a sigh that came from his very soul and whispered, "As much as I hate to continue this farce, I think I must. For the good of everyone involved, most especially my brother."

The duchess rose up and paced away. Her shoulders slumped forward in relief and defeat combined.

"Good," she said quietly. "Good."

Simon hesitated. There was one issue resolved, but he still had questions. Did he dare hope she would tell him what he needed to know?

"What do you know about my life before I came here?" he asked.

She turned to look at him. "Nothing."

Simon flinched, and she seemed to understand his thoughts.

"I hope you'll believe me when I tell you that is the truth. I never even knew your real name, your father kept it to himself, insisting I only ever think of you as Simon. I don't know where you came from."

Simon nodded. He thought himself a fairly good judge of people and he felt that his mother . . . the woman he had thought of as his mother . . . wasn't lying. Not now, when so much had been revealed already.

He moved toward her slowly, easing out a hand in offering. "My name is Henry Ives, Your Grace."

She stared at him, stared at his outstretched fingers. Then she took his hand.

"Henry," she whispered, rolling it on her tongue as if she were trying to understand it. Then she shook her head. "It does not suit you, *Simon*."

He shut his eyes as she pulled her hand away gently. That was as much acceptance as he was likely to ever garner from this woman. And knowing all he did now, it was enough.

"And what of the others?" he asked, tilting his head to look at her.

She hesitated. "The other bastards?"

He nodded.

"Your father was a busy man," she all but whispered as she turned away. "Incapable of self-control, whether he was seducing the lowest of servants or the highest of ladies. He thought it a challenge, and I think he secretly loved spreading his seed all about England. I knew of his conquests, I sometimes even knew that they resulted in children, but I knew nothing else. We didn't exactly talk, if you recall."

Simon nodded. That much he *knew* to be true. His father and the duchess had never been close. As a child, he had judged her for her coldness and respected his father for his kindness.

How much things changed when one understood them. Now he saw his father's behavior as self-righteous posturing and her response as measured considering what she had been through.

"Thank you for telling me all you know, Your Grace," he said softly. "I understand how difficult it must have been for you."

She turned back and stared at him for a long moment.

"I suppose," she said, her voice brittle and low, "that you shall now expel me from this and any other property under your control. You will wish to punish me for my part in this deception. I'm not your mother, after all. You owe me nothing."

Simon stared at her in utter disbelief. It took him a few moments before he found his voice in response to her accusation.

"Madam, you think quite ill of me, I see. Reluctant or no, I would hope you realize you raised me far better than that."

Surprise lit her face. And enough hope to break his heart. She truly had expected no kindness from him at all. He supposed he could thank his father for that; the last duke had shown her little of it.

"This is your home, Your Grace," he said softly. "Your son lives on the grounds. Why in the world would I send you away from him? My brother needs you, that much is clear from speaking to him for less than a minute. He talked about you the entire time I spent with him. If you were gone permanently, he would be utterly lost."

His mother nodded, her shoulders shaking with emotion. "You won't force me away from him?"

He shook his head. "In fact, if you would like, I shall have a dowager house erected on the property closer to his cottage, so you won't be forced to travel so far when you wish to see him. In time, perhaps you could even move him there so the two of you could be together always. Or we could expand his current cottage and make it more fit for you to join him if that is your wish. I think you two have been kept apart for far too long as it is."

She said nothing for a full minute and then she utterly shocked him by crossing the room and awkwardly putting her arms around him. The embrace lasted only a few seconds, but in that time he felt more warmth, more motherly concern from her than he had in thirty years of the lie they had lived.

She pulled away and he let her go. This was all he could expect, he wouldn't demand more.

"Thank you," she said softly, and then she straightened up and her vulnerability was once again hidden. "Now if you will excuse me, it has been a very trying day. I think I shall take a tray here tonight and turn in early. I'll leave you and your future bride to take care of our guests for the evening."

Lillian understood the sendoff as much as he did, and she got to her feet and came to his side. She sent his mother a quick nod as they moved into the hallway, which the duchess did not acknowledge, only closed the door smartly behind them.

They stared at each other for a long time before Lillian gave him a half smile. "If your mother's final dismissal of me is any indication, it seems all has returned to normal."

Simon couldn't help but grin, despite the upheaval of the day. "Yes. She still despises my choice in wife. I suppose that means she accepts *me* in some strange way."

But as they walked up the hall together, Simon couldn't help but look behind him. And wonder what the future would hold now that *all* the secrets were finally out.

Chapter 22

Although Lillian hadn't told Gabby about what she now knew, and she had no intention of ever doing so, it was evident her friend recognized the strain as they shared supper together that night. There was simply an air of melancholy that hung over the table, and the absence of the duchess and her daughter, who had gone to sit with her mother for comfort, made it clear that *something* had occurred. Even Gabby's aunt seemed to feel it, for she picked at her food quietly.

Finally, Gabby broke the silence. "Do you still plan to be married in London when we return?"

Simon lifted his eyes from his plate, and Lillian could have kissed Gabby. It was the first time any attempt at conversation had roused him.

He nodded. "Yes. In fact, I received word from my solicitor an hour or so ago that the special license has come through. The moment we arrive in London, we shall be free to wed."

Lillian nodded absently and caught Gabby looking at her. She avoided her friend's stare, for she could see Gabby was wondering if she had yet told Simon the truth about why she had come here. The fact that she hadn't hung over her heavily, but with so much turmoil, she hadn't found the right time. After they were married, perhaps it would be clearer. Even though the thought of waiting made her stomach clench.

"I hope you'll be very happy," Gabby murmured as she smiled at Simon.

He returned her smile. "You shall stand up for us, I hope."

"Of course," Gabby said. "If that is Lillian's wish, I'd be proud to stand up and witness your wedding."

Lillian glared at her friend. "Who else in the world would I have at my side? Only you and perhaps Lucinda, except I doubt she would come, as she is still in mourning."

Simon frowned. "Lucinda?"

"Lucinda Stoneworth," Lillian explained. "Her husband died a year ago and she is still devastated."

Simon nodded. "Yes, I recall. His brother holds the title now and there was some outrage about it initially."

Lillian nodded.

For a moment the table was quiet and then

Simon cleared his throat. "But it does make one think, doesn't it?"

"About?" she asked.

"About the fleeting quality of life. An accident can change everything, a lie can alter a life, a secret uncovered can change the course of everything after. If we don't seize the moment, it might be gone."

Lillian stared at him, filled with empathy. It was clear to her that they were no longer talking about a friend's tragedy, but Simon's own. And no wonder he would think about it. After all, he was still digesting everything that had occurred. It would probably take years for him to determine his place in the world.

And she would be by his side to help, which was somewhat comforting to her in a strange way. If she couldn't destroy his father, at least she could help undo some of the damage the man had done.

"Lillian, why don't we leave for London tomorrow morning at first light?" Simon asked.

Lillian blinked. "Tomorrow? That is so soon."

"Why wait?" he asked, taking her hands as if no one else was in the room but her. "Haven't we seen what missing a moment can cause? With good roads, it is but a two-day journey. If luck was on our side, we could be married before Sunday luncheon. My mother may not choose to attend, but we'll have Gabby to stand for us and I'm sure Rhys and Anne would come even though they are marrying less than a week later. What do you think?"

Lillian blinked. He was so earnest, so eager to start anew. And she understood why. When he married her, it would be a step toward a future. A future where there were no lies.

Or at least none he knew.

"Yes, Simon," she said softly. "If you wish to leave tomorrow, I will happily go with you."

He laughed and jumped to his feet. "I shall make the arrangements straightaway."

He hurried from the room, and even before she looked at her, Lillian could feel Gabby's eyes on her. She gave her friend a look before she downed a gulp of wine.

"What is happening?" Aunt Isabel asked, her tone too loud for the small room.

"We're going home tomorrow," Gabby said loudly. "His Grace is making arrangements."

"Tomorrow?" Aunt Isabel shouted with a scowl. "I shall have to tell Maggie."

She threw her napkin down and stomped from the room to find the servant. Once they were alone, Gabby's attention focused back on Lillian.

"He loves you," her friend said.

Lillian choked on her wine as she stared at Gabby.

"Love?" she repeated when she was able to breathe properly.

Gabby nodded. "I don't know what happened between you these last few days, and I won't ask because I doubt I want to be involved in it, but something has changed."

Lillian frowned. There was no denying that. What they had seen, what they had said, what they had uncovered . . . it *had* bound them.

"Do you intend to tell him the truth?" her friend asked softly.

Lillian let her arms come up on the table and flopped her head down to rest on them.

"Yes," she murmured, her voice muffled. "I must, I know. But I fear his response, Gabby. In truth, I fear losing him forever."

By mutual agreement, the entire household went to bed early that night in preparation for their journey back to London the next day, but Lillian didn't go to her chamber. Instead, Simon took her arm and led her to his room and she made no move to resist. After that day, after everything that had happened, she wanted to be alone with him just as much as he did.

Still, when the door closed behind them, a sense of shyness filled her. After all, the other times they had been together, there had been a sense of urgency, of passion taking over. Tonight, standing in the middle of his bedchamber with him watching her, she wasn't sure how to start.

"What can I do for you, Simon?" she finally asked as she clasped her hands in front of her awkwardly. "Is there anything you need?"

He smiled slightly and moved forward. Her heart leapt as he did so, her body tightly wound in anticipation of his touch.

"Need," he murmured as he stopped a few inches before her, though he made no move to touch her yet. "*Need.* There are a great many things I need at this moment and after this day, but I think one stands above all others."

She tilted her head. "And that is?"

His fingers came up to gently trace the curve of her jaw and his smile softened. "You, Lillian. You to wash away the ugliness. To make me forget everything but your taste. I need *you.*"

She caught her breath, overtaken by the depth of meaning in his words. Wanting her was one thing, a man could *want* any woman if his animal desires were strong enough.

Need was something else entirely. Need implied a deeper connection, a dependence born of feeling. And she was honored to be the one he turned to in his trial.

And uncertain. But she was determined to give comfort the best she could, so she reached out and slowly unbuttoned his heavy jacket. He made no move to assist, just watched through hooded lids as she slipped her fingers beneath the woolen fabric and glided them along his warm shoulders to slide the jacket away.

It hit the floor behind him in a pile and she immediately went to work on his cravat. It was tied in a complicated knot, but she managed it somehow after a bit of work, then set about opening his shirt button by button. She tugged to get it free from his waistband and parted the fabric, letting it hang loosely as she stared at the expanse of chest she had exposed.

"You are . . ." she whispered.

He arched a brow as she trailed off. "I am . . . ?" he teased.

She glanced up at him with a smile of her own. There was a lighter quality to him, as if he truly was able to forget his troubles in these moments. And if that was the gift she could give him, then she was happy for that.

"You are incorrigible." She laughed. Then she leaned in and pressed a hot, wet kiss to the slope of his collarbone. As he sucked in a breath of pleasure, she added, "And magnificent."

He let her kiss his chest, moving her lips across planes of muscle. She tasted his skin, teased at his nipples, let her fingernails rake across his muscled abdomen.

She felt it affect him. His body tensed as she touched him, his hands formed fists at his sides as he fought not to grab for her and take over. And when she stood up and leaned into him, she felt the hard, thick length of his erection pressing her thigh with insistent pressure.

Her body reacted to that weight, to the scent and taste of his skin, to the warmth of his body as she touched him. She felt hot, her skin too tight, her nipples hard and her sheath tingling and clenching against emptiness as it readied for the joining of their bodies.

She pushed his shirt away, rubbing her chest against his bare one as her touch became bolder, more certain.

"Now let me," he whispered, lowering his lips to an exquisitely sensitive spot behind her ear.

As he nuzzled and kissed the side of her neck, his hands found the buttons along the back of her gown. With swift efficiency, the dress fell forward and he helped her ease it around her hips to a pile on the floor.

He stepped back and stared at her. Her chemise was summer weight, so it was thin and short, revealing her stocking-clad legs up to mid-thigh.

"And you said I was magnificent," he mused as he put his hands on her sides.

He slid them up and down, pulling her closer, closer until their bodies were pressed together. Lillian almost couldn't breathe as he leaned in to kiss her. She met his lips eagerly, parting her own to allow him in, reveling in his taste and the heat of his tongue as he invaded her mouth.

That overwhelming passion she had experienced before returned instantly as the kiss deepened. She felt herself slipping under the spell of it, surrendering to it, overpowered by the feelings and by his physical presence.

But just as that thought filled her mind, he pulled back. In the bright light of the chamber, he stared at her, his lips swollen from the kiss, his eyes glittering with sensual intent and sexual desire.

"I'm afraid once I start with you, I lose all sense of control," he said, his voice rough as gravel. "But tonight I want restraint. I want to take my time."

She shivered. Holding out a trembling hand, she slipped her fingers into the waistband of his trousers and tugged. He stumbled forward, his eyes widening with surprise at her aggressive tactic.

"Unless you are trying to steal control from me, Miss Mayhew," he whispered, his hot breath stirring her hair as she stared up at him.

She smiled. "I rather like the sound of that. Do you think I could steal control from you?"

His pupils dilated and the jade green of his stare darkened. "Mmm, I'd like to see you try."

Instead of responding, Lillian unfastened the top button of his waistband. She kept her stare firmly locked with his as she repeated the action on the others. Finally the pant waist parted. She looked down, staring at the thin line of hair that snaked down and met with the base of his hard erection. Mesmerized, she took him in hand and freed the thrust of muscle from his trousers. It sprang up at attention, warm and hard in her fingers.

"It seems you can steal control," Simon said, his eyes squeezing shut as she stroked down over him once, then twice. "Great God, woman."

She smiled, though she was taken aback by her own actions. The fear and uncertainty she had felt when they first entered the room was gone now, replaced by a wanton confidence inspired by how strongly he reacted to her touch.

She wanted more. She wanted to give *him* more. Her thoughts drifted to the first time they made love. Before he had taken her, he'd readied her with his fingers and then the hot wetness of his mouth. It had been a shocking pleasure when he tasted her so intimately.

Would he like such a thing, as well?

She felt wicked as she slithered down the length of his body, kissing his bare chest and stomach on the way. When she dropped to her knees, Simon stiffened.

"Lillian?" he asked, his voice low and harsh. "What are you doing?"

She looked up at him as she took him in hand again. "Stealing control."

Before he could respond, she wrapped her lips around his length and slowly eased him into her mouth.

Simon bit back a cry as Lillian took more and more of him between her lips. He knew he should stop her, that she was still too innocent for such an illicit act, but somehow he couldn't. Events of the day had brought him so much pain, but this intense pleasure took it all away and made his world revolve around Lillian's mouth and slowly working tongue rather than anything else.

He let his head tip back, releasing a harsh groan as she swirled her tongue around and around his length. God it was good. *She* was so good. A natural at finding the most intensive parts of his pleasure. And she was his now. Forever. He could teach her more, and learn more from her. They could make love like this every day.

He couldn't wait.

Lillian increased the pace of her mouth around him, and Simon tensed as waves of pleasure began to blur his vision and make his seed move. As much as he wanted powerful, pleasurable release, more than that he wanted to be with Lillian. Buried deep within her, feeling her pulse around him.

He pulled back, and she looked up at him with disappointment in her gaze.

"Was I wrong?" she asked.

He caught her arms and brought her to a standing position. Before he kissed her, he said, "God, no. Perfectly right. But any more of that and I won't be able to do *this*."

He swung his arms beneath her bare legs and lifted her. Pressing his mouth to hers, he carried her to his bed and laid her out across the soft coverlet. She settled back, looking up at him with utter trust and desire.

He shuddered with the power of that expression. He had never been with a woman who moved him so completely.

Pushing her legs apart, he moved up her body to cover her. He settled down against her, letting his pulsing cock rest against her entrance without breaching her body.

"We won't be able to do this again until we are in London," he murmured, nuzzling her lips with his. "The next time we do, you'll be my wife."

She shivered deliciously beneath him and he was completely unmanned. He moved forward and slid into her willing body easily. She responded by arching up and he found himself fully seated within her sheath.

"You see, you are *utterly* capable of stealing my control with just the slightest effort." He chuckled, feeling lighter than he had in weeks as he stared down at her. "In fact, I surrender it willingly to you. Just as I surrender everything else."

Her expression softened as the meaning of his words sank in. Then she reached up and curled her fingers around the back of his head. Gently she urged his lips to hers and he began to move within her.

Unlike the other times he'd had the pleasure of her body, tonight he did not allow himself to be utterly swept away. Passion was there, of course, but it was a quieter, gentler passion. He reveled in every slide of his body in hers. He cherished every moan and sigh she made as their bodies tangled in languid fluidity.

Slow and steady, he worked her toward completion. And she let him lead her there, lifting to match his pace, straining as her pleasure mounted. He watched her every reaction, relishing the ever-mounting urgency of her movements.

And finally she tensed beneath him and her tight sheath gripped him as she orgasmed. Her moans filled the air around them, her fingers gripped at his shoulders, her hips slammed up. It was all too much. He let himself go, increasing his thrusts, shutting his eyes as he allowed his own pleasure to wash over him.

And then he erupted, jerking out a few last thrusts as he filled her with his essence.

He collapsed down on her, holding his weight so as not to crush her. Her arms came around his back and she held him, whispering soft endearments in his ear as she smoothed his bare skin.

"I never thought I would have this," she whispered after their breathing had returned to normal.

Simon rolled to his side and gathered her against his chest. He looked down at her, her dark blond locks sweaty and tousled, her ever-changing eyes the same amber color as the firelight.

"I cannot imagine why," he said, smoothing hair away from her face.

She shrugged. "With my past, I'd all but given up on it. The best I could have hoped for was a marriage of convenience with someone who needed a nursemaid for his children."

"Those other men were fools," he said. "*I* was a fool for ever hesitating over a past you had no control over. It seems so silly now, especially considering what we have uncovered about my own life and the lies that brought me here."

She was silent, and her gaze darted from his momentarily. He sighed as he settled back against the pillows and looked up at the ceiling with unseeing eyes.

"Actually, I think I shall applaud the fools who had a chance to win you and let it slip away. If any of them had been able to see past your mother's actions, they might have married you and you never would have come to me. Perhaps it was fate that kept them from you. The same fate that brought you here to me when I needed you."

Lillian sat up, dragging the sheets up to cover herself. "Simon—"

"No." He sat up, too, and leaned in closer. "Let me say this, Lillian."

She opened her mouth as if to refuse, but then nodded, tears glistening in her eyes.

"When this house party began, I never thought I'd discover what I have about myself," he said, trying not to dwell too much on the facts that still burned within him. "That my life is a lie perpetrated by the one man I respected and loved above all others."

A tear rolled down Lillian's cheek, and he caught it and swiped it away before he continued.

"And yet my heart isn't heavy. After all, my future was found here, as well as the truth of my past. *You* are here, and you've been as supportive and caring toward me during this trial as anyone could ask for in a wife. You've never judged or flinched away from the truth that I am a bastard masquerading as a gentleman. In fact, without you, I don't know if I could have faced my brother, my mother, even myself."

"I'm glad I could help," she whispered.

He shook his head. "You did far more than that, Lillian. You saved me in some way. And I—"

He broke off and stared at the woman beside

him. In that moment he realized the sentiment he wanted to express. And it felt right and true and perfect.

"Lillian, you are the only truth I trust anymore. I am in love with you."

Chapter 23

Lillian stared at Simon in utter shock. Then the joy hit her. He loved her. And God knew, she had come to love him, despite her attempts to keep him at arm's length.

And yet the first thing he'd said rang in her ears even louder than his astonishing admission of his heart.

You are the only truth I trust anymore.

Except she wasn't truth. She was a lie, just as everything else in his life was a lie. And he deserved more. Deserved better. At the very least, he deserved to choose.

She had to tell him the truth of why she came here. And she had to do it now.

"Please say something to me," he said with a little chuckle that was more than a bit nervous. "It isn't every day I lay my heart out so."

Lillian touched his cheek. "Simon, what you said, it means more to me than anything in the world. You'll never fully understand how much it means. But I must tell you something."

He tilted his head, clearly confused. "Tell me something? What is it?"

She drew in a deep breath and forced herself to leave his bed. It was wrong to say this while lounging beside him. She searched for her gown and managed to get herself back into it with a little effort.

"You are dressing, so I shall assume what you need to tell me isn't something I shall enjoy hearing," Simon said, his frown deepening.

She shook her head. "I doubt you will, but as we have learned these last few days, sometimes the truth hurts, but it is always better."

He followed her from the bed and grabbed for his discarded trousers. As he pulled them on, he said, "Let us have it then."

Lillian drew a long breath to gird herself for what she was about to do.

"I wish I could say that my coming here was fate bringing us together, as you so sweetly stated," she began, her voice trembling. She forced it to stop. "But it wasn't. I came here with a purpose."

He was silent, his face utterly unreadable.

"A purpose," he finally repeated in a flat tone.

She nodded. The words were so hard to find now, but she forced herself to continue.

"You see, before I arrived, I-I already knew your

father to be a liar and a libertine, despite his exalted reputation."

Simon stared at her, the shock and the beginnings of betrayal in his expression. He drew a few long breaths.

"And how did you know that?" he asked, his voice abrupt as his nostrils flared slightly.

She shut her eyes. "Do you remember when I told you about my mother? That she was prone to fits of sadness, but that it was another person who helped push her over the edge to her death?"

He nodded. "Yes. You didn't elaborate and I did not wish to pry. Not until you *trusted* me more."

She didn't miss his emphasis on the word *trust* and bit back a little sob. "Well, the person who pushed her was . . . it was your father."

He turned away sharply and moved to the window. "What did he do?" he finally asked after what seemed like an eternity of silence.

"As my father lay dying just over six months ago, he confessed to my brother that the Duke of Billingham, your father, he—he tried to seduce our mother. When she refused his advances, he . . ." She made herself say it. "He forced himself on her. In her guilt and shame over the rape, she killed herself."

Simon made a strangled sound as he turned toward her. "Raped her?"

She nodded. "In his last breath, my father begged

my brother to claim his revenge. At that time, your father still lived. I waited for my brother, Jack, to do as he had asked, but he was too like our father. Instead of coming here and confronting the man who pushed our mother to her death, Jack went mad with alcohol, determined to wreck himself rather than feel the pain."

"That was what your father had done when he found out the truth about your mother," Simon said. "He was too weakened by drink to confront my father himself."

She nodded. "When I saw that Jack wouldn't fulfill my father's wish, it was left to me to plot revenge, and I admit that the idea and the thoughts of what had happened to my mother consumed me."

Her eyes squeezed shut and she fought back tears. She would not cry. Not now.

"When Gabby was invited to your country party, we conspired for me to join her as a guest."

"What was your hope in coming?" he asked, shaking his head. "What did you think to gain? The duke is dead, he's been in the ground for months."

She flinched. "When your father died, all the world began talking about him like he was a saint, even as they murmured ugly things about my mother. It enraged me even further. So I came here, determined to find proof of what he was. I hoped to be able to search this home for some kind of detail I could release into the world. I wanted people to hate him, to whisper about him as they did my mother. I wanted to ruin him."

He stared at her for so long that she almost wondered if he had heard her. But then he advanced on her in long steps. "You came here looking for his secrets?"

"Yes, Simon," she whispered, hating the betrayal that now sparkled in his eyes. She had known it would happen, but seeing it cut through her like a knife.

He shook his head. "Well, my dear. It seems you found everything you were looking for and more."

Simon paced away from Lillian, shaking with the force of his horror. Horror that his father had committed such a terrible act against her mother. Horror that Lillian had pretended to care for him while all the time she had been plotting against him and his family.

And now she knew all their secrets. If she chose to, she could destroy him, destroy his brother, destroy everything he held dear.

"Simon—" she said from behind him, and he heard the tears in her voice even before he looked at her. She hadn't moved toward him, but her hands were held up in pure entreaty. "I want to explain."

"You *have* explained," he barked. "What more is there to say? It seems nothing between us was real, only a manipulation to help you uncover what you came here to find."

"It started out that way, yes," she admitted, and now she did move on him. "But almost immediately I began to question my quest. When I met you, when I saw what kind of man you were, I began to doubt that I could destroy you. What developed between us was real, as much as I tried to keep it from happening so I wouldn't have to feel that guilt deep within me."

He snorted at that statement, but she reached for him and caught his arm before he could reel away.

"It didn't work. Eventually I couldn't deny my feelings for you. And when I saw how much you had suffered for your father's actions, when I saw that your pain was just as deep as my own, I knew I could never harm you. Even if that meant letting go of the past."

He yanked his arm free. "And when did you have this revelation? Today? Tonight? This moment? Is that what prompted your confession?"

She shook her head. "No, it was before."

"When?" he asked, praying she would say that

it was long before everything they had shared. He didn't want those things spoiled by this.

"The morning you told me about your father's bastard children," she admitted, her cheeks brightening with splotches of color. "Before we were interrupted and you said that we were to be married."

He shut his eyes, the sense of betrayal almost overwhelming. Finally he looked at her evenly.

"That means while you made love to me, while you heard me pour my heart out, you still intended to use what I said against me, against my dead father, the consequences to anyone and everyone else be damned."

Her eyes squeezed shut and Simon couldn't deny the pain that was reflected on her face. Whatever she had intended when this began, it truly hurt her now.

That was cold comfort.

"I know it sounds terrible," she said. "It *was* terrible to consider taking that kind of revenge against innocent people, but you must understand how blinded by grief and anger I was when I set out on this course. I never knew what made my mother take her life. It was a stab in my heart to hear that a man had hurt her and driven her to the brink when she did not deserve such a nightmare."

Simon winced. He couldn't imagine how horrible a revelation that must have been for her. He was certain it was as painful and complicated as everything he had heard about himself in the past few days.

She shook her head. "I felt compelled to do the thing the men in my family could not or would not. I had to avenge my mother before your father was forgotten and what I revealed no longer mattered to Society."

"So because of your situation, you were allowed to manipulate and deceive me simply because my father was not available to you?" he asked, the ice in his tone not something he had to force.

She shook her head. "No, what I planned was terrible. I know that. But I cannot stand having you think that my feelings were part of some plot. I don't expect you to believe me, but the love I feel for you is real."

Simon scrubbed a hand over his face. Somehow her admission that she loved him hurt more than helped now.

"Half an hour ago, I would have rejoiced to hear you say those words. But now . . . well, I don't know what to believe anymore. Is this part of some master plan or the truth?"

Her chin dropped and her shoulders rolled forward in slumped defeat. "I understand your doubts."

He shrugged, though he didn't feel the disconnect expressed by the action. In truth, this final act of duplicity of the day, this realization that the woman he had come to trust and love had betrayed him . . . that was somehow the worst thing he had endured.

He reached for his crumpled shirt on the floor and tugged it over his head. As he did so, he said, "I'll still marry you, Lillian."

Her head jerked up. "What?"

He sighed. "I'm a better man than my father, I must be. You were compromised and you could have my child growing within you." He ignored the swell of joy that thought brought and continued, "But I am uncertain if I'll ever be able to trust you again."

She nodded slowly. "Yes. I understand."

"Now if you'll excuse me, I have things to tend to before we go to London tomorrow. I shall see you in the morning at our arranged departure time."

She made no move to stop him when he left the chamber. As he closed the door behind him, he leaned back against its surface and expelled his breath in a long sigh. He might have been able to maintain some kind of distance, some kind of control as he spoke to her, but now that they were apart, he had never felt so empty and alone in his life.

*   *   *

Lillian stared out the window as the first rays of sunshine broke in the east. Dawn was here and she was fully dressed. She had been fully dressed for three hours. In fact, she hadn't slept after her encounter with Simon. She had simply paced the floor, running their discussion over and over in her head.

Part of her had wanted to run to Gabby, to sob out her sadness and broken heart into her friend's shoulder. But in the end, she hadn't. She didn't deserve anyone's comfort, and Simon didn't deserve yet another act of treason against him. No, she had made this particular bed and she had to lie in it.

Alone.

That revelation had come an hour before and now she was ready for it.

She exited the chamber where she had hidden after Simon left her and took a deep breath as she looked around. Somehow she doubted he'd returned to his bedroom for it was clear he didn't want to see her.

Moving through the halls, she made her way down the stairs. The noises of servants who were awake to see the party off buzzed faintly in the distance. Lillian hesitated and covered her eyes briefly at the foot of the stairs. She had to be strong. She couldn't weep or be weak. Simon would only

see that as a manipulation and she was finished
with those.

When she was ready, she moved forward again,
walking on instinct to the place where she thought
Simon might have gone last night. When she
reached his father's office, she opened the door and
stepped inside.

He was standing at the window, his back to her.
His shoulders were ramrod straight and stiff.

"I wondered when you would come," he said
softly, without turning toward her.

"You know me well," she answered as she closed
the door behind her.

Now he did turn, and his sunken eyes were as
dark a green as she had ever seen. "Do I?"

His retort stung, but she did her best to keep her
reaction from her face. She deserved his coldness,
even though she missed his regard terribly.

"I've come to speak to you about our arrangement," she said, hoping her countenance was as
unemotional as his, though she doubted she managed that.

"Our *arrangement*?" he repeated, folding his
arms. "Are you referring to our engagement?"

She nodded. "I wanted to tell you that as much
as I appreciate your offer to marry me regardless
of what I have done, I cannot allow it. We shall not
wed."

He staggered forward a step before he could stop himself and stared at her. Her statement had clearly shaken him, for his every emotion and exhaustion were suddenly reflected on his face.

"I beg your pardon?" he asked, fighting to stay distant.

She tilted her head. "I cannot marry you."

"Don't be foolish, woman. You were publicly ruined and we announced our engagement. By now the entire *ton* knows that. If you return to London but do not marry, you'll never be accepted by Society again. Given your family history, you'll likely be shunned entirely."

She wet her lips nervously as he laid out the consequences she had already spent a night considering.

"I realize that is very likely the case, Your Grace," she managed past trembling lips. "But it does not signify."

"Does not signify?" he cried with a bark of laughter. "How do you make that out?"

"What I saw yesterday, Simon . . ." She shivered. "It changes everything."

She moved forward and almost reached out to touch his arm before she stopped herself. He wouldn't want her comfort now and she certainly didn't deserve his.

"You are living someone else's life and keeping someone else's secrets because you are honorable.

You've had so much thrust upon you and I won't be another thing, another disappointment you are forced to bear."

He stared at her, unspeaking.

She squeezed her eyes shut to fight the tears that were threatening to fall. "I think you deserve more in a wife than another person you cannot trust. I love you too much to sentence you to that."

"There could be a child," he snapped, and she winced.

Of course he would turn to that reason before he admitted he wanted her in his life. And after all he now knew, she couldn't blame him for that, but it still stung.

"Twice we have been reckless," she said. "But last night, I did some calculations. I believe it very unlikely that we could have conceived a child."

She ignored the pain that statement gave her.

"But I would, of course, inform you if I began to exhibit signs to the contrary. It would change everything, I know."

Simon shook his head. "Then what of *you*? You'll never have another offer, Lillian. You will likely be put out in the street after Lady Gabriela's father gets wind that you have set aside our engagement."

"Yes." She swallowed hard. "But I would rather ruin myself than you and your family. I would rather live a life alone than one where you forever doubted, suspected, and resented me for my follies of the past. It isn't fair to you."

Now she reached for him, letting her palm rest on his rough cheek for the briefest of moments. She felt the muscle there twitch.

"It isn't fair to me," she finished quietly as she pulled her hand away.

He caught her wrist. "I won't allow it."

"There isn't any choice," she said as she extracted her hand from his. "Good-bye, my love."

He stared after her as she slipped from the room. In the foyer, she found Gabby and her aunt already waiting for her. She said nothing as she followed them to the carriage. If they believed that Simon was to follow directly on his horse, as had been planned the night before, who was she to disabuse them of that notion? They would discover the truth soon enough.

She sank into the carriage seat and turned to look back at the house. There, framed in the window of a front parlor, was Simon. Watching her leave.

And she silently cried as she realized that was likely the last time she would ever see him.

Chapter 24

Simon stared out the parlor window, looking at the spot where he had last seen Lillian three long days before. She was back in London now, the man he'd hired to watch her had reported her arrival. If there was a hint she was with child, Simon would know.

But if she was correct and that baby never came to be, then he supposed he would never see her again.

"Do stop looking out the window like an abandoned dog," the duchess said with a heavy, put-upon sigh. "It is unbecoming of a man of your station."

Simon shut his eyes and swallowed back a harsh retort before he began to pace around the room restlessly. Since their emotional encounter a few days before, Her Grace had returned to her usual disdain for him, as if she had never confessed she sometimes loved him and cried to him about the past. He wasn't sure whether to be happy or furious.

"Simon, darling," Naomi said, watching him. "Please sit with us. And have some of these scones. You have hardly eaten since Lillian departed."

He glanced at his sister and the duchess. They were both staring at him with expressions of either concern or barely masked contempt. He frowned and seated himself. He supposed they each deserved their feelings. He'd been forced to tell them about Lillian's deception, they both had a right to know that they might be threatened by what she knew.

After all, despite her declarations of love, he wasn't entirely certain that she wouldn't reveal everything to the world. His doubt hurt as much as anything else.

"I'm worried about you," Naomi said softly, reaching out to cover his hand before she poured him a fresh cup of tea.

He frowned. "I know. And I appreciate your concern, but it's wasted. There is nothing that can be done about it now."

Not that he hadn't tried to think of something. But the fact was that his world had been turned upside down and the only person he had been able to count on was Lillian Mayhew.

And even that had been a lie.

But that didn't seem to stop him from aching for

her. He had paced the floors every night since her departure, missing her and longing for the life he'd begun to anticipate sharing with her.

"Do stop mooning!" the duchess snapped as she let her teacup come down on its saucer with a clatter. "This is all for the best. That girl was a liar, you are better rid of her. And even if she wasn't, she would have had all the benefit from a match between you. All she would have brought you was financial drain and whispers."

"Mama!" Naomi exclaimed, covering her mother's hand as she stared at Simon warily. It was clear his sister understood the situation was far more complicated.

And that Simon was just on the edge of going mad from the pressure.

"You are correct, madam," he said softly, locking eyes with the woman who had raised him. "Lillian would have gained a great deal from our marriage. She would have had an exalted title, a vast amount of money, and a home for her and for her brother, should he choose to take it."

His mother nodded enthusiastically. "Not to mention that it would have hushed some of the whispers, at least for a while, about her *pathetic* mother's suicide."

"Please, Mama," Naomi said softly. "Now that we know *why* Miss Mayhew's mother took her life, we cannot judge her."

"Can we not?" Her mother spun on her. "Do you not think your father hurt *me*? Or countless others around him? None of us resorted to such dire measures. No, some of us continued in the responsibilities that had been thrust upon us, whether we liked it or not."

Simon stared at her. She was talking about him, of course, the burden of raising him as her own and keeping the late duke's secrets. Her bitterness saddened and angered him in equal measure.

"Somehow you forget, in this tirade about Lillian and her family, that *she* threw away all the benefits you accuse her of trying to steal from me." He shook his head. "I told her I would marry her still in order to protect her reputation. She chose to endanger herself rather than force my hand."

"That is true," Naomi said softly as she looked at him.

The duchess snorted out derision. "She only abandoned her claim because you discovered the truth that the little charlatan was out to destroy us."

Simon spun on her, fists at his sides and heart throbbing with powerful anger. "Let us be clear on this, madam, Lillian *told* me what she had done . . . or once intended to do. I never would have known it but for her confession."

He blinked as his own words sank in. He turned away from his sister and her mother and walked to the window, where he looked down once again at the place where he had last seen Lillian. She had been climbing into a carriage, leaving him and everything he'd offered her as some kind of atonement for intentions she had never actually fulfilled with actions.

"If she truly wished to use or harm me, if her desire for vengeance had really been so strong," he mused, now more to himself than the others in the room, "she could have remained silent. She could have married me and claimed all she could take of my money and influence. As my wife, she would have had unfettered access to all of Father's estates, where she no doubt could have found evidence to her heart's content about him, for I'm sure there are more secrets yet to be uncovered."

Naomi made a soft sound of sorrow, but he didn't turn.

"And then, when the moment was right, she could have struck like a cobra. With the increased position of duchess behind her, she could have destroyed us all with everything she knew, when she had every protection to keep her from being ruined by our fate." He blinked. "But she didn't."

His mother pushed to her feet and strode across the room to him. He turned to face her and found her cheeks red and eyes bright with anger and upset.

"So you wish to laud her as a saint for this?" she asked. "Don't be a fool. That girl is no good and you are well to be rid of her. I lived with the king of the liars for nearly forty years of my life. Trust that I know one when I see one."

Simon stared at her. In some ways, her spiteful words were true. And yet they didn't ring that way in his ears. When he thought of Lillian, he didn't think of her lies, but her gentle support. He thought of how she'd told him she loved him too much to be another burden for him to bear against his will.

He thought of how much he loved her in return.

"Excuse me," he said softly before he turned away and exited the room.

He heard the duchess's voice echoing behind him as he moved down the hallway. "Don't be an idiot!"

He moved to another parlor, but before he could close himself in and think about everything he had said to defend Lillian, Naomi was at his heels.

"Wait, Simon," his sister said. "Please stop."

He faced her with reluctance. "What is it? Or did you come to warn me against continuing to care for Lillian, as well?"

"You know me better than that," Naomi said with a sad shake of her head. "I understand the situation is far more complex than Mother makes it out to be. She is embittered by years of lies and neglect and probably other things you and I will never know or comprehend."

He turned away. "I simply wish I knew if her caustic words of warning were actually accurate."

His sister stepped in front of him, so he was forced to look at her as she took his hands in hers. "What does your heart say, Simon? In the end, that is all that matters."

He pondered that question for a moment. He'd been trying to silence his heart since Lillian confessed her objectives in coming here. He hadn't wanted to hear it, it hurt too much.

Now it roared out loud and strong. It beat with an undeniable truth and desire that he could no longer squelch. And in some way, he no longer wanted to hush it.

"My heart tells me that I might very well be throwing away my one chance at happiness," he said softly. "Lillian may not have had the best of intentions when she came here, but that doesn't change her actions once she arrived. She intrigued and delighted me. And she saw all the ugliness of the past few weeks and never once turned away from it."

"And she had every reason to do so, considering what our father did to her mother," Naomi said with a delicate shiver that spoke volumes. "In her position, I can't say that I wouldn't have done the same."

He nodded. He had thought that, too, over the past few days. "I tried to forget I love her. I tried to stop it. But I can't."

Naomi smiled slightly. "Then hear it. Listen to your heart, Simon. I've found mine rarely steers me wrong in life."

He looked down at her with a smile. "I suppose I would rather regret what I have done that what I didn't do."

Her own smile fell. "Yes. I know that from experience, as well."

Now it was he who caught her hands. "Naomi, what happened to our brother . . . that wasn't your fault. I see that you blame yourself, but you were just a child."

Her eyes welled with tears and he saw, in that moment, how much she held herself responsible for what had occurred. How much she needed forgiveness from someone . . . *anyone.*

"I tried to help him," she whispered, and her voice cracked and broke his heart. "But he was so heavy."

Simon blinked back the sting of tears as he touched her face. "Have you ever visited him?"

She shook her head. "Mama forbade it at first. I think they hoped I was young enough that I would simply forget what had happened. Of course I never did, but later I was too afraid to face him."

"You should go. He *is* happy, Naomi, in his own

way. Seeing that might give you peace. Plus he
would like to have another friend, I think."

She wiped her tears and was silent in contem-
plation for a long while. Finally she sighed, "I shall
make a bargain with you. I'll go see him as you
ask, but only if you go to Lillian."

He shook her hand solemnly. "That is a bargain.
I'll leave for London as soon as the two of us have
seen our brother."

"You'll go with me?" she asked, eyes widening.

"Of course," he said. "Whatever and whoever
I was when I was born, *this* is my life now. And I
wouldn't be a very good brother or duke if I let you
face this alone."

But as his sister hugged him, Simon was thinking of Lillian. And how in just a few days he would
be by her side again. That was when he would be
truly tested.

Lillian carefully folded another piece of clothing and set it in her trunk. Behind her, she heard
Gabby sobbing, but she couldn't bear to look at her
friend, for fear she would cry as well.

"It's so unfair. How can Papa put you out?"

Lillian sighed. It had been a week since they left
Simon's estate and three days since their arrival
in London. In that time, Gabby's father, the Earl
of Watsenvale, had realized that Lillian had been
ruined, but had no intention of marrying.

"Your father is merely trying to protect you, Gabby. My actions will reflect upon you and your family if I stay here."

"But—"

With a shake of her head, Lillian cut her friend off. "I knew this was the likely outcome when I began all this. The situation is no more than what I have created for myself, I cannot complain about it now. Aside from which, your father is not putting me out, the earl has arranged for me to take a governess position."

"In *Scotland*," Gabby wailed.

A shiver rocked Lillian. She was trying not to think about that fact. "Well, I've heard parts of Scotland are quite pretty."

Gabby folded her arms. "Not this part. It is cold and dreary and isolated from everyone."

Lillian resumed fussing with her clothing, if only to have something to do with her hands. "Well, then I shall have plenty of peace and quiet."

At that Gabby grasped her shoulder and forced her to turn. "There are eight children in that household, Lillian. *Eight*. And I have heard some of the servants talking. They say they are hellions. Beasts who have driven two women to the brink of madness."

"You aren't helping, Gabby," Lillian said, pulling from her friend's grip. "There is nothing to be done about it, so I might as well accept it with as much cheer as I can."

Her friend hesitated, and then she wrapped her arms around Lillian and hugged her tightly. "I'm sorry. I'm just so sad that I'll probably never see you again. How can I bear it?"

Lillian hugged her back. "I know."

She was trying not to think of all she would leave behind when she departed England. The loss of Gabby's support and friendship was difficult, yes. But there was also her brother, whom she had not been able to contact yet and inform of her departure.

But more than all of that . . . there was Simon. If she had stayed in London, there had always been the faintest of possibilities that she might pass him on a street or see him in a shop. As painful as that moment would likely have been, at least she would have had a glimpse of him.

But now that was gone.

But as she had said to Gabby, she had created this situation. Every consequence that went with it was hers, as well.

The girls parted, and Lillian wiped at Gabby's tears.

"Please promise you'll forgive your father," she said softly. "He was really very reasonable. He could have easily put me out on the street with no second thought. At least this way I shall have a roof over my head and a little money to support myself. I couldn't have asked for more and I thanked him for his kindness. So should you."

Gabby's mouth twisted, but finally she nodded. "You must write me. Promise you won't forget."

"Forget!" Lillian laughed. "You shall be my only entertainment in that savage place. I'll likely write you twice daily and you shall grow sick of hearing of moors and screaming babies."

Gabby laughed but it was a broken sound. "The carriage will be here at any moment, and I cannot bear to watch it take you away, so I'm going out with Aunt Isabel."

Lillian nodded. "That is best."

"Good-bye," Gabby choked, and then she ran from the room without a backward glance.

Lillian sighed out a shuddering breath, but somehow she managed to keep her tears inside. She had cried so much these past few days, she didn't want more tears. No, she had to be strong now.

Snapping her trunk shut, she looked around the small chamber she had been living in for months. It had never really been home. In fact, the only place she'd felt at home since her father's death was with Simon. Not at his house, but in his arms.

"Stop," she said, gathering up her gloves and marching toward the chamber door with renewed purpose.

Before she reached it, it opened, and one of the Earl of Watsenvale's maids stood in the entryway.

"The carriage is ready?" Lillian asked with a sinking heart. The arrival of the coach was the final toll of the bell of the life she had known and the one she had briefly planned.

"Almost, miss," the girl replied with a little bobbing curtsy. "And you have a visitor in the front parlor."

"A visitor?" Lillian repeated.

"A gentleman," the girl clarified.

Lillian gasped. Could it be her brother? She rushed past the girl and down the stairs. Bursting into the room, she hoped to see her tall, reedy younger brother leaning on the fireplace mantel.

Instead, the man was by the window. And it wasn't her brother. It was Simon.

Chapter 25

"Hello Lillian," Simon said after she had been silent for far too long.

She blinked. This was a dream, it had to be. Simon couldn't be here.

He cocked his head. "Are you going to say something?"

Shaking away her shock, Lillian stepped into the room and quietly closed the door behind her, hoping the servants would take that as a sign that she wasn't to be interrupted.

"Simon," she breathed, savoring the sound of his name. She had never thought to say it to him again. "What are you doing here?"

"In London?" he asked, cool and nonchalant, as if they were no more than old acquaintances who had bumped into each other on the street and talked out of mere politeness. "Rhys and Anne marry tomorrow. I'm standing up for him in the church."

Her heart skipped and she cursed herself. Some

tiny part of her had secretly hoped he'd come for her, but of course that was foolish.

"Yes, I had forgotten," she said, motioning to the chairs. He didn't take one, so she remained standing as well. "Please wish them well for me, if you think they'd like to hear it."

"I shall." He arched a brow. "There are trunks in the hallway. Is the family going somewhere?"

"No." Lillian looked away. "I am. Gabriela's father, Lord Watsenvale, has arranged for a governess position for me. I depart for Scotland almost this moment."

He moved forward. "Scotland?" he burst out, his tone revealing his feelings on the matter.

"It's better this way, Simon," she said with a shrug of one shoulder. "And it should cheer you. If you came here to ensure I wouldn't speak of the things I know, now you can be happy. I won't be in London to do any damage. And I wouldn't, even if I was going to stay."

"I didn't come to London for Rhys's wedding," he blurted out, and suddenly he was coming across the room in long strides that closed the gap between them in a matter of seconds.

She gasped as he stopped just inches before her, filling her senses with his scent, his heat, his presence. How she wanted to reach for him, to touch him, to ask how he was adjusting to all he had been given and told.

But she resisted.

"I came for you," he finished. "I came here for my fiancée."

She opened her mouth in shock at his ardor. It was unexpected, and she wasn't sure how to respond.

"I-I am not your fiancée," she finally said, hating how her tone was small and plaintive. She didn't want him to be obligated to marry her and regret it for the rest of his life. "We talked about this."

"*You* talked," he argued. "And I was too stunned by all I had uncovered about my father, about you, to answer. But I *never* agreed to end our engagement."

"You must know it is best," she gasped, utterly shocked by how wild his eyes were.

"It isn't best," he said, raking a hand through his hair. "It is utterly unreasonable and unfair. And I have enough power to force your hand if I desired to do it."

She cocked her head in surprise. "Force my hand?"

He nodded. "I could take you to court. Hell, I could drag you to Gretna Green and make you agree. It's been known to happen."

Lillian's eyes widened. She drew a harsh breath before she whispered, "And would you do those things?"

The steel left Simon's stare as he grasped her

upper arms and slid her closer. "Only if I must. I've come here to tell you something, to ask you something, and I hope you will listen. Please don't leave, Lillian. I'm asking you not to leave me."

Her eyes stung as she looked at him. God, he was temptation.

"I don't want to," she admitted on a sob. "You must know how this breaks my heart. But the things I did! You told me you could never trust me again, Simon. And I don't blame you for that. But that is no way to live a life."

"Don't you think I know that, having watched my parents hate each other as long as I can recall?" he said with a bark of unhappy laughter. "But we aren't them."

"But—"

He shook his head to cut her off. "Lillian, you lied to me, and I won't say that didn't cut me to the bone. I thought you were the only person left I could trust."

"I'm sorry," she whispered.

"In this past week, I've had a lot to consider. I asked myself why the people around me lied to me. Some lied for greed, some out of obligation and fear, others in a misguided attempt to protect me."

She nodded.

"But you . . . you didn't lie to me because of *me* at all, and I found myself understanding your reasons." He stared directly into her eyes. "My father had a hand in destroying your family in the worst way a man could. I looked at my sister and my brother and I realized that if someone hurt them, I would be ready to do anything to avenge that pain. *Anything.*"

She blinked, surprised by how easily he had summed up her feelings at the beginning of her quest.

"Simon, the fact that you understand my situation means the world to me," she whispered. "But I still fear that when you look at me, all you'll see are the lies."

He touched her face, and she couldn't keep herself from leaning into his palm with a deep and satisfied sigh of pleasure. It seemed like an eternity since she'd felt his skin on hers, even though it had been only a week.

"I won't see the lie, Lillian," he said. "When I look at you, I'll forever see the hand you placed in mine before we entered my brother's cottage. I will see your defense of me when we faced my mother afterward. And the smile I so wished to coax from your lips. I'll see the way you sigh when I kiss the slope of your neck. Those things mean more to me than the other."

"Simon—" she breathed.

He cupped her face gently in both hands. "I don't want the deceit that brought me . . . brought *us* to this place to define me. I will not allow it to define us."

She squeezed her eyes shut. How could she deny him when he offered her forgiveness and love and acceptance? How could she turn away from the one man who had seen his way past all the obstacles between them and somehow loved her regardless?

"So what do we do?" she whispered.

"We swear to be honest from now on." He stepped back and held out a hand to her. "Good afternoon, Miss Mayhew. My name is Henry Ives, although you can never call me anything but Simon Crathorne, twelfth Duke of Billingham. I'm forced to live out the life of a man who cannot be anything more than a child. And that is an honor as much as a curse."

Lillian held back a sob as she took the hand he offered.

"I thought I knew my father," he continued, his voice dropping with emotion. "But in reality he was a stranger. And I have at least two more half brothers who he abandoned. I have vowed to find and reunite them."

She squeezed his hand. "That is a great deal to handle."

"Not if I have a partner." He smiled. "Lillian, I don't know who I am anymore. In fact, the only thing I know for certain is that I love you. And I can't delve into my foggy past or face my future without you."

Lillian swiped at her tears and then smiled shakily. "Hello, Your Grace. I'm Lillian Mayhew. My mother was a sad and troubled woman who your father took advantage of. She killed herself, and it was so easy to blame that entirely on him. I wanted to destroy him and I admit I would have settled for destroying you . . . until I met you and experienced your honor and your love." She moved closer. "And I do love you, Simon. With all my heart."

He dropped to his knee before her, and she gasped.

"Then marry me. And we'll face whatever comes next together. Please, Lillian. I want you and I *need* you by my side."

Her hands shook as she dropped down to her own knees before him. She cupped his cheeks tenderly and stared into those shocking jade eyes.

"Yes," she whispered. "I would be honored to be your bride."

He didn't answer in words, but by dipping his head to hers and kissing her. She wrapped her arms around his neck and clung to him as the kiss deepened, expressing all the powerful emotions, all the love they felt for each other. In that moment she knew they could overcome anything. Everything.

When they finally broke apart, Simon smiled. "With you by my side, I shall become the man I *am*, not the boy taken from his mother. Not the lie my father created for his own greed."

She nodded. "We'll change together."

"Forever," he promised, and his lips met hers again.

Epilogue

One Week Later

The solicitor was American and nervous as he bustled around the untidy office, digging for paperwork. Simon shifted and glared at the man until he felt Lillian's gentle hand on his knee.

He looked at her with his first smile that day. "Thank you for coming with me. I know it isn't much of a wedding trip."

She nodded. "I don't need a wedding trip, love. Only you."

He returned his attention to the shuffling man. He wasn't the solicitor his father had named in his paperwork, but a relative who had taken over the business.

"Ah, here it is. I'm surprised this still exists, the work my uncle did for your father was so long ago," the little man said, turning with a thick file in hand.

"Thank you," Simon said, and then stared at the man.

He shifted and finally said, "Well, I shall, er, leave you to look at that. I'll return shortly."

After he was gone, Lillian smiled at Simon. "I think he'll never recover from the scorn of such a powerful man."

Simon stared at the file in his hand. "I didn't want him here while I read it."

"Don't forget, dearest, it might not contain the names of the other brothers," she said softly. "But we'll keep searching until we know them all."

He nodded and slowly flipped the file cover back.

Some of the scrawls were his father's, others were unknown, probably the old solicitor who had made arrangements for him. Simon scanned through the names, the figures, the particulars with a growing sense of urgency.

Lillian was reading over his shoulder. "It looks like this file only details one of the other brothers."

He nodded. "I suppose that makes sense. My father wouldn't want one person lording over all his secrets. He probably used a very long string of well-bribed people to take care of his 'unsavory business,' as he calls it here."

"As of yet, I do not see a name for the child," Lillian said with a sigh.

He flipped to the end of the pile of paperwork, filled with frustration, but just as he was about to close the file and give up, his gaze caught something in the text. He read it once, twice, rubbed his eyes and read it a third time.

"Lillian," he said, his voice no more than a whisper. "Do you see that?"

She swallowed and met his stare. "Yes. It says that the woman your father sired a son with was the Duchess of Waverly. Rhys's mother. Does . . . does he have a brother?"

Simon shook his head as he read the name again. "No," he finally whispered. "Only the sisters you met at the wedding. If this is true, and by the date I have no reason to believe it is not, then that means . . ." He hesitated, almost unable to speak this unfathomable thing. "That means Rhys is my brother."

A series of images filled his mind. Of how his father had first discouraged him from making a friendship with Rhys. He pictured the duke watching the two boys playing. He'd never made an effort to talk with Rhys, as he had Simon's other boyhood friends.

Perhaps he had done that because Rhys was his son. A fearful and physical reminder that the duke was not the man he pretended to be.

"Simon," Lillian breathed, gripping his arm. "What will you do?"

He looked at her. "It seems Rhys and I will have to have a talk when he returns from his holiday with Anne." He looked back down at the paper again and stared. "Everyone should know who they really are. I just hope my friend will be able to stand the truth."

He closed the file and tucked it beneath his arm. He had no intention of leaving such volatile information with a scatterbrained solicitor like this one. He helped Lillian to her feet, and they turned to leave the office together.

"Simon," she said, as he helped her into their carriage a few moments later and settled in beside her. "Whatever happens, whatever this brings, I hope you know I do love you."

He looked down at her, still amazed that just a look, a touch, from her could soothe even the most desperate of pains. He smiled.

"That means the world to me, Lillian. And with you by my side, I know I can face anything." He looked out at the busy London streets. "Even this."

At Avon Books, we know your passion for romance—once you finish one of our novels, you find yourself wanting more.

May we tempt you with . . .

- **Excerpts** from our upcoming releases.

- Entertaining **extras**, including authors' personal photo albums and book lists.

- Behind-the-scenes **scoop** on your favorite characters and series.

- **Sweepstakes** for the chance to win free books, romantic getaways, and other fun prizes.

- Writing **tips** from our authors and editors.

- **Blog** with our authors and find out why they love to write romance.

- **Exclusive content** that's not contained within the pages of our novels.

Join us at
www.avonbooks.com